Santa's Gift List

NAUGHTY	NICE
The IRS	Peter & Mary Ellen Holiday
Congress	Michael & Janice Holiday, their six kids, too
Dennis Rodman	Jared & Alison Holiday
Raymond Holiday*	Holly

*Note to self: Raymond's resistant,
but has potential. Could take a miracle.
Make sure Holly has Christmas magic on her side.
Also, strategically situate mistletoe.
Raymond won't get away this year!*

Dear Reader,

You're about to meet the last of the Holiday cousins, Raymond, who joins Peter, Michael and Jared. They're four sexy guys with two things in common: the Holiday name and humbug in the heart! But this year Cupid's been working overtime, and by Christmas he's aiming to have the Holiday men singing love songs!

From the creative mind of Linda Cajio comes THE HOLIDAY HEART miniseries. Linda's already taken us through Valentine's Day, Mother's Day and Labor Day. Christmas is sure to be a special treat.

Linda Cajio is a name well-known to readers of romance fiction. She's the author of over twenty bestselling contemporary and historical romances, a past president of Romance Writers of America and the winner of many writing awards. Linda makes her home in New Jersey, with her family.

We hope you've enjoyed the Holiday men in THE HOLIDAY HEART series!

Regards,

Debra Matteucci
Senior Editor & Editorial Coordinator
Harlequin Books
300 East 42nd Street
New York, NY 10017

MISTER CHRISTMAS

Linda Cajio

Harlequin Books

TORONTO • NEW YORK • LONDON
AMSTERDAM • PARIS • SYDNEY • HAMBURG
STOCKHOLM • ATHENS • TOKYO • MILAN
MADRID • WARSAW • BUDAPEST • AUCKLAND

ISBN 0-373-16704-0

MISTER CHRISTMAS

Printed in U.S.A.

Chapter One

"So, what are you wearing?"

Raymond Holiday grinned as the female voice erupted in giggles. Women often called his sports-talk radio show. Most were knowledgeable about the local Philadelphia teams, but some were just flirty, like this one whose come-on had raised an enthusiastic thumbs-up from his producer, Karen.

"Nothing," the caller said in a low tone.

"I love morning drive-time, especially when people *aren't* driving," Raymond commented, while his cohost, Tommy Blanco, hit the Perky sound-effect tape. Lights flashed rhythmically on the massive electronics board in front of them, indicating the large number of callers waiting to get on the show. Raymond ignored the lights, adding, "Are you calling from your bed? Please say yes."

"No, she's standing on the corner in the blizzard," Karen interjected, laughing. "Raymond, get a life!"

That charge came often during his show because of his notoriety as a loner. He didn't mind. Anything for the ratings.

"Okay, so I'm desperate," he replied. "Now, let me flirt a little more with—" he glanced at the computer screen with the callers' names on it "—Tammy."

It figured.

"I thought this was a sports-talk show," Bob Kroger, their resident comedian, lamented in his best President Clinton voice.

"Only when I say so," Raymond said. "Now where were we?"

He flirted with the caller a little more, never quite crossing the line from naughty fun to bad taste. His morning show was a mix of talk—analysis of the local teams, topical skits, silliness about family life, and innocent earthiness. It succeeded in the most competitive radio time-slot because he ensured it had such wide appeal that a husband, wife and kids in the car, driving to work and school, would all find something they liked. So would the twenty-two-year-old single male, who wanted to fantasize about callers like Tammy. Everyone also loved the tales about Raymond's "disastrous" love life. Critics called Raymond a benign Howard Stern. Raymond could live with that.

He moved on to two calls about the professional football team's winning record and signed off with a warning about the blizzard raging outside. When the WRP call letters were announced, along with the snappy goodbye, "That's a wrap on WRP," Raymond sat back in his big, padded chair and let out his breath in relief at another day over.

He removed his headphones and said, "Great show, guys."

Everyone agreed.

"It's really bad out there," Bob said, looking out the window at the swirling cape of snow wrapping around the entire Delaware Valley. Under the comic's exterior, he was a worrier of the first order. "There has to be six inches already, and we haven't even gotten to the worst of it.''

"The store owners must be weeping," Tommy said. "They don't need a blizzard on Black Friday."

"Christmas. Bah, Humbug. And to hell with Thanksgiving, too," Raymond said. "It's all too commercial anyway."

"Bah, humbug, to you," Bob retorted. "When was the last time we had snow like this in November? I can't remember, but it makes you wonder about the rest of the winter. We'll have six feet by Christmas if it keeps snowing like this."

"Well, guys, forget the meeting to plan Monday's show. You all might as well get home while you can."

Raymond didn't follow his own advice, however. He worked in his office, laying out Monday's show himself. The rest of his staff had families to get home to. He didn't.

A good thing, he told himself. He wanted no part of love and commitment—and all they entailed. His cousins, Peter, Michael and Jared, might have betrayed their promise and made the plunge into matrimony and family life. But not him. He preferred to be alone.

When he finally left the station, the blizzard was in full-blown fury. Standing just inside the building's glass front doors, he looked out at the thick carpet of snow, then down at his high-top sneakers. He groaned. Where was Mom to nag about snow boots when one needed her?

"In Florida, living with her sugar daddy, that's where," Raymond muttered.

He bent his head against the howling wind and ventured out into the storm. Snow fell like thick white cotton, obscuring his view from nearly everything. Wind whipped his face and burned his lungs. Cold gripped his body in an ague, shiver-shaking him almost uncontrollably. He only had to cross the street to the station's parking lot, but he wondered if he would make it. This was bad, but especially today. Businesses should be calling this White Friday instead of Black Friday, he thought. Tommy was right; the store owners must be going insane at losing their best business day of the year.

He trudged past a wino curled up at the side of the building—an all-too-common site in any city, including Philadelphia. Damn fool had been there when Raymond had come in at five that morning. One would think the guy would find a steam vent to huddle over—

Something suddenly popped up in front of him—literally popped right out of the air.

"What the hell is wrong with you?" the small woman before him demanded.

Raymond gaped at her, astonished at the way she'd appeared from nowhere. She couldn't be more than five feet tall—if even that—with long, blond hair and blue eyes so wide they reminded him of that angel figurine collection sold in a card store chain. Her features were sharply defined, her cheekbones prominent and her chin stubborn. She wore only a red velvet tunic and wide-legged green pants—both incongruous in a blizzard. Her clothes only emphasized her slenderness. In fact, the biggest things on her were her breasts. Boy, Raymond thought, for a little thing, she sure was stacked....

Without warning she walloped him in the arm with her fist. "Get your mind out of the gutter and get your backside over to that poor man and help him!"

"What?" Raymond asked, feeling oddly disoriented, as if her blow had nearly knocked him out.

"I *said* get over there and help that man! How could you walk by him like that?"

"But he's a bum," Raymond said, without thinking.

"I don't care what he is," she snapped. "Get over there *now*."

He noticed the snow had diminished around the two of them, and they stood in a soft light. The blizzard must be in a lull. He shook off the notion as his mind finally cleared. "Wait a minute, lady—"

Something latched painfully on to his ear. Raymond yelped. He realized she held his appendage in a vise grip of her fingers. She yanked him toward the huddled figure. Raymond had no choice but to go with his ear or risk losing it. He had a feeling she could pull it right off if she chose.

"Now help this man," she said, when they reached the forlorn figure.

"But—"

She tugged on his ear several times, in definite reprimand. "No buts. Now help him!"

The logical part of Raymond's brain told him this woman was crazy—probably more crazy than the bum. Up close, the man looked almost healthy and no older than himself. The gaze that focused on Raymond was sharp and clear.

The woman nudged Raymond in the back to prompt him. He wondered if hc would feel a knife there next, should he not do as she commanded.

"Don't be ludicrous," she said and nudged him again.

"Here's five bucks," Raymond said, digging into his pockets.

"Get away," the man commanded.

"Oh..." The nudge thumped him yet again. "Do you need help? I can get you to a shelter—"

"Go away!"

Raymond felt a positive whack between his shoulder blades when he had only a fleeting thought to do as the man asked. He tried one last time with the bum. "You look cold, buddy—"

"Get the hell away before I have you arrested!" the man told him in frustrated tones. A crackling sound erupted from the filthy-looking clothes. The guy lifted a lapel of his coat and said, "No, Captain. It's some idiot Good Samaritan.... Yeah, I don't think it's going down today, either.... Ten-four..."

"Sorry." Raymond backed up, knowing he'd stumbled onto some kind of police sting. He had no idea who or what was to be "stung," but hoped it wasn't him.

"What was that?" the woman asked, at his side.

It occurred to Raymond that she had disappeared the moment the undercover cop revealed himself. Or at least, he hadn't been at all aware of her presence behind him. "What the hell do you mean, what was that? You saw the man was a cop!"

"No. I mean that thing he talked into."

Raymond blinked, the question taking him by surprise. "A walkie-talkie..."

He realized he was talking to a nutcase. Okay, a beautiful nut case with a body to rival Pamela Anderson Lee's. The woman was out in a blizzard, in pajamas, punching people into random acts of kindness. And she thought *he* had a problem.

Raymond walked faster, to try to get away from her before something dangerous happened. The wind suddenly picked up, and snow blinded him. An army of flakes stung his face as the world dimmed again to a swirl of white.

The woman caught up to him, and the storm lessened considerably. The light brightened, and the individual snowflakes glistened like fairy dust. The air even felt warmer, like a heated glow.

"A walkie-talkie," the woman mused. "How fascinating. Okay, so maybe he didn't need help, but—"

Raymond started forward, distancing himself from her...and plowed back into the storm. He gaped at the abrupt change in weather, then whipped around to face the woman.

To his amazement, she stood in a circle of white light, with only a few crystal flakes falling gently around her. Outside the circle surrounding her, the blizzard stormed unmercifully.

"What the hell...?" Raymond muttered, bewildered.

The woman stepped up to him. The area brightened and grew warmer, while the driving snow nearly disappeared.

"What *is* this?" he demanded, feeling as though he was dreaming.

"No dream," she said, laughing merrily. "You're wide-awake."

"Who *are* you?" he asked.

"I'm an elf," she replied, smiling a very sexy smile. "And I'm over a thousand years old."

HOLLY LAUGHED AT Raymond's dumbfounded expression. The poor soul was in shock. She couldn't blame him. She supposed anyone would be at meeting someone like her.

"Lady, you need help," he said finally. "Or I do."

"Actually, you do," she said, her humor fading a little. "That's why I'm here. I have to help you, Raymond Holiday. You're my assignment."

"Assignment! What assignment?"

"Well, not 'assignment' exactly. I'm your Christmas gift," she corrected, not surprised that she wasn't explaining it well to him. This whole business was nearly unprecedented in the annals of her kind's history. Only once before had elves been sent out into the world, to remind men of their obligation to each other. Those three were heroes for scaring the dickens out of Dickens and getting him to write *A Christmas Carol*. But that had been three elves. She was alone on this one. When the Big Guy wanted something, the Big Guy got it.

"You're early, honey," Raymond said. "*Way* early. And I've lost it. I've got to be dreaming this. Somebody pinch me."

"Okay," Holly said, and pinched his ear again.

"Ouch!" He grabbed his offended ear. "Will you stop doing that! It hurts."

"So sue me." She giggled at the thought.

He stared at her for a long, long moment, then shook himself. "I've been working way too hard."

He turned and walked away. Holly kept pace, his long strides hardly a deterrent. He was an interesting-looking man, she admitted, and wondered where that odd thought had come from. Humans seemed cumbersome and gauche, not at all attractive creatures compared to small, quick-moving elves. Still, his dark hair brushed his collar, and his saturnine features looked almost noble. He could have passed for a lord in her day.

Holly frowned. What lord? What day? Elves didn't have lords in the hierarchy. She shrugged the notions off. Errant thought had no place in what she was doing. This man needed help. Somehow he'd lost his heart—the best part of himself—even if he didn't know it. Some sort of special request had come through, and she was now here to aid him in finding his heart again. She only had until Christmas to do it, too. Talk about pressure!

"Where are we going?" she asked.

"I'm going home," Raymond said. "And you're going to the closest hospital. You're nuts, lady."

"I'll admit I'm going to take some getting used to, but the sooner that happens, the sooner we can get down to business," Holly said.

Raymond stopped and faced her. "I don't know who you are, and I don't care, but get away from me before I call that cop over there. The one *you* thought was a bum."

"So I made a little mistake and thought I could *see* him like I see inside you. Hey, nobody's perfect," Holly said, shrugging. "That doesn't negate the fact that you need help, Raymond Holiday."

"Officer!" Raymond shouted to the undercover cop, who was barely visible in the storm. Raymond could discern that the man was now up and walking away from the radio-station building. "This woman is insane, and she's stalking me!"

"What woman?" the cop shouted back.

Raymond pointed to Holly. "This woman here! I want to press charges *now!*"

"Oh, boy," Holly murmured, knowing what was coming next.

The cop stared, then called out, "There's no woman anywhere around here, you dope! Go home and sleep it off, or I'll have to take *you* in!"

On impulse, Holly kissed the finger that pointed to her. "Guess who's the only one who can see me."

"I *must* be drunk." He walked across the street, gasping when he left her circle of warmth. Holly shook her head and grinned at his struggle against the storm. She caught up with him.

"You'll see," she said. "Well, you'll see that no one else sees."

He said nothing.

"This is a beautiful blizzard," she commented. "It's swirling quite nicely, although you all really aren't equipped to deal with it like we are back home. Now those are blizzards...."

He still said nothing.

"Hey!" She poked his shoulder. "You could at least be polite and reply."

"I'm ignoring you," he said.

"Why?"

"Because you're not there. You can't be."

Holly laughed. "Of course, I'm here. I'm here for you."

He said nothing.

She sighed. She hadn't expected this would be easy and obviously it wouldn't be. She supposed she shouldn't be surprised. This wasn't a lark.

He went to a fenced area, her presence making it easy for him in the snow, and stopped next to a small vehicle. Holly thought she recognized it.

"Is this a car?" she asked, curious. "I've heard of them, but I've never seen one before. We usually know what's going on here, but details like walkie-talkies sometimes escape us."

Raymond turned to face her. "I don't know who or what you are, but go away."

She chuckled. "You sound like that cop."

"It's not real, it's not real," Raymond chanted, getting into the car after fiddling with the handle. He shut the door.

Holly pursed her lips in annoyance. "He needs a lesson in etiquette first."

She walked into the car, steel and plastic no barrier to her. She sat in the backseat but leaned forward, her hands on the front seat and her mouth at Raymond's ear. "It would have been nice to open a door for a lady."

"So open one."

"You, not me." She tweaked his ear.

Raymond grunted and whipped around in his seat. "Dammit! Will you stop doing that!"

"Doing what?" Holly asked. "'It's not real, it's not real.' Remember?"

He grunted again and faced forward. The car gave a bearlike roar, startling her. The vehicle moved of its own volition, first backward, then turning and going forward, out the gate and onto the snow-filled street.

"This is neat," she said, marveling at modern technology.

"This is dangerous," Raymond commented. "I can't even see the road. Nothing's been plowed yet, and I'm going to get stuck before I get home."

"'Tis the season," Holly said, patting his arm. She liked touching him. It felt…right. Yet she knew touching was more dangerous than snow. The enclosed space heightened her awareness of him as a man—an attractive man. "Not to worry. You'll get home just fine. I guarantee it."

RAYMOND CRAWLED INTO his bed, trying to ignore thoughts of the visions he'd been having ever since he walked into that blizzard. He'd left it behind in the living room of his town house for now, engrossed in watching the snow falling outside—a change from her jabbering at him.

He rubbed his face with his hands, hoping to ease whatever the hell his brain had conjured. He must be in a dream—a dream that pinched and poked and chastised, but a dream nonetheless. Maybe he had snow sickness. Maybe if he puked out his guts, she would vanish.

His stomach felt rock-solid calm.

"Damn," he muttered, disgusted by his physical well-being.

He hadn't been off his normal schedule for weeks, but somehow he must be sleep deprived. What else could explain this...elf?

Sleep deprived or nuts, he thought with a shudder. A flipping elf! If he had to hallucinate, the least he could do would be to come up with the Playmate of the Month.

He had, sort of, he admitted, remembering her face and body. Maybe she meant she *was* this month's Playmate—albeit on the short side—but it just came out as "Elf." Okay, so she was on the old side, too, by a thousand years or so, but she was still kicking. And for a hallucination, her touch packed a punch in more ways than one. She smelled like vanilla spice cookies and freshly-made icing. Everyone knew what vanilla invoked in a certain part of a man's anatomy. Even the hint of it certainly worked on his.

He pushed the thoughts away. She was a figment of his deranged imagination. He wondered if one could be deranged and actually recognize it. He hoped so. Right now it was his only explanation for what was happening to him.

He disliked this out-of-control feeling. Normally, he curbed his emotions. People were manipulators, always wanting something for nothing—especially in love. His mother had gotten pregnant by a wealthy man, to gain lifetime support. She'd always been open about it to him, claiming love was unnecessary and financial security was. High-school girlfriends had liked him for being the star receiver on the football team. When he'd dropped the winning pass in the last seconds of the championship game, he'd become an immediate pariah. Nothing in his later relationships with women had led him to feel differently. They all wanted to gain something from him.

Even his grandparents had manipulated each other in their own relationship, especially during his grandmother's affair with another man. He'd been a child then, the youngest of the Holiday cousins, but his grandparents had even gotten them to choose up sides in the aftermath. The summers he could spend with them disappeared in a flash. He'd gotten the message then and there that it was one for one and forget the rest. He did trust his cousins—Peter, Michael and Jared—and the staff of the station, but that was it.

Raymond rolled over onto his stomach, glad that his job demanded so much of his time, enough to preclude dating. Maybe monks had the right idea in shutting themselves away from the world. Maybe they, too, had hallucinations about elves—sexy, female elves.

Raymond groaned and rolled onto his back again. He forced himself to visualize sheep leaping over a fence and finally pushed away the thought of her—although one or two straggled in for an encore. Eventually he fell asleep, without any disruption from his imaginary elf....

Something abruptly shook him awake. "Hey! Hey! That box in there is talking. It's really marvelous, isn't it? That's got to be the television. I know you listened to the radio earlier—and the stereo. Boy, we've heard a lot about television back home. It's even better than we were told."

Raymond blinked in the darkness. He glanced at the clock. Two forty-three in the morning. The voice was back, jabbering away.

A light flashed on, momentarily blinding him. Groaning again, he covered his eyes with his hand. "Turn that damn thing off!"

"But you've got to get up and see this! It's about Christmas."

She yanked down the thick silk coverlet and sheets. Raymond yelped and yanked them back up.

She stared at him solemnly for a long moment, then said, "You're naked, Raymond."

"I was sleeping, dammit!" he replied, clutching the bedclothes to his chin. Heat flooded his face at her having caught him in the nude. Now why should he be embarrassed about a figment of his imagination seeing him naked?

"Butt naked."

"Don't you sleep?" he asked grumpily.

She paused. "Not really. Certainly we wouldn't do it naked."

"Too bad," he muttered, wishing he'd had an opportunity to "discover" her in bed in the nude. Now that would be a treat.

She went on, as if she hadn't heard him. "Time passes differently back home."

"You keep saying that. Where's home?"

"The North Pole."

"That figures." He had really lost it. "Go away, okay?"

He sounded like a broken record, but he couldn't help it.

"I can't. I want you to be happy."

"I am happy."

"No, you're not." She said it with complete conviction. "You only think you are."

Raymond forced himself to disagree. "I am. I promise—"

"Oh, forget that for now." She waved a hand in dismissal and became excited again. "Get up and come see the TV."

"No."

"I'll pull the covers down again," she threatened.

Raymond didn't doubt her. He considered his situation. She didn't go away for the asking. God knows, he had tried. And he wasn't ready to be overexposed again. Maybe if he went along with her, this dream—or rather, this nightmare—of an elf would end that much sooner. "All right. I'll be out in a minute."

"I'll wait."

"The hell you will. If you want me up, you'll get out now."

She giggled. "I don't think it works that way. I've been watching the television, so I know."

But she vanished, leaving him astonished and belatedly rueful about his accidental double entendre.

"The blue channel must be bleeding in on the cable again," he muttered.

He lay on the bed a little longer, pondering the fates and whether to get up or not. Terror that the Terror in Red and Green would pop back in to annoy the heck out of him finally won out. He rose and pulled on a pair of jeans and a sweatshirt, then padded out to the living room.

She sat cross-legged in the middle of the black leather sofa, her tunic and harem pants making her look like part of a Christmas *I Dream of Jeannie* episode.

"Look!" She pointed at the screen. "Everyone's in miniature."

Raymond glanced at the television and snorted in disgust. "*It's a Wonderful Life,* the colorized version. You woke me up for a movie!"

"What's 'colorized'?"

He came around and sat down next to her. What the

hell, he thought. If he was going to play along with a hallucination in the middle of the night and discuss the merits of colorization, he might as well be comfortable. He was awake anyway. "People will take old black-and-white movies and paint colors in them with a computer. See how too pink Jimmy Stewart's cheeks are, and the way the images are fuzzy? At least this channel waited until *after* Thanksgiving to put the movie on."

"I thought his name was George."

"In the movie." The least his figment could do was get the details right.

"There's too damn many of them," she said.

Raymond paused, remembering his first encounter with the creature. "Can you read my mind?"

She gave him a look of disdain. "Think about it."

He thought…about her…about her slowly taking her top off to reveal her breasts…. Would she be anatomically correct? He wanted to find out in the worst way….

She pushed him over on the sofa. Her face was nearly as red as her tunic. "I am. And I'm not that kind of elf, okay?"

"You *can* read my mind," he said. This was one hell of a dream he was having.

"And what a filthy one it is, too. Mind and dream," she said, tucking her hair behind one ear.

One pointed ear.

Raymond swallowed at the sight of that beautiful, shell-like ear rising to a point. It wasn't ugly; far from it. Its delicacy intrigued him. So much so, he reached out and touched the odd shape to see if it was real.

Her skin was incredibly soft, as he ran his finger up and over the point. Not a sharp point, he acknowledged, but soft, too.

"Oh, my," she murmured, her voice low and as sexy as her ear. She sat very still.

"You feel so real," he said, tracing her cheek. How could he touch his imagination like this?

"I am real."

"Elves aren't real."

She chuckled throatily. "A lot you know."

He wanted to learn. For a figment of his imagination, she was charming sometimes. She had a straightforward manner that he liked. "Do you have a name?"

"Holly."

"Holly," he repeated, liking the sound of it. The name fit her.

Fascinated with touching her, he caressed her hair, marveling at its silkiness. Never had a woman's hair felt like this. Or looked like this. The blond strands, as they sifted through his fingers, held a kaleidoscope of colors.

"I think you'd better stop this," she said.

"I don't." He watched her eyes. Beautiful, big blue eyes like shining sapphires lit by fairy dust.

"I do."

She seemed nervous, unsure, almost shy.

He touched her ear again, captivated by its difference. It was still pointed. "I just can't get over how real you feel."

"I told you." She shifted, one leg draping over the edge of the sofa seat. Her foot didn't quite touch the floor. She was tiny for a woman, but loaded with femininity.

Raymond had no clue what he was doing, but he had become mesmerized by her. She had an air of enchantment. Of course, he was dreaming and she wasn't real. But he would worry about that later. Right now he wanted to enjoy this new aspect of his insane day. He couldn't keep his gaze from her, nor keep from touching her. Her

flesh was so warm...and so alive. Although his hallucination claimed to want to help him, he sensed that she
was the real one in need. The urge to get closer overwhelmed him.

She pressed her lips together to moisten them—leaving
them glistening with invitation.

"Don't go there," she whispered.

"Where?" The whole thing was surreal, even as he
leaned toward her.

"What's wrong with me? I feel so strange, all tin-
gling."

"I'll make it better," he promised.

His lips touched hers. She stiffened for just a moment...and then she vanished.

Raymond fell facedown onto the sofa seat. He scrambled upright and glanced around the room, searching for
his hallucination. Only the television blared with any life.
The clock on the wall above it read after three. Time had
certainly passed in proper relation to his conversation with
the elf.

But she was gone.

He had wanted her gone, Raymond thought.

So why did he feel so bad?

Chapter Two

He scared her.

Holly watched Raymond walk along the side street in the city. Everything had been kissed by the snow, leaving a pristine drape behind. People were getting around after the blizzard, the streets having been plowed. Holly was a little sorry to see the white go. It reminded her of home.

Raymond occasionally looked in the small shop windows, unaware of her invisible presence. She hadn't yet revealed herself to him today, last night's kiss having shaken her to the core. Especially after seeing him naked. Naked! Her glimpse had been brief but telling. He had a beautiful body, all strong muscle and dusted with fine hairs in the right places. His sex intrigued her. Males were so vulnerable. She'd never had feelings like this before, as if she had awakened from a long sleep. Her body still tingled and throbbed intimately—such a unique sensation pulsed through her. Did human mortals experience this all the time? No wonder they were so obsessed with life.

She was here to help him—a present for Christmas— not to drool over him like some lovesick elf. Kisses and peeks at naked men were *not* on the duty roster. Unfortunately, she wasn't sure how to proceed after last night's disastrous turn.

Raymond stopped in front of a window display for a department store. Holly glanced at it, then did a double take.

"Hey!" she exclaimed angrily, popping into his presence. "What is this? Iggy Pop's version of Santa's workshop?"

Raymond jumped, startled by her voice. "Shut up!"

"You are very rude," she said, glaring at him. "I see we'll have to work on that, too."

"No, we won't."

People turned to stare at him. Holly giggled. Clearly, he'd forgotten that only he could see her. She could help him with that, but it seemed more fun not to. Besides, he did need a lesson in manners.

"They'll lock me up yet," he muttered. "I can't believe this is happening again."

"Oh, pooh," she scoffed, then pointed to the window. "I'll be damned if I've ever seen an elf use a Walkman radio. And Santa doesn't have red-striped underwear. He likes blue silk, which gives Laundry fits. The stuff is a bear to clean. Who's the lady with him? And what's all that business about giving reindeer peppermint sticks to eat? They get gas from it. Boy, that's a stench you never forget—"

Raymond walked into the store.

Holly caught up with him, although she took a few extra turns in the revolving door first. She grinned as she'd finally scooted into the lobby and over to Raymond.

"Nice ride," she said. The store looked festive with its garland and trees decorated in every color imaginable, just like home. "So what was all that back there in the window?"

He kept walking.

"Hey," she said. "I will *not* be ignored."

Raymond whirled around, right into a rack of overcoats. He reached out and pulled her in among the coats, effectively hiding the two of them from the other shoppers.

"It's Holly, right?"

"Right."

"If I tell you, Holly, will you go away?"

Holly grinned, making no promise she wouldn't keep.

He looked heavenward. "This is one helluva nightmare I'm having. You'd think I'd be sensible and have one that knows who Iggy Pop is *and* a bad attempt at modern whimsy when she sees it."

"Whimsy. Is that what it was?" Holly laughed. "I see now. I thought it was what you thought went on where I come from. Actually, in the light of whimsy, it's very cute and playful—"

Raymond stepped out of the coats. A woman screamed. Holly popped out in time to see the woman's frightened face and to hear him apologize for scaring her.

"You've got to be more careful," Holly admonished him.

Raymond glared at her.

Holly smiled triumphantly. She liked keeping him off-balance. It appealed to her femininity, a rapidly growing dimension for her. She could really keep him off balance if she wanted to. But that would be contrary to her job. Too bad.

"So what are we doing today…? And not *that*," she added, catching his darker thoughts. "You need some shirts, don't you? They're over here."

She took his arm and brought him farther into the men's department where the shirts were displayed.

"No one stared at us," he said in awe, gazing at the other shoppers going about their business. "How did you pull me along like that so no one could see?"

"I do have some finesse," she replied, then shoved some shirts into his hands. "Here, this looks good for you.... And this...and this...."

He dumped them back onto the display. "No one's dressed me since I was fourteen. Besides, they were the wrong size. And pinstripes. I hate pinstripes."

Holly frowned at him. "I was just trying to be helpful."

"Thanks but no thanks." He strolled over to a display of plaid shirts and picked several.

"They might be the right size, but they're awful," she said. "Brown's a bad color for you. Get the green or the red."

"Women always want to make you over in their image," he muttered, before walking into the dressing room.

Holly took up several much better shirts for Raymond and popped out. She intended to pop into the dressing room and continue the fight. But she only half-popped.

Raymond was just stripping off his shirt.

Holly stayed in her invisible state, grateful she could do so and still see. And she was *very* grateful to see him shrug out of his shirt to reveal a pair of well-defined shoulders. She knew she shouldn't look, but she couldn't help herself. She wanted to peek at more, and he unknowingly obliged.

His chest was broad and he had a mat of silky brown hair that arrowed down a flat abdomen, past his belt buckle. His skin was lightly tanned and her hands ached to caress it, to find out if his body was as strong and as touchable as it looked. He began to put on the ugly brown plaid shirt. The human magic he wove suddenly broke.

"Okay," she said, popping in fully. "Brown isn't as bad as I thought."

"Hallelujah," he said, then exploded, "Dammit, Holly! Can't a man have some privacy?"

Holly thought for a moment. "I gave you some earlier, when you were in the bathroom."

His jaw dropped. Obviously, he hadn't considered that she could appear anytime or anyplace she wanted. Not that she had wanted to give him privacy in the bathroom. In fact it had been all she could do not to pop in and see if he looked as masculine and intriguing as he had in the bedroom.

"You wouldn't," he said.

"I *could* have." She smiled. "Aren't I nice? Now, try on the green and see how it looks. Better than the brown, I'll bet."

Raymond sat down on the little seat provided for dressing-room occupants. "I don't believe all this, and yet half the time I'm acting like it's normal. I really must be nuts."

"Just stubborn," Holly said. She held out the shirt she'd picked. "Try this on and you'll see the difference."

"Not on your life."

He yanked off the brown shirt, yanked on his own and strode out of the dressing room.

"Here we go again." Holly sighed. He was more than stubborn. He was a bloody stone wall.

She went after him, dropping the green shirt as she did.

The crumb was at the register, paying for *four* brown plaid shirts. Yep, she thought. Mr. Stone Wall.

"Okay, be obtuse," she said.

"I'm ignoring you," he replied.

"I beg your pardon," the clerk interjected, raising his eyebrows.

Holly giggled. "Just give up, Raymond Holiday, and you'll be fine—" She caught his thoughts. "Now that's obscene. Do you want me to wash your mind out with soap? I can do it, I assure you."

"Thank you," the clerk said, passing over Raymond's bagged shirts.

Raymond walked away. Holly walked next to him, his long strides again no deterrent to her keeping up.

"So what else are we buying?" she asked. "Brown pants? Brown socks? Brown shoes? Brown wallets? Brown underwear?"

"You're a nag."

"Ah, he speaks." She chuckled, pleased to have "nagged" him into a response. "So what are we doing? I know. You're shopping for holiday gifts. For the *Holidays*. Get it?"

She laughed at her own joke.

"I'm hysterical. And no, we're not shopping for gifts. I don't give any."

Holly pulled up short. "Raymond."

He shrugged.

She grabbed his shirt and pulled him behind some shelves. Once they were relatively alone, she demanded, "Now, what is this, that you don't buy gifts for the holidays?"

"It's all overrated," he said, making a face.

"Don't you give to your relatives? Your co-workers? Your mother? For God's sake, Raymond, you have to give something to your mother for Christmas!"

"I send her a check."

"Raymond, that is not a gift from the heart," she said, appalled at his callowness. She took him by the arm and yanked him into a women's department. "You pick something for your mother, this minute. From the heart."

"I think I'll leave this to Oedipus," he replied, looking at their surroundings.

They were in Lingerie.

Skimpy, lacy, satiny, sexy and see-through clothing

hung on padded hangers in front of, next to, and behind them. Holly's jaw dropped. "Gosh, do people really wear this stuff?"

"Oh, yeah." Raymond grinned. "But you don't give it to your mom."

"I guess not." She picked up a strapless thing with cups obviously for breasts and four rubbery clasps hanging from one end. It was sheer black yet oddly stiff in spots. "What's this?"

"A bustier, I think." Raymond's face looked darker than usual. "You wear it."

She giggled as she held it up. "Why don't *you* wear it?"

"No way. The name's Raymond, not Ru Paul."

She held the bustier up against herself and looked down. "Oh, I see how it works now. It holds up your leggings."

Raymond made a funny noise.

Holly glanced up. He stared at the bustier, his face suffused with color. A strange, very pleasurable tingle ran through her veins to pool deep in her abdomen. She felt oddly powerful, yet nervous at attracting his attention— his primitive attention—this way. She bet he wasn't thinking of her as a pain in the neck at the moment.

She had to admit they didn't have anything like this bustier in the...the what? She couldn't quite place the elusive thought of the past, just as she hadn't been able to do with the errant thoughts of yesterday.

"Can I help you?"

Raymond started, snatching the bustier from Holly's hands before the clerk saw it. Holly grinned at his thinking that the garment must be floating all by itself in her hands. Honestly, she was better than that. She could keep things invisible when she touched them, yet allow Raymond to see them.

"I was just looking for a present for my mother," he said.

The clerk, an older woman, raised her eyebrows at the bustier he now visibly held. "I see."

Raymond dropped the bustier onto a display shelf. "No, you don't. I think I'm in the wrong place."

"I don't," Holly said, having fun. "You ought to get that for your mom. Surprise her."

"I ought to—" He flushed and said, "Excuse me" to the clerk before striding out of the department.

"That bustier had promise, Raymond," Holly said as she hurried along beside him.

"Whatever happened to a gift from the heart?" he muttered.

"That's the spirit," a passerby said to him. "Christmas is way too commercial."

Holly laughed. "Christmas is what you make it. Tell him, Raymond."

Instead, Raymond detoured off the main corridor of the store, back to a lonely spot in Furnishings. "Will you go away, Holly?"

"Sorry, no can do."

"This has got to stop. People think I'm a nut who's talking to himself."

"Oh, I can fix that," Holly said and snapped her fingers. "There. From now on no one will hear you when you talk to me. People will still see you, of course, but they won't hear anything you say to me. Try it."

"I don't trust you," Raymond said, just as a shopper came within hearing distance. The woman never looked up from the fake Federal table and chairs.

"Hello, Holly," Raymond said loudly, deliberately trying it.

The shopper was very clearly close enough to hear, but again, didn't acknowledge in any way that Raymond had spoken.

"How'd you do that?" he asked, astonished.

"O ye of little faith. They pretty much gave me carte blanche for this job, so I can manage a few tricks here and there," Holly said. "I'm going to miss watching you squirm around bystanders."

"I won't, believe me." He smiled.

Holly wished he wouldn't do that. His smile made him boyish and vulnerable. He tugged at her heart when he looked that way. And that made her all girlish and vulnerable. This humanity business had its pitfalls.

"Okay," she said, briskly, to dissipate the feeling. "Let's go shopping for Mom."

"Okay."

Whether he felt more kindly since she'd finally, yet reluctantly, solved an embarrassing problem for him, or whether he felt worn down and had acquiesced, she didn't know. But he did Christmas shop in earnest for his mother. Holly got it out of him that his mother lived with a friend in Florida, but that his mother had never married.

He was a bastard.

The poor man, she thought, although bastardy didn't have the stigma it had long ago. Still, it must hurt him. Maybe that was why he was the way he was.

He picked out a nice necklace for his mother in the end, one Holly knew he liked and also believed would please his mother. It should, Holly thought. It cost enough.

"Hope the mail insurance goes in the upper three figures,'' he commented, after tucking his purchase in his inside jacket pocket.

"Mail insurance?" Holly echoed. "What's that?"

"You insure packages you're sending to someone in case they get lost or stolen along the way. That way you can recoup your money."

The essence of his explanation set in. "Do you mean to tell me you're *sending* this to your mother for Christmas, not visiting her to give it to her personally?"

"Christmas is no big deal, Holly."

"Raymond!" Holly exclaimed, appalled with him yet again, a rapidly growing response to this man. "Christmas is a time for family appreciation, to say thank-you and I love you."

"And if you have no family, what then?" he asked. "This whole thing is a farce of commercialization, not about the old-fashioned sentiments you're thinking of, Holly."

"That's just an easy way to be cynical, to excuse one's laziness or to wash one's hands in a so-called noble fashion of one's obligations to one's fellow man...." She spotted a toy department. Children's laughter rang out. An urge to see them overwhelmed her and she dropped the argument immediately.

Entering the toy department was like entering another world for Holly—an old, familiar world of joy and contentment. She walked among the children, watching them try different toys. Little ones oohed and aahed over stuffed animals. Older children tried video games or studied action figures or models. Huge snowflakes and evergreen and ornaments hung like a perpetual christmas shower from the ceiling, giving the department a merry look.

Some children cried or whined, tired from shopping more than anything else. Holly touched them as she passed, giving each of them a little lift of the heart. The crying and whining eventually faded. She cooed at several babies in strollers, who cooed back in delight at her attention. Babies could see her, of course; all totally innocent creatures could. Several older children caught glimpses of her, but children *should* catch glimpses of elves, especially at Christmastime. All part of the magic, Holly thought happily.

"Raymond!" she shouted, waving him into the department. "Over here! If you don't come here, I'll come get *you!*"

She stood with some kids playing a video game, when he joined her. She said by way of greeting, "Isn't it marvelous!"

"I think it's supposed to be ruining kids' social skills," he told her.

"What a crock," she scoffed. "Look at the way these children are encouraging the player. Isn't that social? And kind of them, certainly.... That's it, honey.... Yeah! He hit the shell just right."

She patted the young player on his head, and the boy smiled although he didn't know why.

"Oh, look at the little ones at that house over there."

She hurried over to a cottage made out of heavy, molded plastic. Two preschoolers ran in and out, shutting the door in each other's faces and giggling as they did.

"My turn, my turn," Holly said, running in and out of the house with the kids. She had to shrink down to their level, but that was no problem. She laughed with the children.

"That was fun," she said a few minutes later, returning to her normal size. The children's mother valiantly and vainly called them to her, but the two didn't stop until

Holly touched each of them before the naughtiness got completely out of control.

A little girl, no more than three, tried to throw a soft basketball into a miniature plastic basket, equipped with backboard. The basket was just out of arm's reach for the child and Holly tipped the ball into the basket at the last second. The little girl cheered, while the ball rolled to Raymond's feet.

"Give the ball back to Regina," Holly ordered.

Raymond picked it up and handed it to the child. "You know her name?"

"Making a list and checking it twice, my friend."

"I suppose you know exactly what she's getting for Christmas, too," he said, his voice sarcastic.

"A drop of self-confidence and a dollop of courage," Holly replied.

"What? No toys?"

She snorted. "We're way beyond the toy department. People need more than material things in their stockings. Some kids need sympathy or joy or playfulness or luck, depending on what's upcoming for them in the year. Some kids need a step in the right direction. Some kids need hope in a desperate situation. We work very hard to give them the moment that they need—one they can even ride on for the rest of their lives. Sometimes it only takes a little thing to pull a person up from whatever trouble they're in. We make sure that gift is there for them to find when they need it most. But it's up to them to find it."

"Nice way around your real job," Raymond said.

"He just doesn't get it," Holly muttered, realizing he was worse off then she'd been led to believe.

Regina tried to throw the ball into the basket again. Holly helped it along once more, delighted to play even if she couldn't do more than this. She was further delighted when Raymond handed the ball back to the child on his own. He even smiled that lovely smile again.

"Regina!"

A woman rushed past Holly and grabbed up the child, hugging her tightly. The woman glared at Raymond.

"I was just handing her the ball," he said defensively.

The woman left him with a sniff of disdain for an answer.

Raymond muttered a barnyard curse. "Now people think I'm a pervert. And don't you dare ask what that is."

"Silly. I already know what it is," Holly said, then frowned. "Although...you have been having those thoughts about me—"

"Don't start," he said.

"Okay," she agreed. She took his hand.

"Let's go have some more fun."

Two DAYS LATER, Raymond admitted he actually did have a little fun in the toy department, although he had been careful to avoid more one-on-one encounters with kids. Once mistaken for a pervert was more than enough.

But Holly with the children had been a joy to see—and unexpected for a figment of his imagination. He could have sworn babies saw her; they seemed to look straight at her. But that must be a part of his imagining her, too. Never would he have thought himself capable of conceiving something with a penchant for children. He didn't care for children, had no affinity with them, certainly. Neither did he imagine she would have such a naive spirit. All that stuff she spouted about hope and courage in one's stockings was utter nonsense, of course. Everyone knew Santa Claus was the present machine—and some kids got left out.

He would have thought a Playmate-style dream would

be geared to serving him. Instead, he'd gotten the hallucination all backward.

She had popped in and out all weekend, nagging him about things. At least she hadn't shown up while he was using the bathroom or bedroom, those areas already seemingly off-limits. Still, every time he thought the dream was over with and he was normal again, she would reappear with ideas or questions or simple enthusiasm for whatever he was doing. She was the most upbeat creature he had ever encountered, in dreams or real life.

He'd better wake up damn soon or he would start believing Holly *was* real. That he couldn't afford to do or he might as well sign up for the funny farm. He might have to, anyway.

Thank God for work, he thought, punching up the first caller on the Monday-morning show.

"I have a sighting," the caller said.

"A sighting!" Raymond grinned as Tommy started the wailing-siren tape used for "Sightings." "Sightings" as a regular feature on the show. When callers spotted celebrities—local, national, sports or Hollywood—around the Philadelphia area, they would call with a "sighting." Raymond loved sightings. They always brought the unexpected and that perked the listening public, which perked the ratings.

"So who did you see?"

"You, Ray." The man's deep voice boomed through Raymond's earphones. "In Strawbridge's department store."

A sick feeling curled in Raymond's stomach. "I was shopping. Big deal. When will you people get it straight that I'm no sighting? I need something good, like what Denzel Washington tipped at the Four Seasons Hotel. Now that's a sighting."

"*You* were buying a lace corset," the caller added, undeterred.

The entire studio hooted in delight, no doubt followed by hundred of thousands of car and home listeners around the Delaware Valley. Karen, his producer, wolf-whistled in her microphone, which discharged in his headphones, breaking his eardrums.

"I did *not* buy a corset," Raymond said.

"Give me more on this," Tommy requested of the caller, while ignoring Raymond's signal to cut the guy off.

"It was a black lace one, strapless and very sexy. It had pink bows down the front." The caller laughed. "Man, it was sweet. So who is she, Ray?"

"Yeah, Ray, who is she?" Tommy and Bob Kroger asked.

"I was Christmas shopping for my mom," Ray yelped in his defense.

"Boy, I say, I say. Don't go down that road," Bob said, in his foghorn-leghorn voice. "Oh, boy, don't go down that road!"

"I didn't buy it for my mom!" Raymond snapped, trying to recover from his disaster and frustrated by the nonsense.

"Then who did you buy it for? We've got to hear this. You owe it to your fans," Tommy said, grinning salaciously.

"Yeah, all two of 'em," Bob added. "Me and Tommy. Folks, we need details. Call in and demand them."

"Why did I ever start this thing?" Raymond muttered. "It isn't even six-thirty in the morning and already I'm in trouble."

"You started it because you thought it was fun to catch people unawares," Holly said, suddenly appearing. She lay prone across a shelf above his communications board. "It's great fun, isn't it?"

"Oh, great, you're back, and you couldn't have timed it better," he said, then realized he was *on* the air and talking to Holly.

"Don't worry, the silent speaker is still in effect." She grinned and lifted a finger. "I could turn it off—"

"Hold that thought. Forever." He then spoke into the microphone. "All right, people. I confess."

"Hot damn!" Bob exclaimed. "A confession. Do we have a sound-bite tape for that?"

"Not yet," Tommy commented.

Bob put in the *Godfather* theme. As it played in the background, he used his Godfather voice. "You have my ear, *Don* Raymond...and my finger...and my nose...."

"The corset was for me," Ray said, while the morning crew erupted in laughter again. "Yes, it's my sad tale of woe. I've been so long without a date that I had to see *something* in a corset."

Holly giggled. "You looked very cute, too."

Raymond chuckled at something Karen said into his headphones. "My producer says don't bother calling for a date because *she* looks better in the corset than I do."

"So would Bob Dole," Bob added.

"Would *I?*" Holly asked, looking down as she ran a finger along the edge of the communications board.

Raymond faltered. She was innocent in many ways, yet he could easily envision her spilling out of the corset bodice and her legs in sheer black stockings just begging to be unhooked from the garters....

Holly flushed a very pretty pink.

"I can think of one person who would look terrific in that corset," Raymond said. "But it wasn't me, folks, so I didn't buy it."

"I still like the idea of you wearing the thing," Holly said. "Maybe your listeners would like to know how you looked in it."

"Wear the corset!" Raymond exclaimed.

"Whoa! Whoa! I don't know where that came from, Ray, but it's a great idea," Tommy said excitedly. "I know! Let's take a vote to see how many want Raymond to model the corset."

"Barf bags will be available for everyone," Bob intoned.

"Sorry," Holly said, grinning unrepentently. "My speaker trigger-finger got itchy."

He glared at her. "You can stick that finger—"

"No, no, no. You are on the air," she said, wagging the finger in question as he finished his sentence with no voice at all.

But the rest of the show deteriorated into a campaign for him to model the corset in some public venue. No matter how much he bleated that this was a sports show, the callers ignored him. So did his staff. The final tally was forty-six to seventeen in favor. That didn't count the nearly hundred faxes that rolled in over the three-and-a-half-hour span. When the show was over, Raymond couldn't escape to his office fast enough. Not that hiding away mattered.

It looked as though he would have to wear a corset one day. Thanks to Holly.

"I thought you were an angel of mercy," he said, after slamming his office door shut.

"Oh, not me," Holly said. She sat on the top of his floor-to-ceiling bookshelves, out of his reach. "I'm an elf. We work in mischievous ways."

"Come down from there," he demanded.

"Nope. I'm not stupid. Here's nice and safe. Raymond,

you poked fun at yourself today. You entertained people and made them laugh. It was wonderful.''

"But not at my expense, dammit! I lost total control of my show today.''

"Pish-tosh. You're making too much out of this. It was a little harmless fun.''

"I have to wear a corset. A corset! And you call it harmless fun?''

"I told you before, you'll look very cute.''

"I'll look— I don't even want to think about it. The phone lines were all tied up. How much fun was that for Karen?''

"She laughed the entire time,'' Holly countered from her perch. "And look at what that indicates about your listening public and your ratings. The latter will be *big*. Trust me.''

"I know the show's supposed to be a look into the boys' locker room, but this was ridiculous.''

Raymond flopped into his desk chair, feeling defeated. The oversize padded head- and armrests did nothing to relieve his bad mood. He eyed his personal troublemaker for the longest time.

"You'll look like a man who can take a joke with good grace,'' she said finally.

"I'll look idiotic.''

"Well, it depends on how sheer the corset is,'' Holly replied.

Raymond's temper broke. "We're not discussing corsets or any other undergarment ever again!''

Her mouth turned down. "Okay.''

Unfortunately, her lips still looked very kissable. All of her looked very kissable. How could something so adorable cause so much trouble?

"Thank you,'' she said.

"That's it!" he yelled, realizing she had read his thoughts.

He jumped up and raced out of his office. Three doors down he found what he was looking for. Or rather, who.

Margorie Champers, semiretired sports psychologist, sat at her desk, clearly working on her segment dialogue. The woman did a half-hour show every day.

"Marge, I'm sorry to disturb you," Raymond began, "but I'm...I'm seeing things."

"Really?"

"I think so." He rubbed his face with his hands. "Hell, I don't know what I'm seeing."

"I've got a few minutes." She motioned him in. "Shut the door behind you."

She gave him twenty. When he left, he felt a whole lot better. And he knew what he had to do. He should have realized it before.

He needed a vacation.

Chapter Three

The place was called Aruba. It was steamy and lush.

Holly didn't like it.

"What are we doing in this god-awful place?" she demanded, popping in on Raymond while he stood in the baggage-claim area of the airport. She pulled her tunic away from her body, the heavy material already clinging to her sweaty skin. "It's like an oven in here."

Raymond groaned. "Margorie said I only needed a rest to get rid of you. I leave my show on three days' notice, dammit, and you're still here!"

"Sleeping on that noisy plane was hardly a rest," Holly said, although his attitude stung. She admitted anybody would have problems adjusting to an elf in his life so her feelings shouldn't be hurt by his rejections. "Margorie said you need a vacation because you haven't had one in years. One nap is hardly going to do it, Raymond." She grinned. "Nothing will, as far as I'm concerned. I'm here until you fill your heart with love and can trust people again. Still, a vacation isn't a bad idea. It'll help you to learn to play more."

"Why can't a man have peace and quiet?"

"Not in the game plan." She fanned her face, not at all impressed with the tropical surroundings. The heat penetrated everywhere, even the air-conditioned terminal. *Palm trees, smalm trees,* she thought, finding it hard to believe it was December. Heck, she'd been in a snow-storm barely a week ago. Raymond planned to stay for four days—a "long weekend," he called it. She called it mini-hell. She shouldn't even be feeling the heat. At least, she thought she shouldn't. Maybe her abilities couldn't beat it. "Couldn't you have picked Aspen for a vacation? It's nice there this time of year and *way* cooler."

Raymond smiled as he grabbed up his bag from the carousel. "Maybe you'll melt and I'll be rid of you that way. Aruba is great. My cousin Michael did a nice write-up about this island in one of his columns. Sounded perfect, especially after your whining. Nice to have met you, Holly, but I understand."

He put on sunglasses and went outside to the cabstand.

Holly grunted and followed him.

Outside, the full force of the temperature difference hit her smack between the eyes. She wilted, the humid heat too unexpected for her system. Even her brain felt slow, sluggish. Raymond got into a taxi. He was leaving without her!

"I'll fix this," she muttered, sending out a message to adjust her clothing.

Her tunic turned into loosely woven cotton and her pants grew light and loose. Her boots became flip-flops. She wrapped her hair up, pulling it off her neck, and se-cured it with an icicle. Estimating its melting rate in the heat, she made a mental note to automatically renew the icicle every minute and a half.

Immediately she felt cooler. "Boy, am I dumb some-times."

She popped into the taxi but Raymond barely flinched. He must have been expecting her. Maybe that was a good sign that he was becoming used to her. She glanced at his profile, liking the sunglasses on him and the short-sleeved shirt. He looked even better without the bulky winter clothes.

"Nice outfit," he commented to her.

"Thanks," she muttered, already feeling less cool—certainly less in control since they'd left for the island. She was making a hash of this assignment. Heck, she couldn't even keep him home. Christmas would be here before she knew it.

"So, you come to our island to get away from that nasty snow?" the cabdriver asked with a beautiful sing-sing accent.

"'Nasty snow'?" Holly sniffed. "He lives in an inferno and he thinks he's got it good? He needs to readjust his reality."

"Nobody's more glad to leave that stuff behind than me," Raymond told the driver. "It's terrible back home in Philly. I'm even considering moving down here. Farther south, certainly."

"Raymond, you can't!" Holly could still feel the day's warmth seeping into her bones, despite her earlier efforts with her clothes. She wouldn't make it if he moved here—or even spent time looking to move here.

The cabdriver laughed. "Everyone says that when they first get to Aruba—especially in the wintertime."

Raymond and the driver talked more about the merits of living on a tropical island. Holly shuddered, thinking they talked blasphemy, but she kept her mouth shut. She doubted she would ever truly adapt to a warmer climate than Philadelphia's. She barely tolerated that. She prayed Raymond found his heart within the next twenty-four hours or she would be dead meat.

The hotel was sybaritic in its amenities. Holly followed

Raymond into the lobby, turning in circles so she could stare at the satiny pink walls and plush, low furniture. Striped draperies met high above her head, the material billowing like a sheik's tent. Large pillows lay scattered everywhere. Everything advertised sensuous-relaxation.

"Wow," Holly said, awed by the effect.

Several floors above, Raymond had a bed-sitter suite. It, too, screamed the lobby themes of harem odyssey with its soft pinks, greens and blues. Holly popped out onto the balcony, drawn by the bright ocean. It looked like blue-green snow, making her homesick for long stretches of nothingness. But the heat began to bother her again. She went inside where it was definitely cooler.

Raymond sat on the oversize bed. He stared off into space. "The show's going down the tubes. I know it. They'll screw it up."

"Well, let's go back," Holly said brightly, thrilled with his return to common sense. "Do you want to call the airlines or should I?"

He glared at her. "*You* are the reason I'm here in the first place."

"Me?"

"Yes, damn you. I have to get rid of you."

"Just find your heart again," she told him, "and I'll be gone."

That was her objective...so why had it hurt when she said it?

"I have a heart. A perfectly fine heart."

"No." She went over to him and touched his chest. "You've lost it, I can tell. Why don't we go home? You can find it there as well as here or anywhere. Maybe better."

He flopped back on the bed. "This is one helluva mess I've gotten myself into."

"The sooner you work on curing it—" Holly began.

He sat up. "Great idea."

"It is?" Holly echoed, not liking his sudden change of attitude.

He rose and went to his suitcase. He took out a bathing suit.

"What are you doing?" she asked.

"I can't beat it, so I'll join it. I'm going to lie out on the beach and let the sun bake into me until my bones melt to Jell-O."

Holly shuddered again. "I think I'll stay here."

Raymond grinned. "See? It's working already."

When he emerged from the bathroom a short time later, Holly gasped. He wore only the bathing suit, and the thing looked far skimpier on him than it did being put into and taken out of a suitcase.

"You can't go out like that," she said.

"I'm not going naked, that's for sure."

"Close enough," she murmured.

He snorted and walked out of the bedroom. Holly watched him go, her gaze disconcertingly drawn to his backside. He had a very nice-looking one, all muscled and strong despite his narrow hips. So were his back and his shoulders. He must take his sports seriously, Holly decided, then flushed at her reaction. Why did she keep noticing his body this way? She was getting worse, too.

The suite door closed behind him as he left. The room grew deathly quiet.

She stood by the sliding-glass doors for a while and looked at the ocean, unwilling to pop in and out of the heat. She wondered if popping were her problem. Maybe the instant appearance didn't give her time to acclimate to the warmer weather. It was a *big* change from her home.

Eventually, she opened the glass doors and ventured out onto the balcony. The too-warm air still hit her full face. She muttered, "So much for that thought."

Down on the beach, she spotted Raymond laying on a chaise longue. He *was* baking in the hot sun.

A female form baked next to him, and it wasn't hers. Worse, the woman reached over and touched Raymond's arm, rubbing it to get his attention. The feminine hand pointed languidly at something on the water. Raymond touched her fingers lightly in what looked like an intimate caress.

Fury slammed into Holly's chest like a freight train. The day turned a dark, ugly gray for one long moment. Holly forgot heat and missions and everything else—except separating Raymond from that…that floozy.

She popped straight off the balcony and right onto Raymond's chest.

"Oooomph!" He grunted, as the breath squished out of his lungs.

"Serves you right!" Holly snapped, but she did get off him. After all, in her anger she had miscalculated her pop. She sourly eyed the woman on the next lounger. The female's features were pretty, she supposed. In a haggish sort of way, of course. And the woman's dark hair looked shaggy hanging around her face like that. Her figure, in certain areas, seemed…inflated.

But her clothes! She wore a top skimpier than that strapless bustier and a bathing-suit bottom that scarcely covered her pelvic area. Holly's face heated in embarrassment at seeing so much of another female exposed.

"What do you think you're doing?" Holly asked Raymond.

"I was doing a whole lot better a moment ago," he said, rubbing his chest. He glanced over at his companion.

"Oh, she can't hear," Holly said, sniffing in disgust.

His attention shifted back to her. "I thought you were staying upstairs."

"I...I wanted to try the air," she replied lamely, then added, "So who is *this?*"

"Marilyn."

"Marilyn?" The name rolled over her tongue a little too slickly to suit Holly. "Where did you find her?"

"Right here. She's an account executive with ABM." Raymond smiled and relaxed back on the chaise. "Now go back upstairs like a good elf before you disturb her."

"She can't hear me." Smiling evilly, Holly leaned over the woman's lounger and shouted, "Marilyn!"

The woman never moved.

"See?"

"You're disturbing me."

"Raymond, would you put some lotion on my back?" Marilyn asked, sitting up.

"Sure." Raymond swung his legs over the chair and took up the small brown bottle between the loungers.

Holly was treated to the disgusting sight of Raymond slowly massaging lotion on Marilyn's back. Her blood boiled at the way the woman stretched and purred under his ministrations. Holly wanted to swat Ray's hands away.

Marilyn lowered her suit straps.

"She's undressing!" Holly exclaimed, shocked at the woman's brazenness. Worse, with the woman sitting up and leaning even more forward, Holly could see the back of Marilyn's suit bottom. It was little more than a spaghetti strap going down the crack of her butt. "My God! She's wearing hardly *anything* down there!"

"Relax. She just needs the lotion on her shoulders in case the straps shift. We have a growing problem with skin cancer from exposure to the sun—"

"Well, tell the bimbo to wear some clothes and she won't have to worry," Holly said. "Look! Look down there. You can see half her...her rump."

Raymond smiled. "Yes, you can."

"Lower, Raymond," Marilyn murmured, moaning a little at his rubbing. "I want to be sure you reach every spot."

"And I suppose you will," Holly muttered, wanting to be ill.

"I'm only helping my fellow man," Raymond said.

Holly's thermostat rose higher than the island's. "You are a despicable, salacious, appalling, miserable, scum-of-the-earth rat!"

She popped back to the suite, so furious she wanted to throw every knickknack off the balcony—along with a few chairs, the sofa, and *everything* that belonged to Raymond.

He was hopeless. She saw that now.

And time was running out.

"WHY DON'T WE HAVE dinner tonight?"

Marilyn's expression was hopeful with just the right amount of eagerness. Raymond couldn't remember her last name, despite having spent the past three hours with her.

Raymond hesitated. He hadn't had a real date in over a year. He wasn't sure he was up to one now. The mad rush to begin this vacation trip and the hours spent in the warmth outside had left him tired and short on sleep. He really needed that more than anything. Most important, he doubted Marilyn was his type. She always talked business. He hated business; that was why he'd gone into radio. Still, what else was he here on the island for?

"Sure," he said, remembering Holly's reaction to the

woman. That outweighed the negatives. "Do we need to make reservations somewhere?"

"I'll take care of them," Marilyn told him. "Just come to my room at eight. It's 435."

She left him at the elevators with a wiggle of her exposed behind. He thought of Holly in her simple tunic and pants. She'd looked modest yet enticing. A thong swimsuit left nothing to the imagination, including a too-skinny butt.

On the other hand, Marilyn had chased Holly away.

Maybe for good.

The thought that he might have already accomplished his goal in a few short hours bothered him. He'd been so mixed up from the moment she'd come into his life that he supposed confusing emotions were inevitable.

He entered the suite cautiously. Not a sound anywhere. Certainly not one from a ticked-off elf. Oh, well, Raymond thought. Holly had been attractive as hell when she'd been jealous of Marilyn.

A wet washrag hit him square in the face.

"I was *not* jealous!" Holly snapped.

Raymond caught the washcloth as it dropped. "Why are you throwing things at me?"

"You need cooling off. You must have heatstroke if you think I was jealous of that...that woman." Holly's blue eyes blazed with anger. Her face was flushed and her icicle had melted dead away, leaving her hair half-hanging down her back.

"I think you're the one with heatstroke," he said, tossing the wet material back at her.

She caught it in midair. "Not hardly. That woman is a harlot!"

Raymond laughed. "Not hardly. She's a normal, *alive,* twentieth-century woman."

"Who wears no clothes."

"She wore what is appropriate for the time and place. She's on vacation, for God's sake!" He looked heavenward. "I'm arguing with my imagination."

"I'm not anyone's imagination!"

"I hope not or else we've got a psychopath on the loose. Me."

"Well, at least you're rid of the woman," Holly said.

"I'm having dinner with her." He braced himself for a hundred washcloths. When they didn't hit him, he added, "Alone."

He shut his eyes, expecting a million ice cubes next. Nothing happened.

Raymond opened his eyes. He was alone.

"Okay," he muttered. He looked everywhere—behind the sofa, in the closets and drawers—just to be sure.

He frowned, again left with that odd feeling of emptiness.

Maybe he needed more than an overdue vacation. Maybe he needed a psychiatrist, full-time.

He managed a nap, jet lag catching up to him. Holly still hadn't reappeared when he awoke. He raised his eyebrows at her absence, then asked himself what the hell he was playing at. He didn't know, that was for sure.

The idea of a dinner date was less appealing than before. The meal would start at the time he usually went to bed. Although he was rested now from the flight, he knew he would be yawning in the woman's face by nine-thirty. The whole notion of making conversation with a total stranger was far more work than he was prepared to give. Worse, he could hardly remember how.

A little voice in his head countermanded him. He was on vacation and what else would he do? Watch TV? He could do that at home, and he didn't. Watching television wasn't as charming without Holly's unbridled enthusiasm.

The thought of Holly sent his head spinning.

He definitely needed a date.

When he arrived at Marilyn's room, he discovered her idea of a first date was different from his. She answered the door, her white dress long and about three steps away from sheer. She wore gold trim, gold jewelry and a cloud of heavy perfume. Raymond knew her elegance was a far cry from his khaki trousers and knit shirt.

He stepped inside. Marilyn closed the door after him.

"I thought we could order room service," she said, smiling at him. "I'm sure you're tired from just getting in today."

Reluctance was Raymond's first response. Somehow he felt trapped at the idea of having dinner in a woman's hotel room. Something nagged at him because she looked ready for the Rainbow Room at the Rockefeller Center rather than hibernating in a hotel room in Aruba.

"Ah... You look so pretty tonight," he said. "It seems a shame to waste it. Besides, I'm fine. I had a nap earlier. Why don't we go downstairs to the hotel dining room? I'm sure we can get a table."

Marilyn paused for a telling moment. Raymond had a feeling that he'd just thrown a wrench into whatever she'd had planned for tonight.

"Are you sure?" she asked, her expression unhappy.

"Very," Raymond said, opening her door.

She got her purse, then walked past him. No sugar or spice here, he thought as her musky perfume overwhelmed his senses. He wondered if any reindeer had given to the cause.

He talked about enjoying his afternoon at the beach with her to cover any awkwardness during the ride on the elevator. He wished Holly would see him, to know that he did have a heart; he was doing his best not to embarrass Marilyn. And Marilyn responded well, visibly relaxing. Maybe he'd misjudged her reaction upstairs. Maybe she'd only been thinking of his well-being in wanting a quiet dinner in her room.

The dining room was jammed with guests, but the maître d' managed to find them a table in the back.

"I guess my theory about this hotel not being too crowded was off," he commented.

She nodded. "Room service probably would have been slow, too."

"True. At least we've got something to look at here," Raymond said, without thinking. At Marilyn's mortified expression, he added, "Tell me more about your job. An account exec at ABM fascinates me."

Something had better fascinate him at the moment, because he'd just made a complete ass of himself.

"I'm so glad you like business," Marilyn said. "Like I told you on the beach, it's my job to open new accounts with corporations and distributors. It's very difficult now because we're competing against ourselves by selling to the distributors who turn around and undercut us with the corporates. It's ludicrous! No wonder we're "downsizing." God, I hate that word. I've had enough of their crap, I can tell you. I'd look around but..."

Marilyn's monologue went on through a good deal of dinner as she complained about the state of her company and the business world in general. Raymond wished Holly were here. At least the conversation wouldn't be boring.

The thought appalled half of him. The other half still kept wishing.

"I think marriage is very important, don't you?" Marilyn said.

The subject came out of left field. Raymond realized that he'd been paying no attention to the conversation transition and how it had been made. Not that it mattered. He knew what he wanted to say. "Not really."

Marilyn pursed her lips. They didn't look nearly as cute as Holly's. "Oh, men always say that, but they don't really mean it."

"We don't?" Raymond echoed.

Marilyn shook her head. "Men need women. It's a misguided notion to think that you don't."

Raymond wondered where the woman was going with this. Not anywhere he wanted to go.

"Of course, you want children someday. I know I do. I'd love to have one now—"

Raymond panicked.

"I don't want to work forever. Who does? I'm sick of the corporate climbing and the backstabbing. But I'm certainly not working when I have kids."

Raymond thought of women callers who were often getting themselves off to work and their kids off to babysitters or school. He had the distinct impression they didn't do it to fulfill some inner need—or for fun. Definitely not fun. "Some women have to work, whether they have children or not."

Marilyn waved a hand. "That's their fault for not marrying well. I suppose that happens, though. Raymond, you can't tell me you're not looking for Ms. Right. Everyone's looking for the perfect partner. That's what all this is about."

Marilyn had a glint in her eye that sent shivers down Raymond's spine. He'd seen it before in women who were desperate for Mr. Right. Money and Mr. Right, in Marilyn's case. No wonder she hadn't found him yet. She no doubt scared them off with her aggressive talk about marriage and children and being taken care of. She scared the hell out of him.

"Good," Holly said, popping up out of nowhere. She leaned against the edge of the table.

"Dammit, Holly!" Raymond snapped.

"Holly? Who's Holly?" Marilyn asked.

Raymond glared at the elf in question who made a show of inspecting her nails.

"Damn, I've got a catch," Holly murmured.

"Do you know someone over there?" Marilyn craned her neck to see.

"No," Raymond said. "I was just clearing my throat."

"'Dammit, Holly' clears your throat?"

"Absolutely."

"If you're done having fun, can we go?" Holly asked, scooping up some peas from his plate with a knife. The tiny round vegetables stood in a row on the blade side, as she added, "Outside this hotel, there isn't a damn thing to do in Aruba. I told you Aspen was better. No offense to Arubians, but snow's my kind of scene."

Raymond didn't answer Holly. He had a feeling the Speaker button was on, and he would look like a nut if he did. This is what he got for wishing she was around. He'd wished her here.

"You are a very confusing guy," Holly commented, flipping the knife and catching the peas with the other side of the blade.

"Raymond, is there some woman here that you know?" Marilyn asked.

"Oh, she's a smart one, all right," Holly said. "She must be a reject from Bimbos Anonymous. What's this world coming to, anyway?"

He would kill her, Raymond thought murderously. Out loud, he said, "No, no. I don't know a *soul* here." He remembered Holly's first reaction to mention of dinner with Marilyn. It gave him an idea.

"No," Holly said, the peas freezing in mid-toss.

"Why don't we go for a walk on the beach after dinner?" Raymond suggested, watching the peas unfreeze and land on the knife blade without mishap.

Marilyn smiled warmly—a little too warmly. "I'd love that."

"Oops. Sorry," Holly said.

Raymond heard a commotion behind him, then a warm wet mass plopped on his head. Pasta slid down his face and chest. Marilyn shrieked in horror.

Holly sighed. "Remember. I told you I was sorry."

"Sir, I'm so sorry," a waiter said, his face bright red as he snatched up napkins and dabbed Raymond's face.

Raymond pushed pasta strands out of his eyes. He licked his lips clean, noting it was an Alfredo sauce, before he said, "It's all right. Just an accident. No harm done."

"No harm done!" Marilyn snapped. "It's horrible."

"I don't know how it happened," the waiter said, between dabbing and apologizing profusely. "I had that tray perfectly balanced, yet the plate just slid right off."

"I know how it happened. I know how it happened," Holly murmured in a singsong voice.

I'll bet you do, Raymond thought, furious with her.

"No bet." She brightened. "Well, that's that for the walk on the beach."

The maître d' and several other waiters hustled up just then. Their apologies and cleanup kept him from answering Holly. Lucky Holly.

He glanced over at Marilyn who still looked appalled and embarrassed. "How about if we go up to my room, and I'll clean up, then we can go for that walk."

"Uh...okay." Marilyn's enthusiasm had clearly slipped several notches.

Raymond reassured the hotel staff that he wasn't angry and accepted their offer of free cleaning and a free meal as amends for the humiliation caused him. He made sure the waiter wouldn't get fired. After all, it was hardly the man's fault.

Holly was nowhere to be seen. In the ensuing commotion, she had vanished. Again.

Good, Raymond thought. This whole nonsense had gone too far. He was perfectly fine the way he was. Not a damn thing wrong with him.

He pulled a strand of pasta from his shoulder. Well, almost nothing.

He would take Marilyn for a stroll on the beach in the moonlight and he would drop her off in her room and walk away afterward. And Holly, if she was watching from whatever perch she was on, could stuff it.

OKAY, RAYMOND THOUGHT as he walked onto the nearly deserted beach the next morning. A few swimmers caught his eye but he dismissed them as far too energetic for this hour of the morning.

He'd been stupid last night. Marilyn's aggressiveness had reached an all-time high under the moonlight. The term *man-eater* had risen in his head like a warning flag, and he had managed to extricate himself before he fell further into the trap he'd set for himself. Marilyn hadn't taken it well.

Holly must be laughing, wherever she was.

He glanced at his watch. The time showed six-forty. He was still on his work schedule. He wished he were at work instead of on vacation. This whole thing had been nonsense. Figment or no figment, he couldn't afford to be away from the station. Radio was even more aggressive than Marilyn. Radio people sometimes came back from vacation only to find their sub now owned the job because the ratings had shot up during their absence.

The way the pasta had come down on his head last night resurrected itself. While the image infuriated him, he knew he hadn't dreamed it. So how could a figment do that to him?

He didn't know.

"Hey, big guy."

Raymond spun around. Holly was on one of the loungers. She wore dark sunglasses, a streak of pink zinc oxide on her nose and the tips of her pointed ears. She also wore a green-and-red polka-dot bikini.

A string bikini.

Raymond gaped at the gorgeous, creamy flesh exposed to his view. The top just covered the mounds of her breasts. And the bottom dipped low on a taut abdomen. Her legs could match a model's and seemed to go on forever—an ironic twist to Holly's lack of height.

"If you can't beat them, join 'em, I always say," Holly said, copying his words from yesterday. "Besides, I was sick of huddling next to the hotel's main air conditioner."

Raising her glass, she toasted him.

She shifted her legs. Raymond's knees went weak. He gasped for breath, feeling as if someone had punched him in the stomach.

"There's something to be said for lying on the beach and baking," Holly commented. She lowered the sunglasses slightly to look over their top edge at him. "You have a funny look on your face. Are you okay?"

"I…" His voice cracked. He cleared his throat and tried again, although the whole world felt tilted upside down. "I thought it was too hot for you here."

"You do have a point. Maybe I'll try one of those thong things Marilyn has. After all, one must dress appropriately for the time and place.... Oh! Oh, that feels different." Holly twisted her body slightly on the lounger, enough to reveal one half of a perfectly rounded derriere. She'd changed the string bikini into a polka-dot thong. "What do you think?"

The world swirled wildly, then Raymond snapped. "That's it! We're going home."

"Surprise, surprise, surprise," Holly murmured to herself.

She relaxed in her chair and set the sunglasses back on her nose.

Chapter Four

"Now, this is more like it," Holly commented, as she followed Raymond out of the house and into the dark night.

Snow still lay in dirty piles along Philadelphia's sidewalks and curbs. The curse of civilization, Holly thought. Even the dim light at four o'clock in the morning couldn't make city snow that had been around too long look better. Oh, well. The air was cold and brisk, which was all she cared about. What a pleasure to change into velvet clothes again.

Raymond unlocked his car and got in the driver's side and shut the door behind him. Holly supposed she shouldn't ask for more at the moment than not being in Aruba. She entered the car, *not* bothering to open the passenger door in the process.

"Man, it's dark out," she commented.

"Of course, it's dark. It's four," Raymond replied, smiling slightly. "The world sleeps."

"All but you."

"Tommy better be up, that's all I have to say. He usually slides in at five fifty-nine, a minute before we go on the air. The bum manages to sound like he's been awake and planning the show for hours."

"What's wrong with that?" Holly asked.

"*I've* been awake and planning the show for hours, that's what," Raymond said, driving them down the deserted street. "You can't run a radio show any other way."

"You can't?"

"No, you can't." He launched into a litany of why one couldn't from the need to glean topical subjects for discussion to what skits would go on at what time and when gags should be aired. Holly grinned to herself. At least the man was talking to her.

They'd arrived home from Aruba yesterday, with Raymond still barely speaking to her over the Marilyn incident. Now, had Marilyn been her fault?

Nope, Holly thought. She wasn't the one who had picked up Marilyn on the beach. She wasn't the one who had taken her out to dinner, either. Okay, she was the one who had dumped the pasta on Raymond's head via the waiter. But he hadn't listened to anything she'd said thus far, so she'd had to do something drastic to get his attention. Pasta had been one way.

The bikini had been another.

The kinky swimsuit had felt scandalous to wear, and even more scandalous when she'd looked into the fire in his eyes. She had no idea what had possessed her to change the bottom of the suit into a thong. Only Raymond could see her, so she felt somewhat comfortable. His gaze, however, had turned blazing hot on her flesh. He hadn't looked at stinky Marilyn like that. Not once.

Even now, Holly knew he looked at her differently. It pleased her no end that he did.

"That's why I take care of the show," Raymond said.

"I see." Holly didn't, really, but she liked hearing him

talk. "It's early to be up, even for cows. It must not give you much of a life."

"That doesn't matter to me."

"It should." No wonder he had lost his heart, she thought. He had eliminated most normal contact with others through his job hours.

A notion niggled at her. She pushed it away. Unfortunately, the notion, which had surfaced since they'd left Aruba, refused to vanish.

Raymond needed a woman.

She had thought that if she got love inside Raymond again, he would regain his heart. Marilyn had given her the key. He'd been interested; Lord knew why, but he had been. That had been the first spark of something she'd seen in him. She had watched television, fascinated by the magic it had; and everyone on it emphasized finding mates. Maybe they hadn't said a man needed a woman straight out, but generally men and women needed to be together. She had the distinct impression that nothing else in life really mattered.

She glanced over at Raymond. He was darkly handsome, especially when a smile played around the corners of his mouth, like now. Why did he have to appeal to her on some primitive level? An old pain, sharp like a dagger's point, ran through her heart. The thought of him having a woman in his life hurt. It shouldn't—not at all—but it did.

Holly set the feeling aside. She had a job to do and she would do it.

In the studio, she eyed the overnight hosts as they finished the last hour of their show. She knew Darlene, the woman host, lived with her partner, Dave, but they weren't married. Maybe Raymond would like Darlene.

She popped over to Raymond, who was in another studio with Karen, his producer.

"Do you like Darlene?" Holly asked.

"Excuse me," Raymond said to Karen.

"Why? Did you do something rude?" Karen asked.

Raymond laughed wryly. "No, I... Never mind." He glanced at Holly. "Why do you want to know?"

"Well, maybe if you liked her, you could love her and get married and find your heart."

"As Bob would say, Don't even go down that road."

"Okay." Holly wasn't crazy about Darlene. The woman was too pretty. Holly surveyed Karen, who was blond and plump. Karen had a husband and two kids. No good.

"Don't even think about Karen," Raymond said.

"I wasn't," Holly muttered, feeling caught out.

To Karen, Raymond said, "We run the skit about the coach and the song about the hockey team as soon as Bob puts them together this morning. *If* Bob ever comes in."

"He'll get here before Tommy," Karen told him.

"There's a blessing."

"Be grateful I like these hours because I get to be home with my kids during most of the day."

"I am grateful," Raymond told her. "You're my guardian angel."

"Sure you don't want me to think about Karen?" Holly asked, after listening to their exchange.

"Damn sure." Karen left and Raymond turned his full attention on Holly. "What the hell is all this about, anyway?"

"Well," Holly began, smiling cheerfully, "I've got to help you find your heart again and I'm thinking that maybe we need a woman to do it. Love and all that mushy stuff. But it works."

He stared at her, his eyes wide, as if he saw an elephant sitting on her head. Finally he said, "I'm fine. How many times do I have to tell you this?"

"Until I feel it," Holly replied.

"God help me."

"Why do you think I'm here? My health?"

He grumbled under his breath.

Bob and Tommy came in, and the studio got really busy at that point as the switchover of hosts neared. Holly didn't bother Raymond again, knowing she had no firm ideas about women. Just a notion.

Now if she were human, Holly thought, she might just have an interest in Raymond herself. His personality was dour, but he had potential.

Holly realized she was trespassing where she had no business doing so. These stray, personal thoughts had to be excised. Raymond needed her help, not her...*interest.*

Halfway through Raymond's show, a caller caught her attention.

"And I'm always having trouble with dates, too," the female voice said. The woman sounded pleasant, and young but not too young.

"People just don't understand, do they?" Raymond said into the microphone. "Dates from hell are out there, folks, and I really attract them."

"I understand," Holly said, leaning over her shelf above the communications board. "Hey! Why not date this woman? You two sound like a match."

"I never date callers," Raymond said as Tommy made several comments about dates in general.

Holly wrinkled her nose. "Now that's stupid."

"No, it's not. Trust me. Obsession, thy name is taking a caller out." To the caller, he said, "Tell me your worst date. If it's a good one, you'll get the WRP Wrap gift pack, a valuable prize of cap, mug and pens that we haven't been able to get rid of by selling them.''

The caller giggled in clear delight. "I'm game. A guy took me to a Mexican restaurant, then had an allergic reaction to the food. His face blew up like a balloon. I spent four hours in the emergency room with him.''

Raymond chuckled. "That's definitely gift-pack bad.''

"His mother didn't like me, either.''

"Now that's really bad," Bob chimed in.

"She weighed three hundred pounds and smelled like those menthol-eucalyptus cough drops all the time.''

"Now *that's* really bad," Tommy said, laughing.

"Cough drops are nothing," Holly said. "She should smell a polar bear on a hot day. Now that's bad!''

"See the pitfalls to dating," Raymond said to Holly. "As four famous guys said, 'Let it be.' I'll find my own dates when I want one, okay?''

"I'll do better than find girls with three-hundred-pound moms who smell like cough drops.''

"Yeah, but which way?''

Holly stuck her tongue out at him.

Three cheerleaders came into the studio during the last hour of the show, to plug the upcoming football game— a critical one, evidently, in order for the team to make the play-offs. The three were beautiful brunettes with perfect bodies and perfect hair. Tommy, Bob and Raymond practically drooled all over the women in their zeal to make them comfortable during the interview.

"I'll bet *their* moms don't smell like cough drops," Holly muttered in disgust. She didn't like any of these women. The earlier female caller had had an anonymity about her. Not these three. But she would make the effort. For Raymond. "What about one of these women?''

Raymond shook his head, while saying into the microphone, "I wish I could describe for the people how lovely you three look today. You've got this sweater thing going…. Oh, boy, do you have this sweater thing going!"

"I take it that's a yes," Holly said, trying not to bristle at the way Raymond stared at the three cheerleaders.

"And the jeans. I like jeans," Raymond said, gazing and smiling at all three women equally.

At least he was democratic about it, Holly thought.

"I think they outlawed harems in this country," she said. "You'll have to pick just one."

"I couldn't possibly," Raymond told her and went right back to his staring and fawning.

"Then they're out," Holly said, relieved. If he couldn't choose, he couldn't choose. Who was she to argue with him?

But something had to be done with him. And now.

RAYMOND PICKED UP the square of paper that had suddenly appeared on his dinner plate. He'd nearly dumped his sesame noodles and spinach onto it.

"I almost ruined my dinner," he complained to the air, then began to read the paper. "Hey! This is an ad for The Doll House."

"Right," Holly said, popping into the chair across the table from his. "It says 'Girls Galore.' I figured you could find *one* there, at least."

"Ah…" Raymond chuckled, wondering how to explain The Doll House to her. "I'm sure there are nice women there. But Holly, it's a… Well, it's a naked-dancer place, among other things."

"Naked dancers!" Holly snatched the ad out of his hand. She read through it. "It only says about lots of girls. Look, this Elise has 42DD. You like them…inflated up top, like that Marilyn person—"

"I do not!" he said hotly, astonished by her conclusion about his taste in women.

She merely raised her eyebrows.

"Look," he began, wondering how he got the chore of educating Holly on the niceties of red-light districts. He tapped the paper. "These are the kind of women you don't take home to your mom."

"Not even if she smells like cough drops?"

"Not even. Unless you're a braver man than I."

Holly looked at the ad, then back at his face. "You're very cruel, Raymond."

"Me!" He gaped at her, amazed by her pronouncement. "How am I cruel?"

"You've judged these women and condemned them for something that maybe they can't help. You don't know what brought them to dance naked in these places. They may have no other resources to live on." Holly shook her finger at him. "You should help them, Raymond."

"Me!" He was rapidly becoming an echo chamber with Holly. He could too easily envision the disaster a public campaign to "help" exotic dancers would create. Shuddering, he decided that since everything else usually failed with Holly, he would try reason. "Holly, these women do make a lot of money at this—enough to educate themselves into another career, okay?"

"Oh."

"There are also state and private help agencies for people to get a second start in life. I'm sure they help a lot of naked dancers already."

"Oh."

"I'm only one person, and I don't have the resources for the job."

"Oh."

"So, let's forget exotic dancers."

"But what about a girl to take home to Mom?"

"No, thanks."

Holly glared at him, the determination in her eyes frightening. "You need to find your heart again, and you need love to find it. So you will take someone home to Mom. *Now.*"

"I don't *need* anything!" Raymond said, groaning that she'd missed nearly the whole point. "You have the wrong person, Holly."

"No, I don't. I'm attuned to you."

He waved a hand in disgust and went into his bedroom.

"What about dinner?" Holly called after him.

He knew what he wanted to tell her, but she would only get more ticked. Then so would he. It wasn't worth the effort. "You eat it."

"But I don't need to eat! You do."

He could tell her what else to do with the food, but she would probably wash his mouth out with soap.

Once he was in his bedroom, his stomach growled but he ignored it, not unwilling to go out there and discover what else Holly wanted him to save. He wished he knew what the hell was going on with the rest of his insides, to have brought about this elf. If only he could turn it off. But she looked to be a permanent fixture.

He glanced at the clock. Seeing it was after seven in the evening, he decided to go to bed now. What the heck, he was usually in bed by eight anyway in order to get up at three-thirty in the morning. Doing morning drive-time meant very early hours and a completely different schedule for general life than most others in the world. The odd hours didn't bother him. Neither did the loneliness. He preferred it, in fact, to the manipulations of a relationship. He didn't need a woman—or a family, either. Why Holly was on this track now, he didn't know. Just to bedevil him, probably—and dump another load of pasta on his head like she had after the last "date."

He stripped down to his boxers, just in case Holly "visited." Even though he preferred total nudity, he didn't want any further mishaps like on the night Holly arrived. Leaving the clothes in a pile next to his bed, he made a mental promise to take care of them in the morning. *Early* in the morning, he thought wryly.

"You have to eat," Holly said, suddenly popping in with a plate of food.

Raymond yelped, startled by her appearance. "Stop doing that!"

She offered the dinner plate loaded with the noodles and spinach. "You have to eat."

"Don't you ever come through a door properly and knock first?"

"Too dull. Eat."

He ignored her command. "Whatever happened to the privacy thing you've been giving me in the bedroom and bathroom?"

"This is an emergency. You can't go without your dinner."

"I'll go without whatever I want, dammit. Now get out of my bedroom and out of my life. You *don't* exist!"

Holly pursed her lips, clearly annoyed with him. "I thought we were long past that nonsense."

Raymond gave up. He flopped down on the bed. "Just leave it on the dresser."

He stared at the ceiling. Eventually, the click of china against wood reached his ears. Holly's face appeared above his own. Despite his frustration with her, he was acutely aware of a body hovering over his. The scent of vanilla and spice filled his nostrils. His blood actually pumped harder at her closeness. She seemed so incredibly real.

"Are you all right?" she asked, concern in her voice. "You've been acting funny this evening."

"An understatement," he muttered. "I dream up some elf I can't get rid of—not even with a vacation—and now she's trying to match me up with naked dancers. Freud would have a ball with my head."

"You didn't dream me up. I'm here to help you find your heart and if that's with a naked dancer, then it is. Now be a good boy and eat your dinner. It's getting cold."

Her treating him like a child was too much for Raymond's overloaded brain circuits. He reached up and pulled her mouth to his, kissing her with all the pent-up anger he felt.

She moaned in protest, bracing her hands on his bare chest. Her hands were soft, yet her fingers had a feminine strength. Raymond refused to be deterred. He would show her he was no child to toy with.

Her lips were soft and sweet-tasting, exactly like caramel candy. He coaxed at them, wanting to persuade her to relax and kiss him back. Her scent grew stronger, sending his blood pounding through him. She was so different from any woman he'd ever met.

Holly's mouth and body did relax then, and she kissed him back; tentatively at first, then with growing fervor. He could taste the innocence in her—and the underlying curiosity that slowly grew to passion. Her hands reached up and touched his cheeks, her fingers delicate on his cheekbones.

He pressed her lips open wider, wanting to taste her inner sweetness. She didn't meet his tongue with her own; simply let him explore her mouth. He finally touched her tongue, and again she answered shyly, as if she didn't know how to kiss a man intimately.

He mated their tongues, swirling them together in a challenge. She caught on to the movement and met him with an enthusiasm that left him breathless. He dipped his hands as the kiss took him beyond reason. He found the curve of her waist and the mound of her derriere. He kneaded her flesh with his fingers. She had to be real. She had to be. He could never have dreamed up a woman who tasted and touched as uniquely as Holly did. His own desire flaring, he pressed her hips intimately to his in a perfect fit....

Holly *poofed* out of existence.

Raymond reached out desperately, only to kiss and clutch air. His body deflated abruptly. He dropped his arms to his sides.

"Damn you," he cursed, not sure whether he meant himself or Holly. Both, he admitted. Him for dreaming her up and her for not finishing the job he'd started.

But she had felt so real; as real as any woman, but so much better.

Raymond had trouble sleeping after that, the kiss playing over and over in his mind. He'd had no clue she could do anything like that. She'd felt like...like a gift, a wondrous, magnificent gift. Raymond shook himself mentally, but the image, the feel of her just wouldn't leave his brain.

THREE-THIRTY CAME TOO early. When he sleepily staggered out to the kitchen to make coffee, Raymond discovered his coffeemaker buried in papers. He flipped on more light to supplement the small fluorescent one over the sink. Half his countertop was littered with clippings.

"What the hell is this?" he asked, picking up several. They were all ads for women.

He looked at some more and even more. All of the paper pieces were ads in some fashion for dates. Some were for nightclubs as meeting places, some were for organizations that arranged dates, some were dating services. Others were personal ads, but all were for ways to meet women.

"Holly!" he shouted.

"Shh!" she shushed him, as she popped in. "You'll wake the world."

"To hell with that! What's all this?"

Her face turned rosy. "Well, I kind of thought...after last night...you need help, Raymond."

He glared at her. "I don't kiss that bad."

"Oh, no, no. You... Well, you seemed to really need a woman, human closeness, real bad, so I thought we ought to move forward—"

He flung the papers in the air. "Stop this! Stop this now! I command you."

She hooted with laughter. "Oh, that's good. That's really good."

He stomped out of the kitchen, saying, "I'm getting my shower and getting dressed and getting the hell out of here. Don't even think of popping in on me."

"I promise I won't."

He expected her usual sarcasm, but her tone was almost meek. Her backing down surprised him. He turned and looked at her closely, seeing their kiss in her wide, blue eyes. She looked frightened by it. Raymond knew how she felt. Whatever was happening to him, kissing figments of his imagination shouldn't be a part of it, no matter how real the figment felt.

He showered and dressed without interruption. At the station, the show went well, the craziness produced by Bob and arising spontaneously out of the callers made it an easy morning. He tolerated the occasional questions about when he would wear the corset. The constantly flashing telephone board told him they had hit a ratings well once again, enabling them to dip in and bring up more of the numbers that sponsors just loved.

He admitted he felt very good going into a new sponsor's meeting after a show with that kind of response. He also felt that maybe he had a better handle on his split personality of talking to others and talking to Holly at the same time. She had popped in a time or two this morning, more subdued but still on the "Let's find Raymond a woman" horse. Since she obviously hadn't gone away, he supposed he would have to cope for the moment. Since no one seemed to notice his "Holly asides," he was okay. At least he coped better now than when she'd first popped into his life. A *very* little better, but better.

Their newest sponsor was Delaware Valley Autos, a regional car dealership with five different locations in WRP's listening area. The president of the dealership was a big, beefy man in his sixties. The dealership's advertising director was a woman in her late twenties. Kathryn Stempel wore a black suit that clung to her slender form. She smiled vivaciously at Raymond as he shook her hand. He insisted on meeting all the show's sponsors. He wanted to feel comfortable about a sponsor's reliability before their product was hawked on the air.

"We're happy to be working with you," Kathryn said.

"So are we," Raymond told her, noting she was attractive in a business sort of way. Her perfume was heavier than he liked, but not bad.

"Let's all take a seat and get to the heart of the matter." Charlie Harper, the station manager, smiled, his white teeth gleaming against his dark features. Charlie obviously loved the Gordon Gecko *Wall Street* look and wore suspenders with flare.

Mike Roucher, the program manager, his girth far exceeding the car dealer's, just smiled. WRP's advertising head was also on hand, smiling like a Cheshire Cat. He was clearly pleased to have landed such a big account.

"What we would like is an exclusivity with Raymond," Kathryn said, pulling no punches. "We think he's the biggest personality on Philadelphia radio with the market we're targeting."

"We have a problem then," Raymond said, although he was flattered by her assessment of him. "We're happy to have any general advertising on our show, but I've been the personal spokesperson for Kelborn Motors, your competition, for five years."

"We know that, and we're prepared to pay handsomely to have you as our spokesman instead," the dealer said.

Kathryn added, "We think we have a package that you'll like. We'll give you two cars for your own use—a top-of-the-line model and a four-wheel-drive vehicle. We want you to like our cars. We'll also give you twenty-five percent above your usual fee as a spokesman, as well as double the standard royalty for the ads, and a bonus for a percentage of the increased profits we feel our ads with you on WRP will bring."

"Wow." Raymond admitted he was more than impressed.

"We want to use your face on all our print and billboard ads, too," Kathryn added, her smile growing warmer, more intimate. "There may even be some television ads with you. All our research says you're hot right now."

Raymond realized that in order to have all she offered, he would have to drop his position as WRP spokesman for Kelborn Motors. He couldn't tell people he thought one dealer was the best in the business, then tell them the same thing again about another dealer. People wanted to believe that a spokesperson used a product or service because it was the very best.

But Kelborn Motors had been with him from the beginning of his career here at WRP. He liked Marv Gutman, the owner of Kelborn, but he knew Marv would never give him all this. Kelborn just wasn't that big.

"I've been with Kelborn a long time," he said. "I'm still under contract with them."

"The contract's up next month," his station manager reminded him.

"We aren't asking you to break the contract," Kathryn said. "We're asking you to give us consideration when that contract ends because we think you deserve the best." She grinned. "And that's us."

Everyone chuckled, including Raymond. He couldn't help it. The woman was persuasive. "You're very good."

"That's why I hired her," the dealer said, patting Kathryn's arm. "She's a real go-getter. She's followed up on all the demographics on this and put together this deal herself. She's made me a lot of money over the last two years, so I know she's not steering me, or you, wrong on this."

"Has anyone talked to Kelborn?" Raymond asked.

The advertising director replied, "I have, Ray. Right before the meeting I called Marv. He doubts he could match this offer."

Charlie, the station manager, snorted with disdain. "Marv's been getting a bargain with Raymond for years and he knows it. Change is good, Ray. Real good."

"Not necessarily," Holly said, popping in with her usual bad timing.

Raymond didn't know what to think about this offer. It tempted him with all its perks, especially the television commercials. He'd been toying with attempting a crossover into TV, but the right opportunity hadn't come along yet. Maybe it would if the commercials were successful.

"I don't know," Holly said, sounding just like the little voice inside himself. "How fair are you being to your old sponsor?"

"As fair as he's being with me," Raymond said to her. "This is business, Holly, not an affair of the heart."

Holly harrumphed indignantly.

To the group, Raymond said, "Let me talk to Marv before I make a decision. I owe him that much."

Everyone protested—except Kathryn. She broke through the deep, male voices with her low, feminine one. "I think Raymond's absolutely right in talking with his current sponsor. And I think even more strongly that Raymond's our choice for spokesman. We want the kind of integrity he has, to project itself to our customers."

Raymond smiled at her, really pleased with what she'd said about him. And Holly had thought he had no heart.

"I only said that you'd lost it," his personal elf muttered.

Raymond excused himself to call Marv, who was none too happy.

"I thought we were a team," Marv said.

"We have been." Raymond felt badly at hearing the disappointment in Marv's voice. "This is a pretty big deal they're offering. I can't deny that I'm interested. But I don't want to hurt you, Marv. We have a great relationship, and your support has meant a lot to me."

"I have one showroom, Ray. I can't compete with the new sponsor, even if I do sell BMWs. This is going to hurt me, Ray. A lot."

"Any of the other hosts would be glad to take my place," Raymond said. "Mark on the afternoon drive would be perfect for you."

"I'd just be bumping off his current car sponsor. It's a vicious business, but I won't go down that road." Marv sighed. "I knew this day was coming. This is a good opportunity for you. Real good. I can see that, much as I don't want to. I've been glad to have you as my spokesman for as long as I have, but I'll release your option."

"Thank you, Marv." Something inside Raymond stung as he said goodbye to his sponsor, knowing he was severing the relationship.

"He was a gentleman," Holly said.

"The best."

"I'd tell you not to leave him, but it's a moot point now. He's right. This is a good opportunity for you." She sighed. "I'm taking a page from a gentleman. So is Kathryn. She's nice. I think you should have dinner with her."

Raymond waved a hand. "No more, Holly, okay?"

He went into the other office and announced his decision to join the new team. Everyone cheered, shook hands and clapped him on the back. They took him out to an impromptu celebration lunch. Kathryn let the men talk, but she was hardly in the back seat.

Raymond assessed her, from Holly's viewpoint. Kathryn was nice. She was attractive and certainly less aggressive than Marilyn—but appearances could be deceiving. Still, Holly had urged him to ask her out, given her blessing, really. Maybe he should ask, if just to stop Holly's latest bent toward getting him a woman.

"It would."

He didn't have to look around to know who whispered in his ear. He managed to be alone with Kathryn as lunch broke up.

"Would you like to have dinner with me?" Raymond asked. "No business."

Kathryn paused for a moment, clearly surprised by his invitation. Then she smiled. "I'd love to."

Raymond thought he heard a funny noise, but he dismissed it.

He had a date.

Chapter Five

"Your tie's crooked."

Holly watched as Raymond adjusted his tie. She wasn't satisfied. "It's still not right."

Raymond made a face. "It's fine."

"I think it's the wrong tie altogether."

"It's fine."

"I'll just get you a new one." She headed for his closet.

"To hell with it."

Holly turned around to find Raymond yanking the tie over his head. He flung it on the bedroom floor.

"Now that's a pretty sight," Holly commented, hands on hips.

"Good, because that's the way I'm going." Raymond buttoned his collar, then shook a finger in her face. "One word out of you and I don't go at all!"

"You're the one who asked her out, not me, bub."

Raymond's eyes bulged. He looked ready to explode. His hand sliced the air, as if he were emphasizing something he was saying—only he wasn't saying anything, clearly too angry to do so. A moment later, he turned and walked out of the town house, slamming the door behind him.

"He's definitely on the 'naughty' list," Holly muttered.

She decided he had to be the most difficult man on earth, despite all the rest of the males being pretty much sight unseen by her. No one else but Raymond could be so resistant to a little help. She just wanted his tie to look nice, for criminy's sake. He also hadn't taken her advice about his suit and cologne. She doubted he looked his best, as he should for...

Holly scowled, not liking to think of Kathryn. She didn't like to think of the way Raymond had dropped his old sponsor in favor of the new, either. Kathryn was tied to that—reason alone for disliking the woman.

But Holly knew her dislike was more than objective. She just didn't like the thought of Raymond with a woman. She could still feel that kiss of his and the way it had shocked her down to her toes. She didn't want Raymond kissing another woman that same way.

What was her problem? She was *supposed* to get him to want love, home and hearth, goodwill to men and all that crap.

Holly clamped her hand over her mouth as if she'd uttered, rather than thought, the "crap" blasphemy. She should never have such negativity about her mission with Raymond. This man-woman business was really getting to her.

Holly straightened, squaring her shoulders. She tugged down her red velvet tunic. She was a professional. She would perform her job with an objective and cheerful heart. Ray was off into the world, taking the first step to finding *his* heart.

She wandered around the town house, having nothing to do. Finally, she settled on watching television. Not able to find anything that interested her, despite flicking the remote through all one hundred and eighty channels, Holly finally tossed the clicker onto the coffee table and sighed. She wondered why it was a coffee table when it wasn't made from coffee.

She wondered how Raymond was doing so far.

Popping in seemed appropriate, so she did, pleased that her abilities to focus on him were growing. Raymond and Kathryn sat at a small, secluded table at the Four Seasons Hotel. The restaurant was dimly lit. A string quartet played a lovely piece by Schubert, enhancing the generally intimate ambience.

"Boy, they must have missed paying last month's lighting bill," Holly said, of the darkened atmosphere. "How the heck can you read the menu?"

"I love clams casino," Kathryn said, perusing her menu without any trouble. "I probably shouldn't admit this, but I love clams and oysters raw."

"Yuck!" Holly made a face at the disgusting suggestion. She'd heard the news about the dangers of raw seafood. What was this woman—crazy?

Raymond ignored her, saying to Kathryn, "You're admitting it to the right person. I love them, too."

Kathryn smiled. "With hot sauce?"

"Hot Sauce! Can I barf now?"

Raymond glanced at Holly, then said, "Is there any other way to eat them?"

"Let someone else do it?" Holly suggested, glancing at the tray a passing waiter held. "Is that scampi? Now shrimp would be better, I'm sure—"

Kathryn laughed, interrupting Holly's monologue. "I know a little bar that has the best raw clams. Big cherrystones, but tender inside."

Raymond smiled at her. "Sounds great. How about that for an after-dinner snack?"

"How about that for an after-dinner snack?" Holly

mimicked in a nasal tone. "Oh, that's suave. Be still my heart."

"Shh!" Raymond hissed, finally acknowledging her.

"About damn time," Holly said. "So how's it going? Hey! You actually look good."

He did, actually. Somehow, the completely buttoned white silk shirt worked well with the black, double-breasted suit. He fit right in with the elegantly dressed men in the expensive restaurant.

But Kathryn...

"Couldn't she find a better dress?" Holly asked, frowning. "She's wearing a purple nightgown. And why does she have all that black around her eyes? Raymond, you didn't punch her, did you?"

"No, I didn't punch her," he snapped.

"Punch who?" Kathryn asked, frowning in confusion.

Raymond looked at Holly.

"Okay, okay. I'll be good." She waved her hand.

"Go home," Raymond said. "I'm not playing around with you tonight."

"The duck's very good here," Kathryn said. "So's the veal."

"I'm not playing around, Raymond," Holly told him, while shuddering at the woman's suggestions. The poor little duck and calf. "I just wanted to see how the dinner's going. Not well, obviously. Look at what she wants to order!"

"It's going fine, so you can get going."

"Raymond, what are you having?" Kathryn asked.

"Not duck and veal," Holly announced.

"Goat," he said.

"But there's no goat on the menu," Kathryn and Holly said at the same time.

Raymond looked heavenward for help.

"I keep telling you, help's here." Holly pointed to Kathryn. "Tell her to have the veal, if she must. I heard that duck's too fatty."

"You tell her."

"I can't. You know that."

"I only know you're making me crazy."

"Oh, you're fine."

"I won't be, if you don't go away. I'm schizophrenic."

"Poppycock. You're Raymond."

Raymond folded his menu closed and faced Holly fully. "Look. I'm having a nice conversation with a lovely lady about mutual interests, all of which *you* want."

"You're having a merry-go-round about food," Holly said. "Which would be to anyone's mutual interests. Except mine. I don't eat."

"I think I'll have the duck. Or maybe the chicken Marsala," Kathryn said.

Holly smiled triumphantly. "Big mistake on her part, but my case in point."

Kathryn set her menu down. "I feel like that *I Love Lucy* episode where Lucy keeps changing her order and driving the waiter nuts. You know what? I'm going to have the clams casino, since all this talk of them has given me a craving. And the duck. That's my story and I'm sticking to it."

Raymond laughed. "Duck sounds good to me, too."

"Too fatty. *Way* to fatty. You really need to watch your cholesterol levels," Holly warned.

"I wonder if Joan of Arc felt like this when she was hearing voices in her head," Raymond commented, eyeing her sourly.

"No," Holly said, thinking back. "She just heard them. She never thought about it. Maybe you shouldn't, either."

"They burned Joan at the stake."

"Good point." Holly grinned at him.

He didn't smile back. Instead he told the waiter, who had arrived to take their order, "Two clams casino and two duck."

"You'll be sorry on your next doctor visit," Holly said.

"Maybe I should have the roast beef," Kathryn mused after the waiter left, then laughed with Raymond.

Holly disliked the inside joke between them. "Oh, please!"

"Dammit! Go home now!"

"All right, all right. I'm going." Holly popped out.

She popped inside the same four, deadly silent walls of the town house. Raymond's attitude annoyed her. Honestly, she was only trying to ensure that this dinner was a success.

Kathryn was a terrible choice, Holly admitted ruefully, for Raymond's partner. The woman didn't even wear the right clothes for a December evening. Kathryn's crepe dress had thin spaghetti straps to hold it up, leaving her shoulders and half her chest bare. She would be covered in goose bumps within the hour. A khaki suit and turtleneck sweater would have done the woman so much better. Holly admitted, with great hindsight, that she should have gone to Kathryn's house and dressed *her*. Too bad the woman couldn't see an elf and never would.

A thought occurred to Holly. She popped back into the restaurant. What she found shocked her. "My God! Doesn't the woman have any manners? She's slurping that awful stuff right from the shell!"

"What the hell are you doing back here?" Raymond demanded, clearly furious about the interruption. "I told you to go home."

"Well, I'm just checking on things. I'm glad I did. The woman doesn't have a clue to what a fork is."

Raymond sighed. "That's how you're supposed to eat oysters."

Holly ignored his comment. "I thought she was having clams casino and the duck."

He smiled. "She changed her mind."

Holly eyed him sourly, disliking that his smile looked a little too dreamy and stupid for a grown man. "Okay, so we know now she's a ditz. Let's hurry up the dinner and move on to a more suitable woman for you."

"I think it's charming of her to eat raw seafood on a first date. Gutsy, too. She's not intimidated into refined manners."

Holly hated that remark intensely. She knew this dinner was her idea, but did he have to enjoy himself so much? "Let's hope she's not all gutsy over you."

Kathryn, having no idea she was under discussion, patted her mouth with her napkin. "These are so sweet. I know I shouldn't have gotten them, especially after saying I would stick to my order. You must think I'm awful."

Raymond raised his own raw oyster and swallowed it. Holly winced, especially at his changing his order, too.

"I was just thinking that you were charming and gutsy to order them on a first date," he said.

"As long as I'm not gutsy all over you, that's okay."

Raymond's laughter rang out across the quiet restaurant. Holly wanted to crawl into a hole and die. The woman said nearly the same thing she had!

Holly realized she *could* crawl into a hole, magically speaking, and popped back into the town house.

"Damn. Damn! *Damn!*" she shouted in total disgust with Raymond, Kathryn and the assignment, but mostly with herself.

Couldn't Raymond see that Kathryn was...what? Holly thought for a moment. Beyond dressing badly and inad-

vertently repeating the words of a wise and gentle elf—
namely Holly—Holly couldn't think of any disparaging
words for Kathryn. *Charming* and *gutsy* were hardly ac-
curate, let alone significant.

Then Holly smiled. Of course she had nothing to say
about Kathryn. How could she when the woman was a
blah? One had to *have* a personality in order to be defined.
Kathryn had nothing other than poor taste in clothes and
food. That was the problem. And if she had poor taste in
such essentials as clothes and food, then the poor creature
had no hope.

Holly popped back into the restaurant.

Raymond's fork clattered to his plate at this new interruption. Holly covered it up so the man wouldn't be more
embarrassed. He had enough in dealing with Kathryn.

"So there I was," Kathryn was saying, "with three
hulking offensive linemen and two skittish burros in the
back alley of a Houston restaurant, in one-hundred-degree
weather, to shoot a commercial for a car-wash chain. I
decided then and there that I might be better off thinking
up the deals, rather than carrying out the aftermath. At
least I'd be out of the hot Texas sun."

Raymond chuckled, having recovered from Holly's latest appearance. "I hope we're not doing burros for my
spots."

"Oh, brother," Holly muttered.

Kathryn grinned. "You're safe enough. But I do think
you'd be great on television."

"Really?" Raymond toyed with his wineglass.

"Oh, *brother*," Holly said louder.

"*I'm* having a date here," he said out of the side of
his mouth to her.

"So have one. By the way, her hair's all falling out of
her bun or whatever you call that style on the back of her

head. All those curling tendrils look annoying as hell. Should I pin them up for her?''

"God, no. It's supposed to be that way.''

"Too bad.''

"That's enough of business,'' Kathryn said. She propped her elbow on the table and her chin in her hand. "We can talk that anytime. I'd rather hear about how you got started in radio, Raymond.''

"I'd rather hear about the clams and oysters again,'' Holly commented.

"I subbed for a buddy at my college radio station and liked it,'' he replied to Kathryn, then turned to Holly. "*Please* go away.''

The desperate tone hurt. Holly had never felt more like an unwanted intruder than at that moment. She had only been trying to help him. He didn't have to act as if she were the latest invasion of the Huns, for goodness' sake. Rather than just pop out, she had an overwhelming urge to teach him a lesson he would never forget.

She leaned over the table and planted her lips firmly against his. She could taste the salt of the seafood and the fruitiness of the wine on his mouth. His lips were firm and yet oddly soft. Twin scents of male and cologne filled her nostrils and swirled through her mind.

She pressed her mouth more urgently to his, guided by pure instinct to express what was inside her. Raymond responded, kissing her with a rising passion that sent excitement coursing through her veins. Never had she felt more alive. Never.

She eased away from him. "Good night, Raymond.''

She smiled and popped out.

"ARE YOU SURE YOU'RE all right?''

Raymond groaned at Kathryn's puzzled expression. He

was far from all right. What man could be all right after
a knock-your-socks-off kiss from an elf?

"I'm fine," he lied, knowing he could hardly tell Kathryn differently. He couldn't apologize, either, for his distracted air ever since Holly had kissed him. What could
he say? "I was kissed by an elf, so you'll have to excuse
me?" Hardly believable. He only wished it was. Somehow Holly had managed to thoroughly ruin his date with
that one kiss rather than all her other interruptions.

He walked his dinner date up to her front door. He
kissed her perfunctorily on the cheek and declined her
offer of coffee, knowing it signaled lack of further interest
on his part. He wanted to have more, but Kathryn was
only a nice woman. He felt nothing toward her beyond
that, and it would be a lie to try—no matter what Holly
would say.

She had better say nothing after that kiss, except answer
why she had done it, he thought. He had a lot of questions
about why. A lot.

Holly, however, was not to be found when he returned
to the town house.

"Holly!" he shouted, determined to have this out with
her now.

She didn't pop in.

"Holly!"

He waited and called and waited and called, growing
more furious with each passing minute. Holly did not
make an appearance.

He stomped off to bed, knowing she had conveniently
disappeared before. He must be nuts to be this angry with
an elf who couldn't exist. Not even if little children could
see her—provided they could. He could *imagine* that they
had seen her. Still, he did leave his boxers on for

bed...and he burned all night over that tender-yet-scorching kiss.

He slept in, it being Sunday and he had no show that day. He finally got up at nine, very late for him, and went out to make coffee.

Holly sat on the kitchen counter, legs crossed as she read the morning paper. Without looking up, she said, "You snore."

"I do not," he began hotly, then realized they had more important things to discuss. "Where the hell were you last night?"

"Where you wanted me to be. Out of pocket. So, did you have sex?"

Raymond gaped at her, shocked by the question. He shook himself. "Dammit! I called you and you never did your little pop thing."

She folded the paper and looked up. "Why did you call? Did you need help with sex?"

"No, I didn't need help—"

"Then your sex went okay."

"I didn't have sex—"

"Oh-h-h." She drew out the word, then grinned. "Well, my help would have been useless, anyway. I'm a virgin."

Raymond stared at her, totally astonished and discombobulated. He realized she would lead him in all different directions if she continued to control the conversation. But a virgin!

No, he thought, he must stick to the point. "You ruined the date."

"Me! You and Kathryn were happily chatting away every time I popped in."

"Your interruptions ruined it."

"Impossible. She couldn't see or hear me. Nobody

could. And I covered you up. Okay, once I slipped. But that couldn't ruin anything and you know it.''

He slashed the air with his hand. ''*I* could hear and see you. That was the problem. How could I concentrate on getting to know Kathryn better when you're whining in my ear every few minutes?''

Holly jumped down from the counter and straightened indignantly. ''I *never* whine.''

''You always whine.''

''Oh, pish-tosh. I could not have ruined your date.''

He glared at her and brought out the heavy-argument guns. ''What about that kiss? What the hell were you doing with that?''

A funny expression stole over her face. Raymond couldn't define it. She glanced away from him, then said, ''I was just being polite.''

''You kissed me like you were starved for love and you call that polite? I don't think so.''

''I am not starved for anything! What utter nonsense.''

''I don't think so,'' he repeated.

''Well, you sound like that kiss really bothered you,'' Holly retaliated with her own argument guns.

''Only as a disruption,'' he replied, reminding himself to speak nonchalantly.

''Liar,'' she said softly.

''I'm no liar.''

''Shall I quote your thoughts word for word?''

''Don't bother.''

''Okay. Since we've established that my interruption and my kiss and your not having sex didn't ruin the date, what did?'' She grinned. ''I've been watching *L.A. Law* reruns.''

''God help me.'' He shrugged. ''Well, it doesn't matter,

anyway. Kathryn was nice, but she's not... Let's just say there's no spark.''

"Oh.''

He went over to the coffeemaker and started a pot of coffee. He needed it, he thought, feeling drained from talking with Holly. He felt like something momentous had happened here, only he had no clue what. Better not to think about it, or Holly would know.

"True.'' She hopped back up on the counter next to the coffeemaker and tucked her hair behind her pointed ear. "What's on today's agenda? There are a bunch of Christmas sales and you haven't been shopping for anyone other than your mother. Which I rightly coerced you into, I might add.''

He looked her straight in the eye. "And that's all the coercing you're doing. I don't give Christmas gifts.''

"Raymond—''

"I don't give gifts. I give my staff bonuses and dinner certificates for the holidays, okay? I'm not changing that, Holly. Don't even try.''

"What about the rest of your family? Your father—''

"I never see him. I don't want to.''

"But why?''

Raymond looked at the coffee dripping into the glass carafe. "Because he's never acknowledged me beyond support payments to my mother. I extend the same courtesy to him.''

"Then he's missing out on a wonderful son.''

He smiled. He couldn't help it, but her comment touched him deeply. He knew his father was married and had children, but as a kid, he'd often wished he'd been accepted in some way. Now that he was an adult, he accepted life with its bumps, of which he was one to his father. He wouldn't change it now, if he could.

"Okay, so Pop's a fool and he's out," Holly said. "What about your cousins? You have cousins you like. I know that."

"Yes, but we never do Christmas."

"Never do Christmas! That's appalling!"

Raymond smiled and shook his head at her naïveté. "We're guys, Holly. We're not sentimental, and don't feel the need for a formal relationship, although their wives are putting together something tonight for everyone. They're trying a family thing, but I'm not going. Why should I? Just because the others got married doesn't mean I change my life-style."

"Of course, you'll go," Holly said.

"It's Sunday. I have to get up at three-thirty for work."

"So you'll lose a little sleep. You don't have to stay all night. And you can get something for the kids. From the heart."

He didn't reply, instead watching the coffee finish running through the coffeemaker. His life was good as it was. It needed no fixing. Certainly it needed no vulnerability with its burdens of family obligations. He'd lived without them this long and he'd lived well, too. Raymond poured himself a cup and took a sip of the hot, steaming liquid. The strong taste kicked in to his brain, clearing it.

"Giving from the heart is not sentimental," Holly continued, gazing at him with a pitying expression. "Well, it is sentimental to a certain extent. But it also lets people know you care. That you want to celebrate your relationship to them, that you want to celebrate life. It's not a thing that makes a man less, Raymond. It makes a man more."

Raymond set the coffee down, its taste suddenly off. "Forget it. If you can't see all that's wrong with the world, that's your problem, because no amount of helping me will change things. Hell, I'm going into a monastery. Maybe I'll get some peace then.''

Holly gasped and grabbed his arm. ''Raymond, you can't do that! A monastery's not for you. You'll whither and die there.''

Her strong objection surprised him. Obviously she'd taken his comment seriously. ''I thought it'd be just the thing you'd want. I'd give up everything in the world, including sex. Now *that's* giving.''

''No. Promise me you won't. I don't know why it's wrong, but it is. Promise!''

He patted her hand. ''I'm only kidding. Besides, I'd have no clue where to find a monastery. This is Philly.''

''Thank goodness.'' She covered his hand with hers.

Raymond felt a myriad of emotions wash over him. He could still taste her mouth on his from last night. He wanted desperately to taste it again.

Holly swallowed visibly and moistened her lips. Raymond took it as an invitation. He pulled her against his naked chest. Holly stared up at him. When she didn't pull away, he took that as a further invitation and kissed her.

Her mouth was even sweeter and spicier than he remembered. Her lips parted and her tongue met his in that unique combination of shyness and boldness. Her hands gripped his shoulders, her fingers feeling warm against his skin. Her breathing grew heavy. Raymond ran his hands down her spine. Her flesh was incredibly soft, softer than any material man created. She felt so real, more real than any woman he'd been with before. She felt so right.

As the kiss grew more frantic, Raymond pressed her breasts into his chest. He hated the cloth that was a barrier and yet no barrier. Holly dug her fingers into his shoulders and moaned in the back of her throat. Raymond cupped one breast, marveling at its human womanliness...at the perfection of the satiny globe. Her being virginal made him only want to be more gentle with his exploration. Best of all, Holly didn't vanish this time. Instead, she snuggled impossibly closer, pressing herself into his hand. He ran his thumb over her nipple. It turned diamond hard.

Holly broke the kiss and looked at him in amazement. "Oh! Oh, my."

Raymond stopped. "What's wrong? Did I hurt you?"

Her eyes were wide and still half-glazed with arousal. "No. I...I don't know what's wrong. It all feels so tingly and right."

Raymond chuckled. "You are naive."

"Oh, shut up and kiss me again."

She pulled him back to her and kissed him with a passion that rocked him to his toes. He gave himself up to it. But when he would have touched her further, she popped out. He clutched at air, totally disconcerted.

"Will you stop doing that!" he yelled, collapsing onto the countertop.

"Okay."

She was back, sitting next to him on the counter.

He turned to her. "That's not fair. You get a man all riled up and then you disappear. Literally."

"I don't mean to. I get...scared." Holly's mouth turned down, her face sad. "I'm sorry. I won't pop out on you anymore. At least, I'll try not to."

"Okay." His brain urged cooling, while his body urged sex. God only knew when she would pop out on that. Needing some time to let the body urges cool, too, he asked, "Where do you go when you pop out, anyway?"

"Oh, nowhere, really. It's a funny kind of limbo that seems to last a second or two until I pop in again."

He straightened and asked the question he'd avoided for days now. "Are you really sent by Santa Claus?"

She grinned. "Really and truly."

"The North Pole and everything."

"Yes. It's a four-dimensional existence."

"Like a space alien?"

Holly laughed. "No. Other life does exist in the universe, but everything man thinks of exists on some level. Fiction is all quite real in its way. So I'm real in my way."

He shook his head. "I don't know what to think...except that I'm having a nervous breakdown. How long have you been an elf?"

"I told you before. I'm over a thousand years old." She chuckled. "You're a kid, Raymond, compared to me."

"I'm not even a twinkle in my great-great-great-great-grandfather's eye compared to you. But you're well-preserved. Very well-preserved."

"Thank you." She patted his back. "I'm here to help you, Raymond."

"I think you're here to make me crazy." Especially when she kissed, he thought.

"Actually, that's my pleasure. Now, why don't you get dressed and we'll do some Christmas shopping for your cousins' party tonight."

"I told you, I'm not going."

She raised an eyebrow. "Life will go easier if you do. Trust me."

He realized arguing was useless. Besides, he hadn't won yet with her.

So they went shopping for his cousin Michael's stepkids, all six of them. Raymond shuddered at the thought, but bought whatever Holly suggested. What the hell, he admitted. He had no clue and she was the one with the checked-twice list.

As they shopped, he wondered what he was to do with

her. He was torn between excising her from his mind—for surely he had somehow created her there—and exploring further intimacy with her. He wanted her. He couldn't remember being so confused and dazed over a woman. Then again, he'd never met a woman like Holly before. Who the hell had?

HE DID GO TO HIS cousins' party, even though he had begged off weeks ago, claiming his early hours for work as an excuse.

Michael looked shocked to find him on the doorstep that evening. "I thought you couldn't come, Raymond."

Raymond shrugged. "I rearranged things, but if it's inconvenient—"

"Hell, no, man." Michael reached out and shook Raymond's hand, then relieved him of his packages. "We were just missing you, as a matter of fact."

Raymond felt awkward when he walked into the living room and viewed the cozy scene straight out of a modern Currier and Ives lithograph.

"Not to worry," Holly said cheerfully, suddenly standing next to him. "I'm here."

She had changed into a satin outfit for the party and had wrapped her hair in a French twist, held in place by an icicle. Raymond thought she looked beautiful, right down to her pointed ears.

"Oh, look at the tree. It's marvelous!" she said, smiling in pleasure at the big, seven-foot fir with its strings of colored twinkle-lights and ornaments.

"You're more marvelous," Raymond said.

"Why, thank you, Raymond," Mary Ellen told him. His cousin Peter's wife had clearly overheard the words. "We were just talking about you."

"Sorry." Holly snapped her fingers. "I'm surprised it wasn't already on."

Raymond kissed Mary Ellen's cheek in greeting. "Why do I think I'm now in trouble with Janice and Alison?"

"Because we always are," his cousin Jared said, smiling at his wife, Alison.

"But that's half the fun," Alison said, smiling back.

Raymond shook hands with the rest of his cousins and kissed Alison and Janice. Peter, Michael and Jared had married well, he admitted. They looked happy. So did their wives. That notion didn't motivate him to take the plunge himself; marriage always sounded as though it was constantly doused with cold water.

Amy, Janice's four-year-old daughter, raced in from the kitchen and wrapped her arms around Raymond's legs. "You came!"

Raymond patted the child on the head, not knowing what else to do with her. Amy greeted everyone with enthusiasm. "Yes, I came."

Holly whacked him on the back. "Amy smothers you with spontaneous love, and you can only pat her head? Give her a hug, dingdong!"

"But I never know what else to do with kids," Raymond said, annoyed by her nagging. "And stop hitting me or I'll turn you in for elf abuse."

"I'm not hitting or nagging. I'm getting your attention and telling you what you need to know. Now give her a hug."

Raymond bent over and hugged Amy. The child smelled like butter cookies—not surprising, since crumbs trailed down the front of her dress.

Janice's triplets saved him from further awkwardness with a young child. Cat, despite being a girl, was as tough as her brothers, Chris and C.J. All three were sports-minded, so Raymond always felt more comfortable around them. The older brother, David, and the eldest, Heather, said hello. Nice kids, he admitted.

Curious, he turned to Holly and asked, "What are they getting for Christmas?"

"What they need," Holly said promptly. "Heather gets a dash of calm. She has her upcoming SAT test for college. David needs a little more volubility. There's a girl he likes, but he's scared to talk to her, and she won't wait forever for him. The triplets' stockings will be filled with a kinder, gentler attitude toward your cousin, Michael, who needs it, by the way. And Amy... Actually, Amy doesn't need anything so she gets the usual staple: a soup-çon of love."

Raymond chuckled. "Maybe you ought to skip Amy, then, since she doesn't need a thing."

"Skip!" Holly looked horrified by the suggestion. "No one is *ever* skipped."

"I could debate that," Raymond said, thinking of his grandparents and how his world had dissolved after his grandmother had had an affair.

"Raymond." Holly said his name in the softest of voices. "You needed all those summers with your cousins because of what was coming, so you would remember love and family as an adult. Every Christmas you got a summer as extra special as we could make them, so you had the best memories when you needed them."

Raymond stared at her in astonishment. "That's impossible."

"No, it's not," Holly replied. "Peter, Michael and Jared have found their hearts again. You will, too. By Christmas. I won't fail you, Raymond. I promise. Oh, look! Amy's opening the present you bought her."

"A new Pooh bear!" Amy shouted, swinging the

stuffed animal around in delight. "He can have tea with us, Daddy."

"What's another bear at the table?" Michael said, laughing.

Raymond didn't know what to think about what Holly had said. His summers had always been the most special time of his life, but had they been *made* very special? By elves? He couldn't believe it.

As the party went on, Raymond admitted he enjoyed himself. He chatted with Alison, Jared's wife. A beautiful woman, Alison had an incongruous mass of strawberry-blond hair. She and Jared were still unemployed, a fact that astonished Raymond when he considered how career-goal oriented Jared had always been. But the couple looked extremely happy as they talked about Jared possibly opening his own law office after the New Year, although his cousin seemed in no hurry. Peter and Mary Ellen cuddled so much, Raymond wondered if they'd swallowed some kind of love potion. And Michael and Janice exchanged intimate looks every few seconds.

Raymond wasn't sure what the three couples had found, but he knew for sure it wasn't for him. All his cousins were now vulnerable to pain because of their love. He would take his current life any day of the week over that.

Holly grinned at him when he happened to stand under some mistletoe.

"I get to kiss you, Uncle Raymond!" Amy shouted.

"Look out for the cookie kisses," Peter warned.

"I already figured that one out." Raymond bent down as he accepted his "cookie" kiss. To his surprise, it was sweet in its own way.

He straightened to find Holly next to him, while Amy ran back to her new bear.

"I think I need a chaser," he said, and took her in his arms.

The party went on while he kissed Holly. He vaguely heard the chuckles and conversations, the squeals and yelps of the kids, a part of him awed at how they didn't see what he was doing. But mostly Holly's lips and tongue occupied his attention. She could occupy a whole lot more....

"Uncle Raymond! Who's that lady you're kissing?"

Chapter Six

She wasn't supposed to be seen.

Holly's gut gnawed at her, while she went over the kissing incident at the party the other night. Babies and toddlers, yes, they could see her. But Amy was five. She shouldn't have been able to see her at all, no matter how strong the child's innocence. Amy was innocent, but not *that* innocent.

Nobody had believed Amy had truly seen anyone, thank goodness. Raymond's face had been classic. Never had Holly seen a more surprised look. She would bet her own had matched his for astonishment. Eventually even Amy had believed she'd "imagined" the lady. The triplets had teased Amy for her "imagination." Holly knew better. So did Raymond. Now.

Holly sat on the sofa in Raymond's living room, waiting for him to finish getting ready for work. She debated whether she should go with him this morning. Probably the sighting by Amy had been an aberration. But what if it wasn't? The question plagued her. She'd been told she would be invisible to adults. Maybe Amy was at a "tween" age and things had somehow become mixed-up.

A door closed upstairs in the town house. Holly heard

the footsteps coming down the staircase. She wondered what Raymond thought about her being seen in the flesh.

He came into the living room and grinned. "Anyone going to see you today? I hope, I hope."

"*I* hope not," Holly said acidly, scowling at him and his jaunty attitude.

"I hope so. Then it'll mean that maybe I'm not nuts."

"You've been saying that the last few days." Holly rose from the sofa and paced. "That's the biggest load of—"

"No, no," he interrupted her curse mid-speak, wagging a finger at her. "You're an elf and elves don't curse."

"You should be around on Christmas Eve," she muttered, and finished her curse with a satisfying finale. "What will I do if people see me? It's not supposed to happen!"

"That's what *you've* been saying the last few days," he said. "I only know someone else over the age of three actually saw you. Come to work with me. I want to see if Tommy or Bob or Karen can see you. That would be great."

"It would be terrible!" Holly gasped, horrified at the notion. "We're not supposed to be visible to mankind."

"Why not?"

"I…" She realized she had no answer she could express. "I just know we're not supposed to be."

"Obviously elves are seen occasionally or people wouldn't know about them at all."

She thought about that. "Maybe they were aberrations, like what happened to me with Amy."

"Maybe. If they are, then I'm glad as hell. Sure you aren't coming?"

She shook her head. The truth was, she was afraid to, but she would be damned before she admitted that.

He shrugged. "Suit yourself. By the way, thanks for making me get gifts for my cousin's stepkids. They liked them, especially the soccer set for the triplets. But I suppose you already knew they would."

"The advantages of elfdom," Holly said.

As he went by, he kissed the top of her head. Holly felt that growingly familiar tingle from his touch. She forced it away. Now was not the time for personal daydreaming. She had a crisis on her hands.

After he left, she tried to pop back home once more to check in. She'd tried before with the same result—only she still couldn't get back home.

"Please!" Holly wailed, terrified that she was alone while things were going wrong. Why wouldn't anyone help her? Even just tell her she was all right.

Maybe they were, she thought, trying to buoy herself up. Maybe she couldn't get back home because things were okay. Maybe she was only experiencing an aberration.

She sat for a long time, before realizing she could just sit forever. That seemed silly over only a peek by a five-year-old. She did have a job to do. Her exposure could also have been a reminder from Old Nick that she had better get cracking. Holly brightened. She hadn't considered that angle before, but it would be like Old Nick to expose her in a whip-cracking gesture. She had only a couple more weeks before Christmas to get Raymond straightened out.

"If he flashed me to Amy on purpose, I'll kill him," she said out loud.

She had made some progress, after all. Hadn't she got Raymond to buy something special for his mom? Something with thought behind it? And hadn't she gotten him to the family gathering? And hadn't she gotten him to bring gifts for the kids? And to play with that little girl in the store that time?

Okay, so that had nearly resulted in his being arrested as a prospective child kidnapper, but the point was he had begun to lose his cynicism and play. She had turned him back from that Aruba mess, too. Wasn't she deserving of credit for progress made?

Holly pursed her lips. Progress wouldn't be made with her sitting in the living room. She really needed to be with Raymond. She couldn't be in hiding all the time. What was she? An elf or a mouse?

"Don't think about it," she commented.

With that notion in mind, she popped into the studio, right onto her shelf above his communications board, startling Raymond as she did so.

"Dammit, I wish you wouldn't do that," he said, glaring at her.

She grinned, mostly because no one else noticed her popping in. Tommy and Bob were busy debating the merits of whether the football team could score after getting in the "red zone," whatever that was. Holly assumed it was close to the goal. Evidently, the team had struggled with that aspect of the game in the last match, putting its playoff chances in jeopardy. Karen sat in her booth, beyond a glass panel. The woman fielded incoming calls, and clearly, nothing was disturbing her from that task. All was normal.

"Relax," Holly said, laughing happily. "Nobody saw me."

Raymond uttered the same curse he wouldn't allow her to use earlier.

"No, no," she said, wagging a finger at him. "You're a radio host and radio hosts don't curse."

"I'm laughing out loud," he replied, making a face.

To the others, he said, "You guys see anything unusual in the studio today?"

"You mean about Tommy being dressed in an evening gown?" Bobby asked. "I didn't want to mention it before, but the way the light hits his hairy shoulders... It's a beautiful thing."

"Bob's got a pickle up his nose," Tommy said. "But we know that's normal for Bob. There is that cucumber in Karen's booth—"

A rude noise erupted over the airwaves via Karen's store of sound-effect tapes.

"Sorry, sorry," Tommy said. "I didn't know it was your lunch. *Bon appétit* and hot dog, woman!"

The rude noise erupted again. Raymond and Bob laughed.

Holly smiled, pleased to see Raymond's genuine sense of amusement surface, even if the cause was a crude one. He really did look handsome when he smiled. Holly's heart beat a little faster and her thoughts strayed to the other night when he'd kissed her so thoroughly....

"Hey! What the heck!" Tommy suddenly exclaimed, staring directly at Holly.

Holly cursed and popped out.

In her little limbo world, she could hear Raymond eagerly ask, "What? What?"

"I...I thought I saw someone sitting on your shelf," Tommy said, his voice puzzled. "Hell, what was in that eggnog I had earlier?"

"God knows, but I want some," Bob announced.

"What did the person look like?" Raymond asked.

"I couldn't tell, not really. What was it? A hologram? Is that why you asked earlier about anything unusual in the studio? Do you have some hologram thing going here?"

"No, no. My earlier questions are not related at all...."

But Raymond continued to ask Tommy about what he'd seen, obviously not caring whether it went out on the airwaves. The discussion sparked more discussion about hallucinations.

Holly's insides curdled. She had been seen again! This time she could make no excuse about five-year-olds being an aberration. She had definitely been seen by an adult.

"Oh, Lord," she muttered, scared past her pointed ears.

She tried to go back home. She popped and popped, but nothing happened. Truly being on her own now scared her so much, she felt frozen in limbo. She had heard of no precedents for this in the annals of elf history. In the vernacular of the time, she was screwed. From now on, she would have to be very careful.

"Oh, Lord," she muttered again.

Raymond's show gradually returned to normal, but she did not. Lots of blame went to bad eggnog. Holly knew the eggnog had been fine. The problem was her.

As soon as Raymond walked into his house after work, he called her. Holly hunkered down in her limbo, refusing to acknowledge him.

"Holly, don't do this to me!" he shouted after interminably calling her name.

"I'm not doin' nothin'," she snapped, popping into his kitchen.

"Your grammar is atrocious."

"Who cares?"

"I care." He grabbed her up and swung her around in a circle while chanting, "I'm not nuts. I'm not nuts!"

"Stop that!" She disentangled herself from him. "You never were nuts. I told you that before."

"Yeah, but who would believe you?"

She whacked his shoulder.

"Hey! There are laws against physical abuse."

"You need something to wake you up!" Tears pushed at her eyes. "Raymond, something's very wrong. No one should see me but you."

"Thank God someone can," he retorted. "I really thought I was insane, seeing and talking to an elf—"

"Raymond!" she wailed, feeling overwhelmed by reality.

"Okay, okay." He sighed. "Let me fix dinner and we'll talk about it."

She swiped at the single trail of moisture escaping down her face. She felt miserable as she sat on the counter and watched him fix an omelet for himself. The food smelled good, she admitted, when he slid it onto the plate and added toast on the side. The melted cheese, combined with cooked egg, gave off a wonderful aroma. So did the jelly on the toast. It all woke something long forgotten inside herself.

He took his meal to the little table in the breakfast nook and sat down. Holly popped into the seat opposite him.

"Why is it so bad for others to see you?" he asked, after eating a forkful of omelet.

Holly's insides felt all stretchy and funny. "It's bad because I'm only supposed to be seen by you. I have some residue for little, little kids. But that doesn't count."

"But why only me? Why not let everyone see?"

"Magic's a funny, dangerous thing. It works best in small doses," Holly said. "People would be avaricious if they had magic. They could do tremendous harm in a very short time. Plus, you need a lot of innocence to believe in magic. That's why it works with the youngest of children."

"And Amy."

"Where it shouldn't."

His plate was already one-third gone and nearing the one-half mark. As she watched the rapidly disappearing food, Holly could stand it no longer. When he took yet another forkful of omelet, she reached across and grabbed the fork from him. She put the omelet piece in her mouth.

"Oh, my," she said, awed by the delicious way the food blended on her tongue. Never, never had she experienced anything like the wonderful flavors of food...and yet she had an odd, faint memory of it—one she wasn't able to bring into focus and define. Shrugging it away, she chewed, savoring the tastes, then swallowed, finally satisfying her stomach's urges. "That's so good."

"You sound like it's the first thing you've ever eaten," Raymond commented, grinning.

Holly dropped the fork with a clatter. "I shouldn't be eating at all!"

"Come on. You have all the body parts to eat with." He frowned. "At least you look like you do."

"I do, but we don't need sustenance like humans do. To my knowledge, no other elf ever has."

"But Santa does," he said. "Everyone leaves out milk and cookies for him."

"He's different from an elf. Elves don't eat!" She stared at him, her throat clogged with fresh tears. "What's wrong with me, Raymond?"

He reached across the table and squeezed her fingers. "Let's be logical about this, Holly. You're an elf, right?"

"I know that."

"You're here to help me." He chuckled. "Damn. It just occurred to me that I have my very own elf. Who would have thought?"

"Not me, that's for sure."

"Maybe that's it," he said. "Maybe *I* needed to know you really do exist."

"I already told you I did."

"No. I mean, I needed it proved to me. I'm not sure two little sightings by Amy and Tommy are one-hundred-percent incontrovertible proof, but it's a start."

"I don't want to be seen by anyone else just to prove it to you," she said, taking her hand from his. "It's like… It's like having a Peeping Tom. It's disgusting to be seen by people in the world."

"Nearly five and a half billion people would see you if you were human."

"Thank you, Mr. Population Counter. I really needed to hear that." She shivered, suddenly feeling cold. "Is that a draft? I feel cold…and my belly hurts."

"Here." He pushed his plate over. "With the way you grabbed that fork, I have no doubt eating will help with the latter problem. I'm a little surprised at the first one, though. The thermostat's set at seventy, so it's comfortable in here. And you liked the blizzard and whined constantly about the heat in Aruba—"

"I didn't whine. I just commented." She began to eat the rest of the omelet. It was good, she decided. A thought occurred. "Aruba! I felt the heat there. I thought I was so much a creature of the cold and that's why I noticed it. But maybe my being bothered by the heat was more than that."

He gazed at her. "You might be sick. That's why this is happening to you."

"Elves never get sick," she told him. Elves never got hungry, either, but she was packing it in like a starving woman. Even she could tell that.

By the time she'd finished the plate, her stomach no longer hurt. It was satisfied. She felt a little badly that Raymond had to make himself a new meal, but she marveled more at the exquisite timing of having the food run out at the same moment one's belly was replete. The miracle of human bioengineering, she thought. She would have to tell the gang at the North Pole.

If she made it back.

That notion scared her, fiercely scared her. She knew about the three elves sent to Dickens, but now she wondered if there had been others sent into the world. Maybe they'd never made it back. Maybe they'd turned human and... Someone should have prepared her better for all the things that could go wrong. No one had said a damn word!

She looked at Raymond. He seemed so calm and strong. Certainly he'd handled her and the shock of her original appearance far better than she was handling the shock of her current "appearance."

"I hope you're right about my being seen in order to convince you that I do exist," she said finally.

She prayed he was.

RAYMOND GRINNED at Holly, as she watched the television.

She was real. She had to be.

Others had seen her. Amy's catching them kissing had been one thing, to be dismissed finally when he considered Amy was a child not much older than the little ones who had seen Holly up to that point.

But Tommy! Tommy was as pragmatic a guy as one could meet. That had put Raymond over the edge about Holly's reality.

He stared at her, marveling at her profile. Its delicate lines only intrigued him further.

"Will you stop looking at me as if I've grown two heads?" she snapped, without turning his way.

He grinned. "I can't help it. I've never had an elf in my living room before."

"I've been here for weeks."

"But now you're real."

"I'm beginning to think I liked it better when you thought you were nuts."

"I still do."

"That's no help." She frowned and looked at him. Her cheeks became rosy. "Raymond, my belly feels funny again, but not like before. I have this...urge...down there."

For a brief moment, he thought she meant a sexual urge, then realized the problem was more functional. "You have to use the bathroom."

She gaped at him. "No."

"Hey, food has to go somewhere once you eat it." He paused. "Do you need help?"

"I think I can figure it out by myself," she said primly, rising to her feet. As she walked away, she muttered, "The bathroom! Lord help me, what's next?"

Raymond admitted he didn't want to know. When she returned, he resisted the urge to ask if everything came out all right. This was not the moment to make crude jokes.

Holly sat back down on the sofa, her expression miserable.

"I just realized this all must be a shock for you," Raymond said.

"No kidding," Holly muttered, sighing. "That's really brilliant work by you."

He leaned toward her. "Listen, elf. I'm being nice here, so lose the sarcasm."

Holly's face turned red. "I'm sorry. It's just... I'm scared."

She burst into tears.

Raymond gazed at her, awestruck. She was always so cheerful or tough or stubborn or mischievous, but never once had he seen her sad. Her shoulders shook with her weeping and she covered her face with her hands, as if to catch her tears. Mostly, she just all-out bawled.

He had no clue what to do. Not a single word of advice, not a shred, came to mind that could help her get over her unhappiness. He was no expert on elfin behavior. Who would be? He didn't know what might comfort her, under the circumstances.

Finally, he patted her on the shoulder. "It's not so bad, Holly."

She raised her tear-streaked face to him. Her eyes were red and swollen. Her skin looked mottled from her crying. A tormented elf was not a pretty sight. Raymond had an overwhelming urge to hold her and kiss away her tears.

The tender gesture struck him as alien, not to be done without opening himself up to emotional vulnerability. Not knowing what else to do, he patted her shoulder again in a compromise gesture that gave sympathy but kept him at a comfortable distance.

"Try popping in and out," he suggested. "If you can, then you know the magic's working."

She did, vanishing and returning in a second. "It seems I haven't lost that. I can be seen sometimes, but not all the time."

"I'm sure it's just some kind of quirk in your system," he offered. "Maybe you have picked up an elf bug or something and you'll be back to normal the moment it passes."

"I told you, elves don't get sick," she said, fresh tears welling up in her eyes.

"How many elves are exposed to humans? We're riddled with germs. The type-A Asiatic flu is going around now. That wreaks havoc. It's so virulent that maybe it's affected you in a strange way.''

Holly frowned. "I don't know."

He thought about his very early day tomorrow, then looked at Holly. She needed a distraction, as well as reassurance that she was okay. "Tell you what. Dry your eyes and we'll go out. There's a nightclub not too far from here."

She shrank away from him. "People will see me."

"Maybe not. We can do this as a test, to see if you're working right." He grinned. "This place is always packed, so no one will notice if you pop out or not. And if they do notice, they'll just put it down to the booze. 'Tis the season to be jolly, after all."

"What the hell would you know about 'jolly'?" Holly asked, then shook her head. "Sorry I'm snappy. Okay, I'll try the bar...."

"Or maybe I shouldn't."

He got up and pulled her to her feet, trying to ignore the frisson of sensuality that just touching her hand caused him. Good thing no one could see that, he thought. He let go of her fingers. "If you fall off a horse, you get right back on again."

"But I wasn't riding a horse."

"Same thing. I'll get my coat."

"Better get one for me, too. I think I'll be cold out there, if I'm already cold in here."

He gave her an old, thick, professional team jacket that swam on her slender form. They went outside into the dim night. The streetlamps blazed, illuminating every nook and cranny on the sidewalks as a crime deterrent. Raymond wondered if people would see her or if his coat would just float in midair. To his relief, several passersby looked at him, but not at Holly.

"Brrr!" She shivered. "It's cold."

The temperature had to be at least fifteen degrees warmer than the day of the blizzard. Even the snow had nearly all melted away. While she could pop in and out, her body's sensitivity wasn't good. Raymond said, "Zip up the jacket, and I'll warm up the car."

Inside the car, with Holly beside him, he had light without turning on the interior one. "I think you're okay. At least you've got that circle thing going again. That's a good sign."

"I do, don't I?" She caught a stray snowflake with her tongue. "Tastes right. But why do I feel cold?"

"Chills are a symptom of the flu." What the hell, he thought. It was as good a theory as any other for her predicament.

"But I told you—"

"Elves don't get the flu," he finished. "There's a first time for everything, Holly."

"JUST WHAT I WANT to be doing. Breaking new elf ground."

Club Egypt, the "in" Philly singles bar, wasn't as crowded as he'd expected. Only about five hundred people, most of them in their twenties, were there on this midweek night. Raymond felt like the older, wiser brother of those present. But the atmosphere would do for cheering Holly up.

Rock music boomed through the elaborate sound system, as if intent on blasting every eardrum to deafness.

"It's too loud!" Holly shouted, covering her ears; she'd let her hair down earlier to hide their distinctive shape.

"You'll get used to it," Raymond assured her, even

though his own ears protested the near catastrophic noise level.

"Don't bet on it. People can't see me, can they?"

"Doesn't seem like it," he said, looking around. Neither of them attracted attention.

She waved a hand in front of a couple, who never flinched. "Good. Wow! Look at the way those people dance. It's all bobbing up and down, like those little dog heads in the backs of cars."

Raymond chuckled. In the strobe lights, the dancers' silhouettes did look as if they were going up and down in timed unison. He thought of all the sleep he was losing—even if they went home at eleven—then put it out of his head. One night wouldn't kill him. Maybe he would even find fodder for the show, which would make the outing worthwhile for another reason.

Several people recognized him and teased him about when he would wear that corset, but nobody noticed Holly. He smiled as she looked around in wonder. She snitched an onion ring from a passing waiter's tray.

"I can guess what list you're on for Christmas," he said.

She stuck out her bottom lip. "I couldn't help it. I'm hungry again and it smelled good." She bit into it. "Tastes good, too. If you'd buy me a french fry or something, then I wouldn't have to resort to lowly thievery for a meal."

"Now that would be a miracle." He settled them at the bar and put in an order for a beer and an appetizer. "We'll try the stuffed mushrooms. You'll like them."

"Why? Because you do?"

He chuckled. "Of course."

"Good enough." She pointed to a girl, a beautiful redhead. "She's pretty, isn't she?"

"Yes." Raymond frowned. "You're not going to start that matchmaking nonsense again, are you? Kathryn was nice, but I wasn't interested, and I'm still not interested. When I'm interested, I'll do the work, okay?"

"Okay, okay." Holly made a face. "I was just asking."

A tall, muscular man passed them, his jaw so square it could be a corner. Holly's gaze followed the man, her appreciation obvious. Raymond wanted to jerk her around to face the bar, so she couldn't see the freak of nature. The guy had to be one, with all those bulging muscles.

Holly sighed. "Now he has promise, hasn't he? Definite promise."

Someone squeezed up to the bar on the other side of her. "Sorry, lady."

"Oh." Her face filled with dismay. She leaned into Raymond and whispered, "That guy just saw me."

"I noticed. How do you feel?"

"The same. What's making this happen?"

He had no clue, but that would sound too flip if he said it out loud to Holly. Besides, what else could he say? That he was happy the guy *had* seen her? Very happy. He had more proof that she wasn't a figment of his imagination. "We'll figure out what's happening to you. I promise."

She shivered, despite still wearing his jacket. "Boy, I hope so. And I'm cold again."

He put his arm around her and brought her even closer to him. Their bodies were pressed tightly together. Raymond grinned. "Let's try a little mutual body heat. That might help. It's not really cold in here, not with all these people. I'm more and more convinced you have an elf flu. I just hope you're not contagious, otherwise all these people will be popping in and out of who knows where."

She giggled—the first amused sound she'd made all evening. "That would be fun."

"Only you would think so." But he had to admit, he would love to see people's faces if they did start popping in and out. His own would no doubt be a laugh riot.

Her scent reminded him again of vanilla and spice, like freshly baked cookies. He wondered how she managed that. No matter; she smelled wonderful. He liked having his arm around her, liked the idea that she needed something as basic as bodily warmth from him.

He was very attracted to her, to the effervescence she possessed. He wanted her and now she was real—part of the time, maybe, but real. His earlier comment about doing the work when he was interested came back to haunt him. His body certainly urged him to work overtime with her. He set the thought aside, however, knowing the timing as well as the circumstances were bad. She'd had a shock today, one that matched his own over her. And already he'd gotten far more personal than he ever should have.

He drank his beer to cool himself off, holding the long neck of the bottle between two fingers. It didn't work. His body only felt hotter for Holly. To distract himself, he said, "I must be ten years older than most of the people here."

Holly laughed. "How about me?"

"Oh, yeah." He grinned. "I forgot you were the old lady elf." He leered at her. "You don't look a day over five hundred."

"Thank you." She grinned in return, then ate one of the stuffed mushrooms, which had just arrived. She licked the excess juice off her fingers, nearly killing him with the innocent gesture. "I'm feeling a little better, even though people can see me right now."

Raymond frowned, remembering something. "I wonder. When the bartender gave me my beer, she didn't ask if you needed a drink. She should have, if she'd seen you. She would have, I'm sure of it.'' He glanced at the bartender. ''Can I have a soda for my lady, please?''

The young woman behind the bar glanced over, then frowned in clear puzzlement. ''Your lady friend?''

''Never mind, she's in the ladies' room right now.'' He looked at Holly. ''See? Or rather, see what she didn't see? You.''

''But that guy saw me before.''

''I wonder why.''

''That's the big question.''

He thought for a moment. ''You were cold then. Maybe that's it— No, you were cold when we went to get the car but nobody saw you then.''

She pursed her lips. ''So what the hell is going on here?''

''I'm sticking to my flu theory.'' Standing this close, he was bound to catch the flu or whatever was wrong with her. Life would be interesting if he did. But more interesting would be kissing those perfectly pursed lips.

''But what if it's not the flu?'' Holly persisted, her mind only on one track—not that Raymond blamed her. ''What if it's something more permanent?''

''You mean, if you turn visible all the time?''

She nodded.

''Don't worry about that until you get there,'' he advised her.

''Easy for you to say.''

''I know.'' He rubbed her arm in comfort, finding her easier to cope with minus the tears. Probably it was a man thing, he wryly admitted.

''Probably,'' she said.

''You're reading my mind. That's normal. For you.''

"True." She brightened and ate another stuffed mushroom. "Boy, these are good."

"They're the bane of my existence," a woman behind them said, grinning as she squeezed in to get a drink. "I eat one and I gain five pounds."

Holly gaped at her, then set the mushroom down. "Really?"

"Sure. They look innocent, but those suckers are loaded with fat." The woman got her drink and moved on.

"This in and out is killing me," Holly said glumly.

"I know."

He wondered what would happen if Holly were to become permanently real. She was living with him now, but where would she go? What would she do?

A whole avenue of endless responsibility opened up before him. He'd been responsible only for himself, for most of his life. His father had been nonexistent, and his mother had made sure he'd been dressed and fed, but that was it for parental responsibility.

Faced with the possibility of caring for Holly forever made his stomach curl. He pushed it all away, even as he dropped his arm from around her and stepped back, needing the distance.

"What's wrong?" she asked, frowning at him.

"It's late," he said, shoving his hands into his pockets and deliberately thinking only of his extremely early morning. "I've got to get up in a few hours for work."

"But we just got here," she said.

He was glad she hadn't seemed able to read his thoughts now. While he hadn't asked for her to be in his life, his reaction to the prospect of her being around for a long time shamed him. It would have hurt her unnecessarily.

He shrugged. "This is a lot of the reason why I don't have people in my life. I have odd hours, a demanding job. It takes a special person to accept it. I have to go. You can stay if you want."

Her frightened expression only made him feel worse. He realized he sounded callous. She didn't need that.

He put his hand on the small of her back and guided her away from the bar. "Come on. This isn't the Christmas-elf crowd."

Relief washed over her face. "Hey, I may not be a Christmas-elf-crowd person anymore."

He didn't say much on the way home, although Holly talked about the bar and its singles-seeking-singles clientele. The whole process mystified her, which wasn't surprising. He didn't ask about elves' dating habits.

He knew she chatted on to cover up her nervousness about what was happening to her. He knew he only answered in monosyllables, because the thought of her as a permanent responsibility disturbed him still. And that only shamed him all the more.

"Thank you," she said gratefully, when they were inside his town house again.

"You're welcome." He felt he had to give her a little perk from the evening. "At least we learned that sometimes you're seen and sometimes you're not."

"And it's growing. If only I knew why, I could stop it."

Her face changed, and she opened her mouth wide in a yawn. She immediately clamped her hand over her mouth, her eyes wide with surprise. Finally, she lowered her hand. "Don't tell me. That was a yawn because I'm tired and I need to sleep."

"Okay, I won't tell you…but I'll take the sofa and you can have the bedroom."

"What *is* this?" she moaned, spinning in a circle.

"You'll feel better in the morning," Raymond offered lamely.

"I'm *not* sleeping," Holly announced and popped out.

Raymond gazed about the empty room, then shook his head and went into the bedroom. After he'd stripped off his clothes and gotten into bed, he lay with his hands behind his head, pondering the recent changes in his life—pondering what to do with Holly if she was suffering from something more than an aberration or the elfin version of the flu.

Maybe the powers that be had decided to make Holly visible to show him that she was real. If so, then he believed, and gratefully, too, that she existed. If so, it meant he was sound in mind and body.

He heard the television go on downstairs. Holly must have popped back in from wherever she'd gone, to *not* sleep in his living room. He grinned, having a feeling that she would lose the battle with the Sandman eventually. He wondered if that guy existed, too.

Unfortunately, he won her battle against sleep. When his alarm rang at three-thirty for work, Raymond swore he hadn't had more than an hour's worth of sleep.

"Damn," he muttered, dragging himself into the bathroom.

He emerged from his bathroom and bedroom, dressed, barely awake and not refreshed. The television was still on, playing a late, late showing of *Miracle on 34th Street.*

Holly lay prone on the sofa, her eyes closed, her mouth slightly open in sleep. She was out like a light, he thought in amusement. Raymond shook his head and smiled. So much for *not* sleeping.

He took the remote control from her nerveless fingers and clicked off the TV. She looked so forlorn, as if she were trying to curl up into herself. Something plucked at his heart. He went up to his bedroom and pulled the silk coverlet from his bed, then came downstairs and put it over Holly, very gently so as not to waken her. With care, he tucked the edges between her and the sofa back. Holly snuggled deeper into the warmth the coverlet provided.

Something flipped over in Raymond's heart. She was so beautiful, so strangely different from any woman he'd ever known before—and incredibly sexy. Unable to resist, he leaned down and kissed her cheek.

A slight snore erupted from Holly's mouth.

Raymond grinned and straightened. He sobered, however, when his brain reminded him of her possible permanency in his life. He didn't want to be responsible for another person—elf or not. He wasn't equipped to handle it, for one thing. He had no desire, for another, no matter how attractive she was. Holly was from another...another something. She did not belong here. It would be better for her, and him, to get her back where she did belong.

Only how to do that?

Raymond sat down across from Holly and stared at her composed face, wondering how to help her return to her world. Ironic, he thought, remembering that *she* was supposed to help *him*. He sat up, as a notion struck home. Maybe that was it. Maybe he needed to allow her to "help" him. Once her requirements were satisfied, she would go back to where she came from.

Regret surged through him. He told himself he was being foolish. Holly was sexy, but there were dozens of sexy women within a five-block radius, who had fewer strings attached to them than Holly. Holly was loaded with strings. Anyway, who knew what getting physically closer would set off? Better not to find out, he admitted; he only needed a wake-up cup of coffee to convince him of that.

Deciding he would get coffee and a bagel at the all-night convenience store, he crept out of the town house so as not to disturb her. Poor elf. But he would be a good little boy and get her back on track.

The urge to be bad—very bad—reared its ugly head. He ignored it.

Chapter Seven

Holly screwed up her courage and popped into Raymond's radio show.

She settled on the shelf above his electronics board and held her breath, waiting for Tommy or Bob to see her.

Nobody said anything, however, about her presence. Not even Raymond.

"Hey!" she said, annoyed that he hadn't acknowledged her bravery in showing up.

He kept chatting with a caller about whether the football team's assistant coach was a complete moron or not. Evidently certain of his decisions from last week's game were under scrutiny.

"Hey!" she said louder, poking Raymond in the shoulder.

"And thanks for the call," Raymond said, pressing a button. He glanced up at her. "Hey, yourself. I'm on a phone call here."

"You hung up," she reminded. "But I'm finally here. Do you think anyone can see me?"

"Looks safe so far," he said, smiling.

Hope rose inside her. "Maybe I did have a virus and it's over now."

"How did you sleep? Again?"

She looked down and muttered, "Okay. I ate breakfast again, too. Happy now?"

"No. Not for you. Don't worry."

She still had no idea what had caused her sudden visibility. She knew exactly how Raymond must have felt when she'd appeared into his life. Frightened and bewildered and insane—and in that order—covered it.

In the few days since feeling her first need to eat and sleep, she'd had continued urges for the same. She'd also felt the urge to be clean this morning. Not that elves weren't clean, she acknowledged, but they didn't *need* to clean themselves like humans. Much as she hated to admit what it might mean, she had braved the shower—and loved it. The water had run over her flesh like silk over velvet, and the soap had felt satiny on her body. She'd felt so good that she had decided to venture out of the house and try again. She planned a bath for next time, once she got Raymond to buy her the stuff that would make bubbles.

She listened in on a few more conversations—one from a woman caller. Although the voice sounded young and flirty, Holly had no desire to fix Raymond up with her. Those days were over. But she did have to get back to her job, to help him find his heart.

Only how?

He had been sweet the past few days, giving her balance in her turmoil. He'd suggested solutions and encouraged her to get out, like last night when he'd taken her to the bar. He'd even thought she was ready to be left there. She had panicked at that, but his confidence in her had been a boost.

Her stomach growled when she thought of the delicious stuffed mushrooms she'd eaten there.

"Forget it," she told herself.

While Raymond took calls, one of the city papers at his elbow caught her eye. An article on the front page announced the shocking news of a church's Christmas toys having been stolen the night before.

"How awful," Holly murmured, picking up the front section to read the article fully.

"He's a moron," Raymond said, his voice rising. "He doesn't have the special team players ready for the games, and the Cowboys ran back two touchdowns on kickoffs, last Sunday. That's outrageous. He should be fired—"

"Raymond," Holly interrupted.

"Not now. I'm on a roll," he said, then went back to his microphone. "Does he have blackmail photos on everyone in the front office? Is that why the team hasn't fired him yet? It's been two years. *Two* years! This guy has been costing us games for that long and now with our play-off chances in jeopardy—"

"Raymond, you have to help these people."

Raymond blinked, clearly taken off his current cause. "What?"

Holly tapped the paper. "You have to help these people."

He frowned and glanced at the article.

"Hello?" the caller said.

"Hey, Ray. Did you zone out?" Tommy asked, chuckling.

"No." Raymond turned back to the microphone. "And thanks for the call."

He pressed the button, cutting off the caller.

"Hey!" Bob yelped. "That poor guy just got on. Mike from Havertown, call us back and we'll put you straight through right away."

"What's with you?" Tommy asked, putting his hand over his mike so the audience couldn't hear.

"Gremlins in the brain," Raymond said, glaring at Holly.

She grinned, feeling almost back to normal. A little mischief never killed anybody. Well, almost never. She pointed to the newspaper article. "You need to help these people, Raymond."

He opened his mouth, closed it, then opened it again. "Okay."

Holly grunted in surprise at his quick acquiescence. "What? No argument?"

"I've got a show to do." Which he did, without further disturbance on Holly's part.

In his office after the show, he said to her, "Okay, so I'm to help that church. What do I do?"

"I don't know," Holly replied helplessly.

"You're the expert here. You've got to have something in mind."

"Hey, I only come up with the mission. You have to execute it."

Raymond shook his head. "Now I know you're still sick, since you can't come up with anything."

"I got through the show unnoticed, didn't I?" she said, proud and relieved that she actually had.

"Not quite. They noticed my talking to you, even if it was considered a 'zone out.'"

Holly waved a hand. "Semantics. So how are you going to help them?"

He picked up the paper, having brought it into his office after the show. He read the article, then said, "Easy. I'll send them a check for a hundred dollars."

"Raymond!" Holly exclaimed, appalled at his quick solution.

"Two hundred?"

"Money does not cure everything."

He laughed. "Boy, are you out of touch with real life."

"Thank goodness." She focused on the actual problem. "The church lost many toys, something a couple of hundred dollars won't cover. And they'll have the added work of shopping for the toys all over again. But you could help them two ways by shopping for the toys yourself."

He gaped at her. "I could what?"

"Shop for the toys," she said right in his face.

"How come I do the added work but the church doesn't? Maybe if they locked their doors properly they wouldn't have lost the toys in the first place."

"You're being semantical again."

"Is 'semantical' a word?"

"Who cares? Look, just go buy a bunch of toys and take them to the church today."

He eyed her for a long moment. "And that would make you happy? You'd feel like I was on the road to finding my heart by doing that?"

"Yes." The question, however, struck her as odd. Maybe not so much the question, but the way he asked it. She felt as if he had set a trap. Nonsense, she thought. Yet the sensation did not go away.

"All right, then," he said, leaning back in his chair and smiling.

This seemed too easy to Holly, especially after the way he had fought her very existence. Maybe her being seen had truly convinced him to cooperate. She hoped so. She wanted to see Raymond happy—even if it meant she would go away forever.

What more did she want? Holly mentally shook herself. She couldn't lose sight of her purpose, which was to help Raymond—no matter what it cost her emotionally. She had a feeling it might cost her a lot. She would make sure it cost *him,* she decided mischievously.

"Let's go toy shopping," Holly replied with determination.

The toys proved more expensive than she'd considered. When they returned to his office with their purchases, she looked with dismay at the pitiful pile several hundred dollars had bought.

"It's not enough," she said sadly.

"It has to be," Raymond told her.

"Well, it isn't," Holly said, glaring at him. "They have more kids than this to give to. I just know it."

"Makes you wonder if the thieves had to back an eighteen-wheeler up to the door to get them all."

She whacked him on the shoulder. "That wasn't nice."

"And hitting me is?"

"I needed to get your attention."

"You're an elf!" he exclaimed. "What's *not* to get my attention?"

She grinned wryly. "That's true, but making jokes doesn't solve this problem. There aren't enough toys."

Raymond sighed. "Holly, you have got to get a clue about real life. I can't buy thousands and thousands of dollars' worth of toys to replace every one that was stolen. No individual can do it unless he's making thirty million bucks a day like Bill Gates."

"Then let's ask him," Holly said eagerly.

Raymond looked heavenward. "I don't know the guy."

"We'll need to find someone who does, then—"

"Holly! This is what *I* can give, okay? The church will have to call on other resources for more toys. They have them, trust me."

"This isn't in the spirit of the season," Holly warned.

"It's in my spirit."

"That's the problem."

Raymond put his hands on her shoulders. "Holly. I'm not Joe Do-Gooder and I never will be."

"Can we get him?"

"Holly!"

"Okay, okay. Jeez!"

His gaze turned from resolve to something more...earthy. Holly swallowed, suddenly feeling shy and yet very feminine. His hands were strong and firm on her shoulders, sending a frisson of sensual energy along her veins. Only he could create such a joy, a recognition within her. No elf could understand this need to be close, she thought. Then why did she?

"I don't want to kiss you again," he said.

Her insides shrank with disappointment. "Okay."

She tried to look away but she couldn't. His gaze held her captive. He leaned down and kissed her. She immediately fit her lips to his. Their tongues swirled together and she pressed her body against his. So hard, she thought, wrapping her arms around his waist. So lean. Kissing made her feel alive. Everything was incredibly vivid whenever he kissed her. She loved the unique taste of his mouth...the fierceness and the gentleness of his lips...the masculine scent of his cologne...the heat of his skin...the way their hips pressed together so intimately. She loved it all.

He eased his mouth from hers, then stepped away. "I don't want to get involved with you."

"Oh." His words hurt. She wasn't sure why they should.

Her pain must have shown on her face, for he said, "Holly, I'm not a man who wants a relationship with anyone or anything. It's not you. I wish you understood the rules of relationships. But maybe it's good that you won't be here long enough to have reason to know them."

"I'll be here just until Christmas," she said.

A funny look came over his face. "That's right."

Holly drew in a deep breath. She might not know what the man-woman rules of play were, but she knew when a situation called for elfin pride. "We'd better take the toys to the church."

"Right."

Holly followed glumly when Raymond left his office, with their several bags of toys. In the hallway Charlie, the station manager stopped him. He gave no sign of acknowledging Holly's presence. It didn't perk her up as she thought of her conversation with Raymond.

"Off for the day, Ray?"

"After I detour to this place." He set down a bag and took the article about the church out of his coat pocket. "You've lived in Philly longer than I have. What's the best way to get here?"

"Why are you going there?"

"I've got some toys for them, to make up for the ones stolen," Raymond said.

"You!"

"See how bad you are?" Holly piped up, not able to resist.

Raymond ignored her. "Okay, so I don't have a soft spot normally. What's the best way?"

Charlie told him, adding, "You think they need more toys?"

"Tell him yes," Holly hissed.

"Probably," Raymond conceded.

"I'll take up a pool here at the station," Charlie said, his voice excited. "And I'll call some of the sponsors to help."

"Wonderful!" Holly exclaimed, clapping her hands. "We can get more toys."

"I can't buy more toys," Raymond said in exasperation.

Charlie grinned, hearing him. "We'll send a couple of the interns shopping. Not to worry. Hell, they're still kids themselves. They'll know what to get."

"I just love this," Holly said.

"We'll buy the toys and have a photographer to go with you," Charlie added, rubbing his hands together. "It's a great press opportunity for the station. And for you. We'll set it up for tomorrow."

"What's a 'press opportunity?'" Holly asked.

"I don't want a *press op*," Raymond said. "I just want to take my toys and go the hell home."

"Nonsense. This will be great! You'll look really good, Ray. Mr. Philanthropy. Who'd have thought."

The station manager walked away, still talking to himself about the "press op."

"What the hell is a press opportunity?" Holly demanded, hands on hips.

"A mess," Raymond said in disgust.

"Now that clears it up for me."

"They take pictures for the newspapers," Raymond said. "They create another article about the church's loss, this time making me look like Santa Claus."

Holly burst into laughter. "You? Santa? Oh, that's priceless. I can't wait to see this photo op."

"I don't want to be Santa Claus," Raymond snapped.

She giggled. "Looks like you've been crowned. But we're getting all the extra toys we need, now. Think of the children you'll make happy. You'll be giving a beautiful gift from the heart, Raymond."

"Not when I think of all the fuss it's created."

"You can make a sacrifice for a good cause." She grinned at him, delighted with this turn of events.

"Don't say I didn't warn you," Raymond said.

"Oh, pish-tosh." Holly waved a hand in dismissal at his pessimism.

Lord, the man gave Scrooge a run for his money—and that was saying something.

RAYMOND LOOKED AROUND at the toys piled to the ceiling in his office and groaned. What a sight at five in the morning. The station must have gone on a buying spree last night that would have made F.A.O. Schwarz happy. In fact, it probably did. Now, he had to get all this to the church after his show this morning.

"Isn't it wonderful?" Holly exclaimed. She sat on top of a pile of large, boxed trucks, her eyes shining with excitement.

"That'll fall," he warned.

"Naw." She swung her legs against the boxes. The tall pile never moved. "See? I'm okay."

She looked so happy that Raymond took it as a good sign. She clearly thought she was accomplishing her mission. His heart didn't feel any better, however. It even felt a little worse at the thought that she was on her way to vanishing forever. It was what he wanted, wasn't it? It was what she needed. It was what had to be.

"We need to wrap these," she said.

He gaped at her. "Wrap them! Are you nuts?"

"I believe that's your department." She frowned. "What's wrong with wrapping them? The kids should have the fun of tearing off the paper and making a mess for their folks. That's half the joy of Christmas."

"A pragmatic elf," he muttered. "Just what I needed."

"Yes, I am, and yes, you do. We'd better get started. Where's the wrapping paper?"

"The church might not accept them if they're

wrapped,'' he said, thinking quickly. ''They need to know what's appropriate for a child's age. They don't want to be giving Monopoly to a three-year-old.''

''Oh.'' She grinned. ''Got out of that one, didn't you?''

''Just what I was thinking,'' he said.

''I know.''

Her smugness grated on his nerves. It shouldn't. She was entitled to be smug since her mind reading was clearly in perfect working order.

''I've got a show to do,'' he said.

For four hours, he tried to forget his upcoming afternoon chore with the toys, but the trip stayed in the back of his mind all through his show. He had a sense of doom about the entire thing, especially knowing he wasn't doing it for the most altruistic of reasons.

The station manager was waiting for him afterward in Raymond's now empty office. Charlie was entirely too gleeful and it wasn't from generosity of spirit.

''We've got a van loaded with all the toys, and I've called in the news stations. Channel 10 wants to cover it.''

''It's too much,'' Raymond said, feeling used by the man.

''This donation is good for us. What's wrong with that?''

''I'd rather do this quietly.''

Charlie was silent for a moment. ''Raymond, I give you a lot of space here because of your ratings, but it only goes so far. You understand?''

Raymond stayed silent for one full minute. At last, he said, ''Sure.''

''Good.''

The manager left. Holly popped in. ''Who the hell died and left him king?''

"Santa ought to wash your mouth out with soap," Raymond said.

"Hey, we're all big elves here." She looked down at her feet. "I think I really am getting bigger. My pants look a little short."

Raymond glanced down. The wide-legged green pants did seem on the high-wader side. He shrugged. "You insisted on washing them the other day. They probably shrank in the water."

"They felt cruddy," Holly said. "Granted, they never had before, but they couldn't have shrunk. They're magic."

"Then they shouldn't have needed washing at all," he told her.

"I suppose." She changed the subject. "That boss of yours is really pushy."

"He's the boss. He's allowed to be."

"I'll make sure he gets a bushelful of niceness in his stocking this year."

"Don't. None of us would know what to do with a nice boss." He sighed. "I'd better go and get this over with."

"This is not an attack of the Huns, Raymond," Holly said. "You're supposed to feel good about it, dammit."

"I feel good," he lied.

At the church, the television station's camera crew stood next to the freelance newspaper reporter and photographer on the front steps. The building was located in the middle of the Badlands, as the neighborhood was known—a lone haven in a drug-infested area. A slew of church officials also stood on the steps. All had broad smiles. Raymond got out of his car after parking it around the corner. He preferred his personal vehicle not to appear in any photos or film. It made him feel less exposed.

He shook hands with the minister and his staff, their

gratitude so genuine he couldn't help but feel good about helping them out with the toys. The cameras rolled and clicked, while the newspaper reporter took notes and the TV reporter did her intro in four takes. The station got its credit and the sight of all the toys being unloaded did add to Raymond's growing sense of goodwill about taking up Holly's "suggestions."

"Too bad we have no funds to wrap the gifts for the children," the minister said.

"See? I told you," Holly said, popping in.

Raymond looked at the minister, conscious of the TV camera recording the discussion. "Can't you get the locals to donate the paper or the funds?"

The man bristled. "Does this neighborhood look like it can afford to spare money for wrapping paper?"

"Yeah," Holly added. "Hey! I think I'm feeling better."

"What if you're not?" he whispered out of the corner of his mouth to her. "Aren't you taking a big chance in being here? What if you suddenly turn visible and are on TV?"

"Good point." Holly popped out.

At least he'd gotten rid of the nag.

"I heard that thought," her voice said.

"I'm sorry," Raymond told the minister, while thinking even darker thoughts about Holly. "We didn't think about wrapping paper."

The church people said nothing.

Raymond dug out his wallet and handed over all his cash. "I hope this helps."

Everyone laughed and smiled at his offering.

"It does, son, it does." The minister winked at him, clearly knowing full well he'd trapped Raymond into it. "Bless you and have a Merry Christmas!"

The television reporter signed off after that. So did the cameras. Raymond shook hands with everyone again and left. As he walked away from the church, he noticed two kids, no older than Michael's Amy, standing on the sidewalk. They stared wide-eyed at him.

"You from Santa Claus, mister?" one asked.

Raymond smiled. "I'm just trying to help your church."

The kids' faces split into big grins, and they talked together excitedly about what they might get from the toys. Suddenly Raymond's spirits lifted and he didn't mind the way he'd been maneuvered into donating a van full of toys—and money for paper to wrap them. The effort seemed more than worth it, at the sight of the kids' anticipation of a nice Christmas.

"See?" Holly said, *very* smug this time as she popped in. "I told you so."

"So you did." Okay, he thought. She'd been right about the need to do it—and about feeling good afterward.

His happy mood lasted until he rounded the corner, to where his car was parked. The tires on the side facing him had been stripped off, the thieves not even courteous enough to put the car on cinder blocks. The vehicle wasn't listing, giving him a big clue that the tires were probably missing on the other side, too. The passenger-side window was smashed in, and as he got closer, he saw his glove box had been broken open. His one unit-radio and CD player looked tampered with, big scratches marring its front. The good news was that the equipment's antitheft device had obviously worked. The bad news was that his car alarm hadn't. They must have bypassed it, somehow. To add to the insult, the driver's seat had a long rip down its back.

"Merry Christmas?" Holly murmured sheepishly and popped out.

Raymond cursed as he stared at his vehicle. Fury shot through him at the boldness of the thieves—and at their timing. His nice little spirit lift had winked out faster than Holly had. He thought about returning to the church to report the assault on his car, but decided the media people would go crazy for the story's negative ending, which would hurt the church. Instead, he flipped open his cellular phone and dialed 911. He reported the theft, then called Charlie.

"You owe me a new car," he said, and explained what had happened.

The station manager roared with laughter. Raymond was not thrilled.

"Stinker," he muttered. "Send one of the interns to get me."

When he finally arrived home that night, after spending hours in the police station, Raymond was too tired to be angry. He flopped down on the sofa, his face nestled in the cushions.

What a day, he thought. *What a flipping day.*

The scent of vanilla and spice reached his nostrils. A finger eventually poked him on the shoulder when he didn't move. "Raymond? Are you okay?"

"No, I am not okay," he said, turning his head to the side to speak. He didn't look directly at her. He just couldn't.

"You did a nice thing today."

"I spent most of the day in the police station. And I was the victim! That was not nice."

"Now don't get upset."

He turned his face into the seat cushion to keep himself

from yelling at her. That was the only way he wouldn't get "upset."

"Raymond?"

Go away, he thought.

"You don't really mean that. Raymond? I'm sorry about your car. You warned me it would be a mess. I guess it was."

He sighed and turned to her again. Her contrite expression was sincere. He admitted her heart was in the right place, even if her judgment went wacky. At least she hadn't tried to fix him up with a woman. She was improving.

"My car getting ripped-off wasn't your fault," he conceded, turning to face her again.

"I still feel bad about it."

"Thanks."

"You look tired."

"I am. Filling out seven thousand police reports takes a lot out of a person."

"Seven thousand!" She whistled. "That is a lot."

He half smiled, albeit very reluctantly. "It's an exaggeration of speech, Holly."

"How many did you really have to fill out?"

"I don't know. About five or six different forms."

"Five or six! How can you make a big deal out of five or six?"

"Because," he began angrily, "you have to get interviewed and you get bounced around from person to person, none of whom knows what to do with you until finally someone gets disgusted and they give you another form to fill out. They get annoyed when you don't have your registration and insurance numbers because those things were stolen out of the glove compartment. And then they forget to tell you they're done with you so you can go home. Finally you say to hell with this and you go home anyway. I did.''

''Oh.'' She thought that over for a few moments. ''Would you like something to eat? You'll feel better. I know I do.''

''I'm too damn tired to eat. I could use a drink. There's a bottle in a cabinet in the kitchen. Dewar's.''

''Okay.''

She came back a few minutes later with a bottle but no glass and no ice. He realized he'd forgotten to ask for them.

''To hell with that, too,'' he said, sitting up. He took the bottle from her, opened its screw cap and took a hefty swig. The fiery alcohol burned a satisfying path to his stomach, leaving the slight aftertaste of liquid peat. ''Now I feel better.''

Holly sat down next to him on the sofa. ''I wish I did. Why do I make a mess of these things?''

''Hell, honey, I don't know. Talent?'' He offered her the bottle. ''Here. Try a little Dutch courage, as they say.''

She took the bottle and sniffed the open neck. She recoiled. ''That's strong!''

''It's Scotch. A good brand, too. Here, I'll take it back.'' He put his hand out, but Holly held the Dewar's away.

''I didn't say I didn't want any. I'm feeling almost as bad as you over your car.'' She took a big gulp...and coughed violently.

The Scotch fell from her nerveless fingers as she gasped for breath. Raymond retrieved it before it spilled its precious contents. He grinned at Holly's watering eyes. ''You sip it, like tea.''

''Oh, sure. I'm real knowledgeable about *that*. Here.'' She snatched the bottle from him and took a little sip. She didn't choke on it, although her eyes seemed to bulge slightly. "There. Better?"

He grinned at her. "For your sake."

"You know, this stuff isn't bad once it's not trying to kill you." She pursed her lips and studied the amber liquid. "It's got a nice burn to it."

"It'll kill you if you drink enough of it," he said.

"But we're not doing that."

"Nope. We're only drowning our temporary sorrows for an evening." He frowned at her. "I don't know if you should even be drinking liquor. You're an elf. Your anatomy's different."

She glanced down, then took another sip—a bigger one this time that didn't choke her, either. "My anatomy looks no different than yours."

"Your anatomy is *way* different than mine and it looks damn fine, too. But that wasn't what I meant." He took the bottle and drank from it. Normally satisfying, the burn didn't quite reach the new sensations now swirling in his gut.

Holly reached for the bottle and drank from it. He took it from her again, swigging more Scotch down. The bottle went back and forth several more times. Finally Holly asked, "Does my anatomy look better than Kathryn's?"

The bottle exchanged hands once more. Raymond drank from it. "Oh, yeah."

"Really?" She looked pleased She also looked very rosy in the cheeks. "What about What's-her-name in Aruba?"

"What about her?"

Holly took the bottle again and drank from it. "Boy, you can grow to like this, can't you?"

"Moderation is the key, lady. Moderation in everything.'' He grabbed the bottle and eyed its much-lowered contents. ''We're definitely moderating.''

He had himself another good swallow of good Scotch. She nudged him.

''The bimbo from Aruba.''

''Definitely better.''

''What!''

''Yours, not hers.''

''Good.'' She smiled slyly and put her hand over his, guiding the Scotch bottle to her mouth. Because she didn't have total control, some of the fine whiskey spilled out around the edges of her lips when she took her drink. She choked and laughed while pushing the bottle away. ''I think I'm done.''

Raymond watched the amber liquid dribble down the creamy flesh of her neck and throat. ''I don't think I am.''

He leaned forward and pressed his tongue to her skin, lapping up the spilled Scotch. God, he thought, never had he tasted anything so intoxicating in his life.

''Do that some more,'' Holly whispered.

Chapter Eight

Holly shivered in delight as Raymond pressed biting little kisses along her throat. Her head spun. This was so much more pleasurable than eating and drinking, she thought.

His scent, unique to him, swirled through her brain, already imprinted and remembered so well. She was all fuzzy and warm as if the Scotch had created a soft fire inside her. Her limbs were languid and heavy. They couldn't seem to move on command, but hesitated as if not quite sure she'd asked anything of them. That sensation, combined with the sensations Raymond created, only added to the marvelous lethargy.

When she could no longer resist the urge to have his mouth and tongue on her own, she touched his cheek and lifted his head. He stared at her, those brown eyes of his glazed with desire for her. Holly was female enough to recognize it and feminine enough to glory in it.

"Kiss me," she said. "I love it when you kiss me."

"I think you're drunk," Raymond replied. "I think I am, too."

"Oh, stop yakking and just kiss me."

He did. His mouth was a fire that ignited her own. She wrapped her arms around his shoulders and gave herself up to the kiss. She felt his breath on her cheek. She tasted his tongue with hers. She wanted to be like this always, in his arms, kissing him. To hell with helping him, she thought. *She* needed the help now. She *had* to experience everything her body was crying out for. She had to experience him. Just once. Once wouldn't hurt, wherever it led.

His hand covered her breast and she moaned in the back of her throat. Her blood quickened in her veins. It pooled and throbbed deep in her belly. She clawed at him when his thumb rubbed her nipple. She wanted him to touch her bare flesh. She wanted to touch his.

The notion emboldened her and she pulled his shirt up. Her palms spread along the hot skin at his waist. His muscles were hard, his body lean. She could just feel his ribs hidden under his flesh. Touching him only enhanced all the sensations he created inside her. She wanted to touch him more and began to pull his shirt over his head—or tried. Somehow the garment wouldn't go between their nearly-touching noses while they kissed.

She stopped kissing him.

"What?" he asked in bewilderment, his voice hoarse.

She giggled and pulled the shirt off his shoulders and down his arms, trapping him. "I've got to get your shirt off."

"Wait." He put his hands over hers. "Maybe we should stop."

"But why?" she asked. Out of the corner of her eye, she saw the fine dark hairs on his chest that arrowed down past the waist of his jeans. The idea of stopping seemed utterly ludicrous.

"You don't know what you're doing."

"I'm taking off your shirt, and I hope you'll do the same to me. You'll show me the rest, I'm sure." She peered at him in growing disappointment. "Or maybe you don't want to."

He chuckled. "I'm dying to."

"Okay, then." She pulled his shirt the rest of the way down his arms and flung it behind the sofa. She eyed him happily. "Raymond, you're very beautiful. Are all men this beautiful?"

"Holly, Holly, Holly."

"What? What? What?" She touched his chest, amazed at the way the silky hairs tickled her palms and the hard wall of his muscles sent shivers of gratification through her. "Oh, I know, I know. Do I know."

"Holly." He kissed her under her ear, finding a spot that sent runnels of delight along her veins. She felt as if she'd been shot out of a cannon. He whispered, "We have got to stop this and soon. I'm only a man and you're an...elf. A very sexy elf. We don't belong together."

She didn't want to hear this and so she kissed him soundly on the lips. She poured every emotion, all her senses, into the kiss. She touched him everywhere she could, taking delicious revenge from his moans of need and his frantic response to her boldness.

She knew she was victorious when he flipped off her tunic and kissed her bare breasts. Holly almost died from the amazing kaleidoscope of sensations spinning deep in her body.

"See?" she managed to say in breathless pants. "You talk too much, Raymond."

He lifted his head and kissed her. "I talked for you."

"I'm a big elf. I know what I'm doing."

He laughed, then sobered. "Holly, we're both half-drunk and we're not thinking straight."

"I know what I want. I want you."

She pulled him down onto the cushions, tired of talking,

She only wanted to taste and feel—to feel him in the most intimate of ways. Elves never experienced this special kind of closeness. Never had the whisper of an urge for intimacy. She'd watched enough television to know this sex thing was a compelling act to breed and procreate. Elves had no need to procreate. They simply existed. But, boy, someone had left the best piece of the puzzle out, and now she had found it.

Something told her she ought to be more afraid of this than anything else. But she wasn't afraid. How could she be afraid of something that felt so right?

His hands turned frenzied, coursing all over her body. They swept along her hips and thighs, nearly touching her in the most intimate of places. Her body urged more from him. He grasped her pants and slid them from her legs. Cool air swept over her nakedness. She tried to cover herself, instinctively embarrassed to be seen so.

He pushed her hands aside and kissed her at the junction of her thighs. "You're perfect."

"I am?" She smiled, suddenly not embarrassed and very pleased to have pleased him. "I know you're perfect, too. I've seen you before."

He chuckled again.

If being with him had felt right before, now she knew being naked with him went beyond perfection. She couldn't believe humans had had such an amazing secret. If she were to lose this—if she ever got back home again—then she wouldn't want to be an elf any longer.

He stroked her hidden folds and she forgot everything, even to breathe. Nothing worried her as she gave herself up to the need he created. No one else could wreak such havoc within her except Raymond.

"I shouldn't," he whispered, perspiration breaking out on his skin.

"Yes, you should," she told him and stroked him in kind.

He moaned her name, stretching them both along the length of the sofa while they explored each other. He seemed to have a sixth sense about the moment when she needed more and pressed himself into the cradle of her thighs. His body was heavy—almost smothering and yet comfortable at the same time.

Holly's breath caught in her throat when he probed her soft inner flesh and she had a moment of hesitation, a fear of the unknown. Never had she felt so emotionally vulnerable. But then a surety, a rightness about their being together, washed it away.

She pressed herself into him, absorbing him into herself. Her body stretched and adjusted with a magic of its own.

Raymond groaned. "You are so perfect. So incredibly real. Am I hurting you?"

"Oh, no. It's wonderful," she murmured, stroking his back. "I think I need you, Raymond."

He smiled against her shoulder, as if she'd said something amusing, and then he began to move. The rhythm surprised her, and she followed her body's urges and matched his. The movements grew faster and faster. Her yearnings increased. She could no longer bear them. She needed something more. And more and more. She needed it now.

Her body reached another plateau and began to release itself in a wild, throbbing pleasure that pulsated along every inch of her flesh. Holly cried out in her ecstasy. She clung to Raymond as wave after wave rose and flung itself over her. She felt him stiffen and moaned her name as his body throbbed inside hers. She knew he felt the same extraordinary thing as she.

Holly let it take her into its soft, velvet blackness. Her only anchor was her body wrapped around Raymond's own.

RAYMOND SURFACED FROM the most intense, most delicious and most emotional pleasure he had every experienced. Holly clung to him, her unique perfume of vanilla and spice imprinted in every fiber of his being. He realized they had fallen asleep for several hours after making love....

What had they done?

All the satisfaction left with a whoosh of common sense. She had been drunk and not thinking straight. She had never experienced intimacy before, and he had taken her quickly on the sofa. She deserved far better. She was an elf, and he had followed his own urges, ignoring any complications he could cause. He hadn't used protection, either. While his health was good and hers clearly was because of her virginity, what if a pregnancy occurred?

Now that was complicated.

"I'm sorry," he whispered.

"I know," she replied, opening her eyes.

He hadn't considered that she would be aware of his thoughts. His concerns had surfaced so quickly, he hadn't been able to suppress them. Still, he was glad she could read his thoughts. Her magic hadn't been affected by her loss of innocence—something neither of them had considered.

"Holly, this wasn't fair to you," he said. "You've never been intimate before. You're an elf so you don't understand what sex even means between two people. And I didn't protect you from a pregnancy. You deserved so much better—not a guy like me. Hell, I'm not even doing this right."

She gazed at him for a long moment, then kissed his cheek. "Thank you. But I wanted to do this, so I'm responsible for what happens to me, although I won't get pregnant. Who ever heard of baby elves? I have regrets, but this was so wonderful they don't seem to matter." She paused. "Raymond, is it okay to say it was so wonderful?"

He chuckled and relaxed. "Oh, yeah."

She grinned and rubbed his shoulders as he lay on top of her. "It was wonderful. Boy, the things we're missing back at the North Pole. We had no idea about sex. Well, we sort of do, because we're aware of the world, but we didn't know it felt this good!"

Raymond had a vision of elves everywhere getting the word about sex and turning the North Pole into one big orgy. He burst into laughter. "Holly, you kill me."

"Oh, I hope not," she said, adding shyly, "Would it be possible...could we do this sex thing again?"

"Sex maniac," he told her, tugging the tip of her pointed ear.

"Is that bad?" she asked so earnestly he had to laugh again.

"No. Not with me."

"Good." She sighed. "So could we?"

He wanted to. He needed to make love to her properly this time, for her sake.

Holly's eyes widened. "You mean we did it wrong? Oh, let's do it right, Raymond. It must be beyond awesome when it's right because it's awesome now."

Raymond chuckled. "My prowess is secure. But I was thinking of things like a comfortable bed, not a cramped sofa. And a little more care on my part to give you more pleasure."

"You couldn't possibly give me more pleasure."

He kissed her nose. "Thank you, but I think I can. I know I can."

"Oh, my."

"And we need protection, just to be safe. That's upstairs with the bed, in the nightstand."

"Okay." She popped out.

Raymond fell face first the few inches to the sofa cushions, landing with a thud. The roughened upholstery scratched his naked skin. His body shrank at the abrupt loss of her nestled warmth.

"I'm up here with the bed and the protection!" Holly called out.

"I'm down here naked as a jaybird with my face in the sofa," he muttered in disgust. His words were muffled by the seat cushions.

"Raymond!"

"All right, all right!" he yelled back, sitting up. The Scotch bottle caught his eye. He thought about a drink to steady his shot nerves but booze had gotten them into trouble the last time.

He pulled on his pants and climbed the stairs. He knew they needed to talk. Despite the bed and the protection, sex had all kinds of complications for them. Ones she had no clue existed.

But all rational thought left him when he saw Holly lying under the covers of his bed. Her blond hair spread out across his pillows and her smile beckoned. She looked so innocent and so delicious that he couldn't *not* consider making love to her again.

"Oh, that would be wonderful," she murmured.

"I thought so, too."

He shucked his pants and crawled under the covers with her.

"I'M HUNGRY," Holly announced in the wee hours of the morning as Raymond got ready for work.

Raymond stopped fixing coffee and glanced over at her. "You feel okay?"

"I have a headache. Is that normal after sex?"

Raymond laughed. "No, although many people have used headaches to avoid sex."

"Why? It's wonderful!"

He grinned. "I'm extremely glad you think so. But you probably have a headache from the whiskey. I have one, too. We drank too much and now we're paying."

"Then, other than paying for drinking, I feel marvelous," she said, putting her arms around his waist.

She liked touching him. In fact, she wanted to drag him back into bed and touch him all over again.

She still couldn't get over the incredible new feelings racing inside her. Oh, what she had missed out on! She hadn't known how human sex would affect her—well, she did now—but she'd had no idea what she might have risked when they made love, or whether she had risked anything at all. Her magic seemed to be intact so far. She didn't feel differently, magic-wise, so she doubted it would be more skewed than it already was. Feeling such well-being, she was positive even her earlier problems had to be on the mend. She just felt too damn good for it to be otherwise. Well, maybe her hunger hadn't quite been sated. But then, she had worked up an appetite.

And she doubted elf and human physiology matched closely enough to make a baby. No elf had ever had a baby. She wasn't sure exactly where elves came from. From magic dust, she supposed. Elves did not arrive in the human way, that was for sure.

"Since you're hungry, I guess you're not over your elf

flu yet." He rubbed his forehead. "I didn't get enough sleep, either."

She giggled and hugged him. "You didn't get any sleep. Your choice, if I remember. I was trying to be good. I wish we could go back to bed—"

"You're insatiable, elf," he said, groaning. "Holly, I have got to go to work!"

"Poo." She sighed and let go of him. "If you must, you must. So what's for breakfast?"

"Whatever you want to make. I've got to go in a few minutes."

She glanced at the clock. It wasn't quite five in the morning. "Couldn't you be late for once?"

His expression would have cut stone. "No."

"Okay, okay. You can't blame an elf for wheedling." She grinned at him, undeterred by his dark look. "I'll pop in after breakfast."

"I don't know," he said dubiously.

"I'll be good," she promised. "I only want to be near you. Maybe something nice will happen to help you find your heart."

"Holly, my heart's fine."

"Oh, no. It couldn't possibly be," she replied. "It doesn't feel like mine. Raymond, you need to have joy. Like this. I'll help you, don't worry. Today, I feel inspired."

"God better help me, then." But he chuckled.

She thought it was a start.

He gave her a parting hug and kissed her goodbye. His gesture satisfied Holly temporarily. Raymond had been alone too long to be more demonstrative. He had "demonstrated" enough, as it was. More than enough. She still tingled from it. And she was a little sore, too.

"Forget a bath," she said out loud. "This was a hundred times better."

After a breakfast of pretty much everything in the refrigerator, Holly decided to look for Raymond's Christmas decorations. She would put them up after visiting the studio. It was getting on to Christmas, after all, and one needed the trappings to enhance the mood.

Only Holly couldn't find Raymond's decorations in any of his closets. Not a single wreath or red bow to be had.

"Don't tell me he doesn't even put anything up!" she muttered, hands on hips.

She popped into the studio to lecture him on the importance of mood-setting paraphernalia.

"What the hell!" Tommy yelped while Bob shouted an obscenity.

They stared at Holly, shock in their eyes. Holly stared back at them for a horrifyingly endless moment, then popped out. She popped into the town house.

"No!" she wailed, as Raymond's familiar kitchen came into focus. She had not only been seen again, but she hadn't popped into that invisible-yet-aware state where she could eavesdrop on the aftermath of her appearance.

Fear shot through her at the evidence of her lack of control. This couldn't be happening to her. It couldn't.

She stood frozen for the longest time, before she pulled her shot nerves together and tried again to pop into the studio unobserved.

"Hey!" Bob shouted. "She's back!"

Holly looked helplessly at Raymond, who gaped at her. She popped out again...and again right back to the town house.

"It's not working!" she shouted, this time trying to get back home.

Thoughts jumbled through her. What did this mean? Everything was all wrong. It couldn't be an elf flu. Her head felt ready to explode from her shock. She held it, terrified it would do just that. Maybe it was some kind of flu. Hell, she thought. She needed help desperately. She had to find the answer to what was happening to her.

Again, she focused with all her might on home, but like before, nothing happened. She was still on her own—and in worse shape than before!

A ringing startled her, and she screamed before realizing it was the telephone. She'd never used the device, never answered it when Raymond wasn't home, so the damn thing didn't have to scare her to death.

"Stop it!" she shouted, as it rang a fourth time.

The telephone clicked dead and the answering machine came on. Raymond had the answer message turned down, but she could hear the voices of the callers. Raymond said it screened his calls so he could hear them and then decide if he wanted to talk with whoever was on the other end of the line.

Suddenly Raymond's voice came over the machine. "Holly, are you there? Pick up the phone. I've only got a minute."

"I'm here!" Holly ran for the receiver. She picked it up. "Raymond!"

"Holly, pick up the phone."

"I did!" Why couldn't he hear her?

"Holly, pick up the flipping phone!"

"But I did!" she shouted, tears running down her cheeks.

"Push the Speak button on the receiver!"

She found the correct button and pressed it with shaking fingers. The line came on. "Raymond! I'm visible and you can read my mind!"

"I guessed. Never mind. Holly, I only have a moment on this break. Are you okay?"

"No!" she cried. "Everyone saw me. Twice!"

"I know. I don't think this is an elf flu."

"Why is this happening?"

"I don't know, but we'll find out. Right now, everyone thinks you're an elaborate joke with cameras and I'm the one doing it. That's okay. You stay put, and I'll get home as soon after the show as I can."

"That's easy because I can't go anywhere! I can't even pop halfway now, like I could before." She began to cry as her emotions and her panic overwhelmed her.

"We'll work on it when I get home."

His voice sounded so sure and so confident that she took heart from it. From him. Sniffing back tears, she said, "Okay."

He said nothing for a moment. Holly felt words forming in her mouth but she couldn't say them.

"I have to go. Sit tight until I get home. Bye."

She set the receiver back on its stand and went over to the sofa. She sat down on the edge of the cushions—the cushions where she had experienced the most marvelous thing in the world. She sat tight.

SEVERAL HOURS LATER, when Raymond arrived home, she was still sitting tight. He was no sooner through the door when she flew into his arms. "Raymond! Thank God you're here!"

"It's okay." He patted her on the back. She clung to him, needing his strength. "Holly, let me get my coat off."

"Oh." She released him and helped him off with his coat, saying, "I can't believe this. At least earlier, I was around for a while before someone saw me. But this time...I couldn't even trust popping back in to see if it would happen a third time!''

"Did you try going anywhere else?" he asked.

"Just back home. I couldn't, like before. And then I sat tight like you said."

"Literally?"

She frowned. "I didn't move off the sofa, if that's what you mean."

He grinned.

"This is not funny!" she wailed, bursting into tears.

"No, I know it isn't. Let's sit down and figure this out."

They sat on the sofa, but not together. Holly frowned again, this time at the distance between them. She scooted closer to him, wanting his warmth for comfort. He was the only solid and real thing in this disaster. He was the only one she knew, the only one she could depend on to help her.

"Did you eat?" he asked.

She looked heavenward. "What kind of question is that? Who cares if I ate?"

"Because the last time you were hungry, you were seen."

"That's right." She felt as if they were on to something. "I did eat much earlier. Maybe that was it. Okay, I won't eat again."

Her stomach growled loudly.

"You may not have a choice in the matter."

His smile held more amusement than sympathy.

"I wish you weren't so happy about this," she grumbled.

"It could be worse."

"How?"

He thought for a moment. "Good question."

His stomach growled.

Holly grinned reluctantly, despite her panic. "I guess we'd both better eat."

They made some sandwiches—another new taste treat for Holly. She wished she could enjoy it more; she wished she wasn't enjoying it at all.

"There's got to be a logic to this," Raymond said finally. "If we can figure out what it is, we'll have the cause. That makes it easier to find the cure."

Holly grasped at it. "Okay. So what's logical about it?"

"Hell, I don't know. Let's try and remember what you were doing when you were seen before. That's what the detective books do when they're trying to find the murderer." He intoned, "What were you doing on the night in question?"

"But I didn't murder anybody!" Holly exclaimed.

"I'm just joking around to lighten the mood."

"You are sick. You know that?"

"Holly, it's irony. Never mind. What were you doing when you were first seen?"

This irony business confused her still, but Holly thought about his serious question. At least she hoped it was serious; she understood it. "I was kissing you."

"Oh." He looked surprised, as if he'd forgotten. "That's right. Amy saw you. Then Tommy did, but you weren't kissing me then."

"No. And I wasn't the other times I was seen, in that bar."

"And you weren't kissing me this morning."

"No, I wasn't." She flushed, remembering the night before. "Not right then. So where's the logic in this?"

"I don't know." He ran his hand through his hair. "Magic isn't logical. Is it?"

"Yes, it is," Holly said, sipping her tea after the meal. Raymond had made it for her, and she liked it better than coffee. It gave her an ancient comfort. "Three laws govern magic. Law number one says one cannot make magic unless one *is* from magic. Law number two says one's strength in magic is governed by one's place in the hierarchy. And law number three is that laws numbers one and two are absolute."

"Okay," he said, frowning. "What do they mean?"

"I would think they're self-explanatory."

"Not to me, nonmagical creature that I am."

"That's true. Number one means you, as a human, can never make magic because you don't come from magic. Number two means a wizard will always beat an elf in magical abilities but not necessarily in chess." She smiled at having made a little joke. Lord knew, she needed one. "And number three says one and two are all there are to the laws of magic. I don't think we'll find what's happening to me in the laws."

"Not unless a wizard is messing with you." He whistled. "There really are wizards?"

"Sure." She frowned at him. "Why wouldn't they exist?"

"Beat any of them at chess lately?"

"No. Thank goodness. It really ticks them off."

"Why do I think I'm missing out on a whole new realm of the universe?"

"Because you are. Raymond, this is not helping me." She sipped more tea.

"It's tied to the eating-and-drinking thing," he said. "But how did that all start?"

"With kissing?" she suggested. She wished he would take her in his arms and kiss this latest disaster away.

"Maybe they want me to continue to see you," he began. "Not that I'm having any doubts about you being real."

"No. Maybe. Wait." She gazed at him. "It was last night."

He stared back at her, saying nothing.

"I should have realized before," she continued, as her theory grew. "But I was so upset this morning that I wasn't thinking straight. No matter how you try and look at what happened before, you only have to look at last night to explain what happened today. How could it not? It was the only thing different. But it was a *huge* thing."

He glanced away from her, then back but not quite meeting her gaze. "I suppose we could dance around it some more, but that's all we'd be doing. I think you're right. I'm sorry."

"It's not your fault, Raymond." She smiled sadly. "I made the choice and I take responsibility. I should have realized there would be a price to pay for human intimacy. That's not your fault, either. I'm here to help you and I forgot myself. I'm sorry, Raymond. But I don't regret being with you. It was wonderful."

She expected him to agree with her, but he said nothing.

"Raymond?" she queried, her insides tensing.

"I guess I'd better say it now."

RAYMOND STARED AT Holly, the words choking him. How could he make her understand the reality of adult relationships? He would have to.

"Holly, you're right," he began. "What we did was wonderful. But humans—men...and women—take pleasure in the moment. It doesn't imply a long-term relationship. Or even desiring one. You didn't know that when you and I were intimate. You couldn't understand—not where you come from."

She frowned. "I don't understand any of this."

"It means... Holly, I like you. I think." He grinned wryly. "I don't want to see you hurt, but I can't give anything to a relationship with you."

"Because you have no heart. Yes, I know that, Raymond."

The matter-of-fact way she said it bothered him. His only concern, when everyone had seen her, had been for her well-being. He'd had to use every ounce of control to keep from running home to her. The urge was even stronger after he'd heard the terror in her voice and her tears. That instinctive reaction of caring unnerved him. He knew himself. He knew it wouldn't last. But he wasn't the monster she made him out to be. "I'm not heartless, Holly. If I were, I would tell you to get out."

Her lip quivered. "But where would I go?"

"That's the point, isn't it?"

She drew in a breath. "I'd just come right back, Raymond. I have to help you. In fact, if you did that... Well, I'd have to ask for overtime to get the job done."

She patted his hand. Raymond felt like a little kid who'd just had a temper tantrum, only to discover Mom wasn't buying into it.

He tried again, wanting to be straightforward and honest with her. "Holly, having sex does not automatically mean we love each other and we'll be together forever."

"Oh, I know that. I'm only here until Christmas, anyway." She crossed her fingers. "If all goes well."

He gave up. She didn't understand what he truly meant, and he doubted she would ever grasp that he was incapable of meeting her emotional expectations. If she ever did, she would be very hurt. He could do nothing about that. He'd tried to warn her.

But this visibility business brought up another concern. "Holly, what if this condition of yours is permanent?"

"I don't want to think about that," she said firmly.

"You can't stick your head in the sand," he replied.

"Why would I do that?" she asked.

"It's an expression. Ostriches stick their heads in the sand when they don't want to face trouble."

"Actually, they stick their heads in the sand to cool off, and then can't hear trouble when it sneaks up on them," she told him. Suddenly she gaped. "I get it now. Okay, I won't stick my head in the sand to not see trouble coming."

"I think it's already here," he muttered under his breath. Louder, he said, "You have to think about your future and what will happen if this is permanent. What will you do?"

She said nothing for a while, clearly mulling over her situation. Her demeanor changed and she seemed to grow outwardly stronger. "Look. I have until Christmas to fix you up. That's...how long?"

"A week."

"Oh, boy. I'll know then what my future is. In the meantime, I'll go about my work." She pointed a finger at him. "That means you, Raymond. I feel better."

"I don't," he muttered, feeling like an ostrich with its head in the sand.

"I won't pop in anywhere until I know for sure I won't be seen by anyone but you."

"I'm thrilled." But he was relieved she wouldn't be popping in anywhere. It had been enough to handle when she hadn't been seen.

She looked at him solemnly. "And we can't have sex."

Somehow, in all his concerns to try and point out that

they would have to terminate their relationship before it started, she had understood the crux of the matter.

And that bothered him more than anything else.

He couldn't fathom his mixed emotions about her. Why should he be hurt when she rejected him? What else could it be when she told him, in no uncertain terms, that he had been a one-night stand of elfin curiosity and she was out of there by Christmas? Now *that* was rejection.

He ought to be relieved, he thought, if not downright clicking up his heels with joy. This whole thing had gotten out of hand—with an elf. An elf!

Only that didn't matter when he looked at her and her face satisfied something deep inside him. Nothing mattered when he played over and over their lovemaking— the innocence and the exquisiteness of it. He imagined never experiencing her again, never taking their being together in lovemaking to its furthest exploration. His heart sank, and oddly, never had he felt lonelier.

Holly gazed at him. He wanted to wipe the earnestness from her blue eyes. He wanted her to feel exactly what he was feeling. He realized she couldn't make out his thoughts, for if she could, she would know his anger at her.

"I absolutely agree," he said at last, forcing himself to smile. "Sex was a big mistake between us. We know that now."

Her expression went blank.

"I've moved on," he added, just for good measure.

Chapter Nine

Holly wasn't happy when she yawned.

Hunger and chills and sex and now exhaustion were all involved in her distorted abilities. She couldn't get home, although she'd tried several more times since Raymond had returned after her disastrous appearance in his studio.

She had also tried popping into limbo, but that hadn't worked. She had to have a destination—which, she discovered, had to be attached in some way to Raymond. Boy, had he been surprised when she'd accidentally popped into the garbage can when he'd taken out the trash. Not a thrill happenstance, but she'd gotten a bath of out it. That had been nice, even though she shouldn't have felt as though she needed one.

Now she sat in front of the TV in Raymond's shirt and sweatpants. They hung past her feet but that was okay. She liked wearing his clothes, even if they were too big. Somehow they made her feel more feminine and closer to him. She needed to feel close to him, for in spite of being outwardly calm, she had never felt so alone.

Raymond had gone to bed earlier. She glanced at the stairs, several things he'd said still puzzling her.

What had he meant, that he'd "moved on"?

She sensed some undercurrent in his words on the subject of no sex, but she hadn't been able to grasp his thoughts. Another of her magic abilities lost. Boy, she had really screwed up.

"I won't think about that," she said tersely.

She was scared to, even though she felt like one of Raymond's ostriches.

She never should have experimented with human things. This was a punishment for that. If she'd only thought instead of panicking, she would have recognized the root of her problems. If she'd even thought before trying sex...although she didn't know what she might have done. Missing out on the most marvelous sensations she'd ever experienced seemed more wrong than not being a good little elf.

While no one had told her she shouldn't experience human sensations, even an idiot elf should have realized sex was forbidden territory. If the first rule of magic said one could not make magic unless one was magic and the third said the first was absolute, then the opposite held for her. One could not make human unless one was human and that was absolute, no doubt. No wonder she was all scrambled.

But what the hell did it mean that he'd moved on? Moved on from where?

Holly popped into Raymond's bedroom. She peered through the darkness at him. All she saw was a big lump in the bed.

"Raymond?" she whispered, trying not to think of when she'd been a lump in the bed with him. A very active lump.

"What?" His voice was strong and clear, as if he hadn't been asleep.

"Were you asleep?"

"No."

She glanced at the clock. The hour was late—for him. "You should be asleep."

"Holly, what do you want?"

She paused, her brain totally blank. "I don't remember."

"Then go away so I can sleep."

He sounded angry with her. "Are you angry?"

"No. Just go back downstairs, okay?"

"All right."

She popped back downstairs. The sofa seemed lonely somehow and cold despite the little nest of quilts and pillows she'd made for herself. She tried to get cozy and watch television, but comfort eluded her.

She remembered her question and popped back upstairs. "Raymond, what do you mean, you've moved on? Are you leaving home?"

"I ought to. I've got the only house with Grand Central Station as a bedroom."

"Is that sarcasm or irony or an expression?" she asked.

"It's frustration. Holly, you shouldn't be in this bedroom."

"Why?"

"Because I'm trying to sleep, for one thing. And because we made love in here. It's awkward to have you here now."

"But we made love on the sofa and you didn't say anything about that."

"Because you have to sleep somewhere and a bedroom's more intimate with a man and a woman in it. More personal."

"Oh." She didn't quite grasp the difference so she said, "I wanted to ask you what you meant when you said you've moved on? Where are you going if you're not leaving home?"

"The nearest Marriott Hotel. Holly, do we have to discuss this now?"

"I don't know," she mused, trying to interpret how she felt inside. The question burned at her. "I think so."

He sighed. Loudly. "I couldn't get a shy elf. I couldn't get a wise elf—"

"I'm very wise," she said, bristling.

Dead silence greeted her.

"Sometimes," she added. "Forget what kind of elf you got and just tell me what you meant!"

"I meant... It's an expression, Holly. A euphemism for saying goodbye."

Her stomach lurched. She felt physically ill. She might never have experienced it before, but she recognized it. "Then you are leaving. Or you're kicking me out."

"Neither of us is going anywhere, Holly. This is my home and you have nowhere else to go. But listen. It's not you. It's me." His voice sounded as pained as she felt. "What we did was wrong. You really didn't know what you were doing. Making love was encouraging you about a future with me. Even without you being an entirely different creature, I don't want anyone in my life right now. I'm content. So when you said we won't have sex anymore, I was trying to say I understood what you meant."

His explanation bothered her deeply. It hurt. She wasn't sure why it should. Her time here was limited. She would be going home soon. She hoped. She was, she thought. She *was*. Raymond had only said he shared the common-sense decision of no sex. "Then why didn't you just say it that way?"

He didn't answer at first. "Because it sounds temporary, encouraging, to say I understood. I wanted it clear that it's final between us. We're not seeing each other anymore.''

''We're not? Are we being struck blind? Why can't we see each other?''

''I mean, we will only be friends from now on. No sex.''

''Why didn't you say that?'' She frowned at him, even though he was in deep shadow. ''You're making me very confused.''

''Holly…forget what I said before. I'm saying it now.''

She tried to read his mind but it was still closed to her. She realized how often she had taken her cues from what he really thought as opposed to what he said. That upset her more than losing some of her abilities. She sensed, too, that he wasn't being honest about something. Clearly, he didn't want closeness; and that saddened her. Why was he so afraid of closeness?

She was determined to have the answer.

She shivered. ''Raymond. I'm cold.''

''Do you want the bed?'' he asked, his tone exasperated.

''Sure.'' She slid in and snuggled against him, needing his body warmth.

''Holly!'' He shot off the mattress.

''What? Don't you want me to have the bed?'' she asked, completely confused now. ''Raymond, you get on the 'naughty' list by offering things and then taking them away.''

''I meant, I would give the bed to you, not share it *with* you. We had this discussion before.''

''We did?'' She really couldn't remember. ''You probably used some euphemism I didn't understand.''

''No kidding. Okay, you have the bed and I'll take the sofa.''

"But there's room for two here." She patted the place where he'd been lying.

"I thought we'd had this discussion, too. You were the first one to say no sex."

"Who said anything about sex? I don't want sex." She did, but she was terrified of what might happen next. "Do I have to spell it out for you? *I've moved on.*"

"Damn you, Holly!"

"What? What?" She glared at him. "I'm beginning to think those words mean something more than you said they did."

"Holly, I can't share the bed with you. It won't stay innocent."

"You mean we'll have sex?"

"Yes, we'll have sex!" He paced at the foot of the bed. "Holly, you can't just turn it off like a sink faucet—or am I being too euphemistic for you?"

"No. You...you can't turn your faucet off with me?" That notion pleased her no end.

"Can you?"

She thought about it. She liked his closeness. It comforted her. She loved his touch, despite what had happened in the aftermath. She *would* want intimacy again. She would have great difficulty resisting him. "I guess my faucet's dripping, too."

"Somehow that doesn't sound so great. Never mind. You take the bed, and I'll go downstairs and try to get some sleep."

"Oh, no. Now that I understand, I'll go downstairs. It's your bed."

"All right." A long time passed before he said, "Holly. Go downstairs."

"Oh!" She got out of bed and popped downstairs. The sofa hardly looked inviting. Another question occurred to her, one that had rummaged around inside her during their discussion. She popped back into his bedroom. "Raymond?"

He cursed loudly. "Dammit, Holly! I *have* to get some sleep."

"I know. I just had a quick question. Do you tell other women you've moved on after you have sex with them?"

"That's my business, not yours—"

"You do, don't you. Why?" Although it hurt even more to think he had, she felt she was on the verge of discovering why his heart was closed. If only she could unlock it, she could help him and be back to normal.

"Holly, go the hell downstairs and go to sleep."

"But, Raymond—"

"Holly!"

"I'm going," she muttered, popping out. When she popped into the living room again, she said, "Sheesh! Ask a simple question."

But that was the problem, she thought. If the question was truly simple, she would have her answer and she would be back home. At this time of year, they never had enough hands.

For the first time, a little voice inside her asked her what she was going back for.

IT WAS ALREADY DARK when Raymond walked through his front door.

Exhaustion rode him hard. Today was not the day he'd needed to attend a special station-strategy meeting for the coming year. He had only wanted to catch up on the sleep he'd missed because of Holly's all-nighter discussion.

Never had he been asked to poke inside himself so much as she had asked of him. He could only partly blame her remembered presence and her lingering scent for his inability to sleep. She made him think too damn much. She made him question, even crave, what he didn't trust.

"Where have you been?" Holly demanded, coming in from the kitchen.

"I'd say you sound like my mother," he said. "Only she never asked where I'd been as long as I wasn't in trouble."

"So were you in trouble?"

"All day." He rubbed his eyes, gritty from lack of sleep. "I'm wiped."

"I've heard of that one. You're tired."

She grinned at him, and he didn't feel quite so tired. Holly exasperated him, maddened him, but somehow she got under his skin.

"I made dinner," she said. "Well…I'm trying to."

Fear curled through his stomach and not because he might have to eat her concoction. "Trying to?"

She shrugged. "I was bored. I can't pop in to be with you, in case people can still see me. I can't pop anywhere else but with you. The television really is a boob tube after a while. I mean, how many talk shows can one see about people sleeping with their boyfriend's brother? Boy, this sex thing can really get out of hand, can't it?"

"Tell me about it," he muttered.

"Okay—"

"Never mind." He waved a hand to stop her before she started. She had a cockeyed enough view of most things without venturing down that road. "Just tell me what you did to the kitchen."

"You'd better see it."

Wednesday's words from the first Addams Family movie came to mind: *"Be afraid. Be very afraid."* He followed her into the kitchen—and gasped.

Dark batter dripped from cabinets and walls. Something

black smoked on a tray in the open oven. Bowls and platters and pots and dishes and pans cluttered every counter and table surface he owned. Raymond swore he couldn't see a square inch of open space. The smoke detector lay smashed in the middle of the kitchen floor. Boxes accompanied it—so many boxes, she must have emptied every one from the pantry closet. A haze of smoke and the stench of burned food hung like a pall over the room.

He stared at her, trying to figure out in his shock how she had managed such a disaster. "My God! How did this happen?"

Holly's mouth turned down. "I'm sorry, Raymond. I was just trying to make dinner. Chicken and noodles and a cake. Things got a little messy. Doesn't anyone realize how vague those directions on the boxes are?"

"Holly!" He swept a set of muffin tins he hadn't even known he owned from a chair. They clattered to the floor. He stared at them, then sat down heavily, his legs refusing to hold him upright any longer. This was too much, he thought, feeling his patience with her beyond the breaking point. "Dammit, Holly. How could you do this?"

"I was hungry…and I wanted to be nice.…" She sniffed, clearly holding back tears. "But the mixer went crazy on me, and the chicken package didn't say anything and I had to guess. And that damn thing kept shrieking at me. I killed it, but I'm not sorry I did. And the noodles all stuck to the pan. Nothing went right, and I feel more useless than I did before. I'm really sorry, Raymond. I'll clean it all up as soon as I figure out how."

She looked as depressed as his kitchen. Raymond's fury abated a little. "I appreciate what your purpose was, and damn straight you'll clean it up because I won't."

"I will," she replied eagerly. She paused. "You're not going to help me?"

"Nope." He stood. "I'm going to get my dinner from the Chinese place around the corner. You want some Moo Goo Gai Pan? That's as far as I'll go."

"I don't know what it is," she said.

"Me, neither. That's why I never order it." He sighed, feeling as if sighing was all he'd been doing since she'd entered his life. "I'll get you chicken and noodles since that's what you were all fired up to make when you fired up my kitchen."

He went over to the cabinets at his sink and took out the spray cleaner and a sponge. "Use this on the mess. Rinse the excess out of the sponge occasionally and put that burned chicken down the garbage disposal. On second thought, leave anything for the disposal to me. You'd probably grind up a body part by accident."

"But Raymond—"

"We all have to face up to our messes, Holly."

"Then why won't you face up to the mess you've made of your heart?" she retorted.

Her words caught him by surprise and his anger boiled over. He shoved a finger in her face. "Don't you even dare start that crap, you understand me?"

She eyed him for the longest time, then pressed her lips together and nodded. He had a feeling she was biting back words in an effort to be more gracious than he in a fight. He had a feeling she was winning.

He left her to her mess and went back out into the chilly evening. The brisk air barely cooled him, but eventually the aroma of spicy beef and ginger sauce at the Chinese restaurant pointed him in the direction of his lost equilibrium.

Holly had the ability to drive him insane.

After getting their takeout, he returned to the house and stood in front of the door. He didn't enter right away, afraid of what other disaster he might find. At last, he girded his loins—euphemistically speaking—and went inside.

Holly was on her hands and knees, pushing boxes around the floor. Her elfin derriere faced him and he forgot his frustrations as a surge of desire rose up in his very real loins. How she could turn him from anger to need, he didn't know. He only knew he wanted to taste her yet again. She was all the dinner he wanted.

She looked up, her gaze brightening when she spotted the brown carryall in his hand. "Dinner?"

He found his voice. "More appetizing than this."

"I hope so." She got up and washed her hands at the sink. Raymond pushed away his baser thoughts and cleared a place at the table for them both. He sorted through the packages. Holly opened the ones set out for her. She frowned. "What's this?"

"Chicken Lo Mein. Translated, it means chicken with noodles. I also got you won ton soup. That's pork and noodles."

"Okay." She took a spoon and tasted her soup. "This is good. Better than anything I can make."

"*Cleaner* than anything you can make."

"True."

"Holly." When she looked up, he said, "Please don't do anything anymore while I'm gone, okay?"

"Raymond, I can't just sit here, day in and day out, and not do anything."

"I know." The "day in and day out" sounded ominous. "I'll set you up with things to do. Things you can handle."

"I suppose." She smiled at him. "Originally, I wanted to put up some Christmas decorations, but I couldn't find them. Actually I wanted to do that yesterday and that's why I popped into the studio, but we'll leave the rest unsaid. Where do you keep your decorations?''

"I don't. I don't have any."

She looked heavenward. "I knew it. I just knew it. Raymond! How can you get into the spirit when you don't have decorations? They make everything so pretty and they make you feel good. No wonder you're a mess."

He was stung. "Hey, lots of people don't put up Christmas decorations. A lot of religions don't believe in Christmas—''

"But they believe in their own feasts and celebrations, and they enhance the mood with appropriate decorations."

"So Santa ignores them."

She gasped at the suggestion. "Never! That's an awful thing to say. I've told you before, everyone gets their gift of need. No one is missed."

"So what have I been getting all these years?"

"Hope, Raymond. You've been getting hope."

HOLLY DRIED THE LAST POT and put it on the now clear and clean counter. She sighed. What a fiasco!

She'd thought she would be helpful and nice when she'd had the idea to make dinner. Something had seemed to surface that urged her to do it. But everything had gone wrong. Especially that stupid smoke detector. It had refused to stop beeping. Okay, so she'd burned everything, but she'd thought she would go mad from the smoke detector's noise and had finally pulled it off the wall. Maybe she shouldn't have taken her frustrations out on it, but she had been beyond reason by then.

She glanced at the clock. Past midnight. Another useless day, she thought. A worse-than-useless day. No wonder she was having so much trouble with her abilities.

She'd lost sight of her objective—Raymond's heart. And time was running out.

She threw the dish towel on the counter and went into the living room to lie down. Sleep eluded her, despite the weariness in her bones. Holly took it as a good sign. Not a good sign, however, were the images racing through her brain.

She had to refocus on her objective—but how?

On impulse, she popped into Raymond's bedroom. She could see him in the darkness. He was asleep. She thought he looked wonderful, his face composed and relaxed. All the lines of cynicism were smoothed away for the night. She wondered what he dreamed. Did he dream of her?

Probably as a nightmare, she thought ruefully. He'd gotten her started on proper human cleaning technique and had left her to it—as a reminder not to do it again, he said. She was duly reminded, although she wished she'd had a wizard handy. One snap of the fingers and the kitchen would have been spotless. That ability was beyond her ken, when her ken was working.

She thought about his reaction last night to her being in the bedroom, but she hadn't felt awkward. She'd felt comforted. Conceding his point about the bed itself, she'd settled down against the wall nearest his bed and watched him sleep. She wondered if anyone had ever noticed how beautiful a man he was. Probably a lot of women had.

That wasn't the avenue for helping him. She admitted she couldn't encourage him with another woman again. Not after they had made love. The words sang through her, and her current predicament faded. She cared for him; she admitted it. She *must* help him.

A little voice rose up inside her, reminding her that if she achieved that goal, she would be gone from him forever.

She knew "forever" in a way a human would never grasp. To be without Raymond cut her own heart to pieces. To never, *never* have his touch again... To never feel his body on hers so intimate, so wild... Holly shuddered with pain. If she failed in helping him find his heart, she might stay as she was. With him.

She steeled herself against her desires. She would help Raymond find his heart, and she would go back and be content that she had. Even into forever. He had so much capacity to love, and to give him that ability would be the greatest gift.

But how?

She racked her brains for ideas she hadn't tried yet. Nothing came to mind.

"Hell," she muttered. "In the story, those three clowns made a new man of Scrooge in one night!"

Of course, they hadn't had a "thing" for Scrooge. Now that would have been interesting. Holly grinned. But when she thought of the intimacy she'd experienced, she sobered. She wanted nothing more than to go to him now and make love again. But she couldn't. Not for his sake. That was the ultimate reason.

She sighed and leaned her head back against the wall, closing her eyes. She was so tired—that human need she should not have. But she was just so damn tired....

"Hey."

Raymond's soft voice reached through the thick layers of sleep, pulling Holly to awareness. She opened her eyes.

"Hey," he said again. He sat on his haunches before her, his hand on her shoulder.

"Raymond," she whispered and touched his cheek, rough with the beginnings of a beard. She felt as if she were dreaming.

"Were you here all night?" he asked.

She nodded and closed her eyes. "I was watching you sleep."

"Why?"

She forced her eyes open, forced herself to think. "Because I wanted to."

He smiled.

She sat up and kissed him before he could stop her. "I wanted to do that, too."

He stroked her cheek. "You shouldn't have."

"Oh, I know."

She did know. She remembered her thoughts while she watched him sleep. They grew stronger until she had needed to kiss him.

His fingers caressed her skin and she turned into his touch, kissing them and marveling at his warmth.

"I'm sorry I made you clean up the kitchen by yourself."

She smiled. "I'm not. I promise I will be good from now on."

He smiled back, still stroking her skin. Their amusement turned sensual.

"You shouldn't be here," he said, his voice hoarse.

"I wanted to be. I like watching you sleep."

"I don't think anyone's ever done that before."

His face loomed closer in the darkness. She could see the flare in his gaze. His mouth touched hers in the sweetest of kisses. Holly stretched up into it, giving herself to the magic he created. Raymond was a magnificent creature.

He rose to his knees, pulling her closer and pressing her mouth open. She met his tongue in a swirl of intimacy that sent her blood flowing richly in her veins.

He eased his lips away to kiss her cheeks, her eyelids,

the sensitive points of her ears. Holly buried her face against his bare shoulder.

"We shouldn't be doing this," he said.

"I can't think why."

She could, but she shoved the cautions away, not willing to make a liar of herself.

He chuckled and rested his forehead on hers. "There isn't anyone like you, Holly."

"Good. I wouldn't want to think you could kiss another me."

"I wouldn't want to."

She smiled and touched his lips again, allowing herself to indulge in holding him and being held by him. His body made hers feel complete, as if parts of herself had been missing for a long, long time. His closeness satisfied hungers she hadn't known she had.

When he tried to disentangle himself, she tightened her grip, not ready to let him go. "No. Please. I can feel your heart beating against my body."

He relaxed against her. "I can feel yours."

His hands stroked her back, his palms hot through her velvet tunic. "I can't resist you. I know I should."

"I'm glad you can't," she told him. "You make me feel so right, Raymond. I'll never have this again. Never. I want you more because I know what I'll miss."

One more time, she thought. Once more wouldn't hurt any more than before. She still had time to get him right. That wouldn't be interfered with. Just she would pay the price.

It was as if she had unlocked the floodgates between them. His kiss was fervent and demanding, filled with need for her. His hands touched her breasts. Her nipples tightened and ached. She dug her nails into his shoulders as if she could keep him forever with her.

She didn't stop him when he gathered her up and laid her on the bed. She helped him strip away her clothes from her body. She pressed herself along his length, accepted him into her inner flesh and moved with him until she cried out from wave after wave of pleasure washing through her. She absorbed his own cries, absorbed his release and made it her own.

She didn't regret a thing. How could she?

She loved him.

RAYMOND LAY WITH HOLLY in his arms and watched the clock's digital numbers change to four forty-five. He should be on his way to the radio station by now.

He didn't want to move from Holly's warmth. Moving meant he had to face the reality of what he'd done. *Again.*

When he'd awakened to find Holly curled up on his floor, sleeping, he had been so touched by her explanation. He'd been so overwhelmed by her sleepy contentedness that he hadn't been able to resist kissing her or touching her or making love to her. *Again.* Somehow his own lack hadn't seemed to matter. He'd only wanted to be with her one more time.

Caution, far too late, reminded him that he had no business at all being with her like this. God only knew what it would do to her now. Hadn't she suffered enough after the first time? He'd *taken,* he thought. Selfishly he'd taken because of his need for her. She had been willing—more than willing. But that shouldn't have mattered. He'd been wrong.

He wished he felt wrong. Holly felt extremely right.

Knowing he had to get up, Raymond finally eased away from her and wrapped the covers around her so she would be warm.

He did four hours of sports-jock radio, letting the frenzied pace take control as it always did. But his heart was a jumbled confusion. He didn't know what to do about Holly.

Not that he ever had. But he didn't see how he could live with her platonically, and she was in no position to fend for herself. Protest at the thought of releasing her rose up so quickly he thought he would choke on it.

"Face it," he muttered after the final wrap of his show. He had woman trouble.

Three hours later, he sat in his favorite city-center bistro and looked at the only people in the world he thought could help him.

"Thanks for coming," he said to his three cousins, Peter, Michael and Jared. If nothing else, maybe he would get insights into how they had failed to stay safe from love.

"Anytime," Peter said. "I'm just wondering what this is about."

"I'm not," Michael announced, while perusing the menu.

"Me, neither," Jared agreed. "Not after he showed up at the family party, last minute. Something was happening with him. I had the feeling it was just like it was with the rest of us."

"Oh-h-h-h," Peter said, like a lightbulb going off.

Together the three said, "Woman trouble."

Raymond gaped at them. He'd never said a word about women when he'd asked them to meet for lunch. He'd only said he had something important to discuss. "How did you know?"

"We've been through this before."

"It's about time, too. I'd hate to think you escaped."

"If she's anything like Mary Ellen, just lie down and

surrender now. Believe me, you'll save yourself a lot of grief.''

This last was from Peter. Jared, the practical one, got practical. ''So, who is she? Do any of us know her?''

''No.'' Raymond wondered how to explain Holly. The truth wouldn't do. ''None of you know her. She's... unique. Very different from other women.''

''Hurdle number one down,'' Michael said. ''Of course, she's different and unique. There is no woman in the world like Janice.''

''She's stable, Michael. That's a first for you.''

''See?''

''Alison has many layers to her,'' Jared commented. ''I'll never find them all. She's the most mysterious woman I've ever met.''

''Mary Ellen beats all others, hands down.''

The three got into a wrangle over the unique qualities of their respective spouses. Raymond could see their pride in their wives. But this wasn't what he needed. ''Guys. My situation's different. I shouldn't be involved with Holly, yet I can't—''

''Keep your hands off her?'' Peter finished, with a knowing grin. ''Mary Ellen shot me in the butt with an arrow. I can tell you reams about not getting involved.''

Michael and Jared chuckled.

''Janice was all wrong for me.''

''I had plenty of reasons not to get involved with Alison. Especially when I found out about Alison.''

''What did you find out?''

''Guys.'' Raymond felt frustrated...and the butt of his cousins' amusement. ''Look. It's just a strong physical attraction, isn't it? Just gonads?''

Peter laughed. ''Gonads have a way of knowing what

you need for life before you do. You can't mess with them, Raymond. Believe me, I've tried.''

"Commitment is a marvelous thing," Michael told him. "It steadies the heart and feeds the soul in ways you can't yet imagine. Don't let it scare you."

"But the first time I saw Holly, even though I wanted her, I knew it wouldn't work. It's not love," Raymond said forcefully.

"There's not a thing wrong with love at first sight," Jared replied. "You look at her and you feel your entire world is turned upside down. No other woman will ever satisfy so many aspects of yourself. You *know*."

Raymond stared at all three. They had no clue what they were talking about. He'd tried to explain, but he must have failed. He tried one more time.

"Holly has unusual problems. She's a…foreigner. She doesn't have a person on earth who's a relation or a friend. She's…dependent on me. It's not a position I can be in. It's not my nature, I've told her that. She's leaving at Christmas anyway, if she can get her job done. She's probably leaving whether or not she finishes on time—not that I agree with her job."

"She sounds like a hit man for the Mafia," Jared said.

"Or she's hiding kids from you," Michael added.

"It's definitely chemistry," Peter declared, apropos of nothing.

Raymond groaned. "Guys, this isn't helping."

"What does your heart say?" Peter asked. The other two nodded.

Raymond paused. "I don't know. According to Holly, I've lost my heart."

The three just smiled.

Chapter Ten

"I was very good today," Holly announced, when Raymond came in the door. "I didn't cook a thing."

She had made sandwiches but she didn't tell him that.

He smiled, although he seemed distracted. "That's good."

"I did go outside."

Raymond froze, half shrugged out of his coat. "Why? what happened?"

"Nothing bad," Holly assured him. "It's just..." She sighed in defeat. "Everyone saw me."

He stared at her, just like the people had. "Everyone?"

She nodded. He knew what it meant as well as she did. Their second lapse into lovemaking had made it worse for her.

"I'm sorry," he said.

She smiled. "I'm not."

Oddly, she wasn't. She'd half expected complications. She would work with them.

"Holly, you shouldn't go outside without me. You don't know where it's safe and where it's not. You walk a block or two the wrong way and you can be in trouble real fast."

"I think I'm in trouble now. People really stared at

me." She glanced down at herself, then back at him. "I'm not exactly dressed the same as people here."

He finished taking off his coat. "No kidding."

"Raymond!" she exclaimed, exasperated. "I've worn out this outfit. I need clothes. Now."

"But... Okay." He put his coat back on. "Let's go."

"I didn't even have to argue," she said proudly.

"If I don't take you clothes shopping, you'll probably go out and do something disastrous."

"I'd try not to," she said, in a small voice.

He laughed and reached into the foyer closet. "Why can't I stay mad at you? Here. Take this jacket for now. We'll get you a new one today."

Holly buried herself in his spare jacket and followed him out the front door. She smiled to herself. This was really nice of Raymond, even if he was avoiding something "disastrous" on her part. She would try to be nice in return. She would only get a few clothes and a few Christmas decorations. She would slip those in when he wasn't looking.

Raymond decided they would walk to the store. She noticed people glancing at her, this time casually rather than from curiosity. Being seen didn't bother her as much as she thought it would, she admitted. The lovemaking had been worth it. And she was with Raymond. She pressed herself closer to him as they walked.

She wanted to talk with him about their lapse last night. She want to reassure him that she had no expectations from him. She loved him for what he was: a good man who had lost his heart.

Funny, she thought, as they moved around a group of shoppers, but she wished they were doing something other than shopping. Like being in his bed, above all other things. What would more lovemaking make her do?

She shivered. Her chill had nothing to do with the weather. "I thought we would take the car."

"There's a big mall three blocks over and two blocks down," he said, putting his hand on her back to keep her close. "Don't try this on your own."

"I won't," she answered, grinning. Their closeness pleased him.

The surroundings looked familiar.

"I've been here before," Holly said, recognizing it was the same way he'd gone when she'd persuaded him to buy his mother a Christmas gift.

"That's right." He chuckled. "You drove me nuts then."

"It's a gift." She sighed. "Or it was."

"Don't worry. You've still got it," he whispered in her ear. His breath sent shivers of delight down her spine.

The Christmas-shopping fervor was at full pitch. Holly realized she was looking at it from the other side of the mirror. She found the festive air still enthralled her, but from wonder rather than from familiarity.

"You probably need jeans," Raymond said. "And sweaters and shirts. And socks and underwear. Nightgowns and a robe. And slippers."

"But I like wearing your T-shirts when I sleep," she protested.

A funny expression came over his face before it cleared. "Yes... Well, okay."

But the first thing in the women's department that caught her eye was a dress. The most sensual and feminine of all dresses. It was pure white with lace and sparkles everywhere.

"Oh, Raymond," she breathed, staring at the beautiful gown. She stepped up to the display. "Look at that dress."

Raymond hung back. "It's a wedding dress, Holly."

She immediately stepped back to him. "Oh."

"People would really be staring if you wore that to take out the trash," he said.

"I'll bet." She wrinkled her nose. "Is that one of the things you have for me to do?"

"It's about your speed right now."

"I guess." Her real speed was to find his heart. Or it should be. She was still working on that.

She got herself fixed up with jeans and sweaters, after trying on several to determine her size. She liked looking at the result in the mirror. She especially liked the way the soft mohair sweaters, with their pastel colors and big, cowl turtlenecks, skimmed her body.

She came out to show Raymond. "Look. Isn't this pretty? Can I have all of them?"

Raymond's gaze seemed focused on her breasts, unencumbered under her sweater. "Oh...sure. We'd better get to the lingerie department next."

She grinned. "I remember that. There's a corset there you're hot for."

"This time *you* will hold the corsets, so I don't get into trouble." He scowled. "Hell, I still have people telling me I welshed because I won't wear one."

"Well, you did welsh."

"Holly!"

She laughed, feeling very good. Sometimes it might be better not to worry about the future and just enjoy the now.

In the lingerie department, the saleswoman piled Holly's arms with lacy brassieres.

Holly looked at the contraptions. "Why do I have to wear these?"

"Gravity," the saleswoman said. "Get a head start against it while you can."

Holly looked at Raymond for translation.

"Wear them for the sake of men everywhere," Raymond said. "Trust me."

"I do." She did, and in more than clothes. She headed for the dressing room.

"And Holly..."

She turned.

"Don't come out to show me how they look."

"Why...?" she began automatically, before realizing she would be half naked in front of him and everyone else. "Right. I'll just make sure they fit."

She went into the dressing room and removed her top. She stared at the first bra, wondering exactly how it worked. She should have asked.

"Oh, well," she said and tackled the problem head-on.

Holly looked at the results in the mirror, after finally giving up all efforts to hook the bra. She couldn't reach it. How could anyone when the ends hung right in the middle of her shoulder blades? One would think the manufacturer would design them to be longer or something. And even though she'd put her arms in the armholes, the cups insisted on trying to wrap themselves around her neck. Now this was a "coal in the stocking" naughtiness if ever she'd seen one. And she had seen many!

She tugged the cups down, to get them over her breasts. They snapped right back to her neck.

Cursing, Holly took it off and tried another bra. The same thing happened with each one. In disgust, she yanked on her tunic and went out to the merchandise area.

"How did you do?" Raymond asked.

"None of them fit! Not even close. They were all up

here." She sliced the base of her throat with her hand. "It's ridiculous! Do women really wear these things?"

"Did you have it on right? The woman was pretty sure about your size."

She eyed him sourly. "What do you think I am? An idiot?"

"I refuse to answer on the grounds I might incriminate myself. Here comes the sixty-four-thousand-dollar question." He pointed to the plastic female-form display above a rack of bras. "Did you have it on like that?"

Holly stared at the bra on the display. "I thought I did. Maybe I didn't. It was all up around my neck."

"Maybe you had it on upside down. Go try again."

Holly felt the heat rush to her face as she studied the bra display further. She knew he was right. "Boy, am I dumb."

"Naw. You're just a novice. At least you didn't come out here to show me."

She glared at him. "I'm not *that* dumb."

He raised his eyebrows.

"I'm not," she muttered, walking back into the dressing room.

As she did, she overheard the saleswoman say to Raymond, "She doesn't know how to put on a bra?"

"She's been...out of touch," Raymond replied. "It's a tragic case."

"Oh, poor thing."

"I'll 'out of touch' him," Holly vowed.

She resolved her lingerie problem and also managed shoes, coat, and "outerwear accessories," as the sign called them. By the time she was finished, she had three very large, very filled shopping bags. She carried one, and Raymond carried the other two.

"Okay," Raymond said, looking pleased. "You're all set."

Holly nodded. She wished she felt "set." Yet every time she saw the fancy-dress department, she couldn't help wanting one. Every fiber of her being craved it. They were so pretty, like butterflies on hangers.

They were two steps from walking out of the store when she pulled up short. She turned around and started back.

"Holly!" Raymond exclaimed, catching up to her. "What are you doing? What's wrong?"

"I need a dress," she said.

"No, you don't. Come on, let's go home."

"I *need* a dress." She stopped and faced him. They stood in the aisle, the Christmas shoppers jostling them as they passed by. Holly didn't care. She had to get Raymond to understand. "I have to have a dress, Raymond. A pretty dress. Please."

"But you're not going anywhere to use it."

Tears pushed at her eyes. "That doesn't matter. I need a dress."

"But..." He looked at her. "All right. But only *one* dress."

She leaped into his arms, kissing him soundly and accidentally whacking three people with her shopping bag. "Thank you! Thank you so much, Raymond."

"It's okay," he said, after apologizing to Holly's victims. "Let's just get you a dress before you hurt more people."

She spent the rest of the afternoon trying on dresses in the exclusive designer department, a pleasure almost as great as making love. Almost. She truly wasn't that dumb. But it was wonderful to see herself in each outfit and how each one made her look the same and yet different. She even felt different in each one. The black Chanel suit gave her a no-nonsense appeal and made her feel powerful. The Carole Little jungle print urged her to be playful. The short Versace dress was sexy and the Donna Karan pantsuit was coolly elegant. But the silver lamé, floor-length gown with an open back was the ultimate in sensuous luxury. She felt as if she were the most beautiful woman in the world in it. It clung to her body like a second skin. She didn't wear a thing underneath it; lines showed if she did. The only horrendous thing about the dress was its price tag.

Raymond gaped at her when she came out of the dressing room in it.

"It's beautiful," she whispered and turned around so he could see it from every angle. "I feel like a present ready to be opened."

Raymond's gaze was like fire on her body. She could sense the heat he sent her way. "You're beautiful, Holly. Stunningly beautiful."

She smiled, then sighed in resignation. "I'll go take it off."

He nodded.

Eventually she came out with a nice dress, one that made her feel good and one that looked good on her. One that satisfied her urge to have a pretty dress. It might not make her feel spectacular, but she could wear it to take out the trash.

"This is the one you're getting?" he asked.

"Sure. I like it."

"But what about the silver one?"

She looked heavenward. "Raymond, you can't take the trash out in the silver dress, either. Even I figured that out."

He was silent for a long second. "Go get the silver dress."

Holly's breath caught in her throat. Her heart beat faster. "Raymond—"

"Go on." He nudged her back toward the dressing room.

"Oh, Raymond." She kissed him gratefully and ran to get the dress.

Before they left the store, she also managed to buy some perfume and makeup to add to her purchases. The saleswoman in the makeup department even did her face, although Holly was careful not to allow the woman to brush her hair back and accidentally reveal her ears. Raymond just grinned.

"Finally," he said, after they left the department store and headed toward home. "My credit card is smoking."

"I have to get me one of those," Holly said, as visions of shopping danced through her head. She tightly clutched her bag with the silver dress inside.

"Holly, you have no job and no income. You can't just get a credit card."

"You can't?"

"Well, they do give them out to just about anybody, but you have to pay the bill when it comes in. That's what you need the job and the income for."

"You're going to have to pay for all this, aren't you?" She frowned now that she was faced with reality. "I guess I really didn't think about that part of it. We'd better take all this back."

"No." He patted her back and smiled. "It's an early Christmas gift for you."

"Even the silver dress?" she dared to ask.

"Especially the silver dress. In fact, I think that's a Christmas gift for me."

She snorted. "You won't even wear the corset for your show."

"Don't start on that."

"Can you spare a dollar for a cup of coffee?"

Holly stopped and surveyed the man blocking her path. He wore no hat or gloves against the cold. His coat was ripped in several places and ill-fitting. He held himself strangely, all stifflike. Add to that his long, raggedy beard and hair, and his rheumy red eyes, and Holly knew the man needed help.

Raymond started to walk past him, unseeing, but Holly pulled Raymond back.

"Can we help you?" Holly asked the poor man. "Can we take you to a doctor or to your home?"

The man backed up, fear coming into his eyes. "I don't want no doctor, lady. I just want a dollar."

Holly frowned. He looked as though he needed more than that, but the man was sure of himself. "Raymond, give the man a dollar."

"Thanks, lady," the man said.

Raymond didn't reach for his money. "Holly, it's not good to give the guy money. He won't spend it on coffee. He'll use it for booze."

"No, I won't," the man protested.

"You're holding a bottle under your coat already," Raymond said. To Holly, he added, "He's just bumming for the next bottle."

"No, I'm not!"

"Raymond," Holly began patiently, undeterred by his words. "You don't know that for sure. Your kindness to the man today could start him back to a better life. You just never know. He'll use this dollar to feed himself, won't you?"

"Oh, sure, lady."

"I'm talking to Sally Sunshine," Raymond said, fishing in his pocket. He pulled out a dollar in coins and handed them over to the man.

"Thanks, buddy."

"Now use that for food or coffee," Holly told him as he moved away to make the same request of another pedestrian.

Raymond sighed and shook his head as they moved on. "Holly, honey, you are too trusting. Don't believe everything that people tell you."

"But what they say might be true, so you have to believe people."

"You could use a dose of cynicism."

She shivered. "No, thanks, but you could use a little less."

"I'm surprised you didn't have me drag that man to the nearest shelter."

She smiled wryly. "I did learn after that police guy. Besides, he wasn't helpless. He's capable of making a choice on how to live his life. Not like the children with the toys."

"You amaze me," Raymond said.

"Good." A memory came up and smacked her in the face. "We have to go back to the store."

"What! Why?"

"We forgot Christmas decorations. We have to have decorations...a tree, garlands, holly. Hey, that's me!" She giggled.

"Holly!"

"Oh, come on." She tucked her hand around his elbow and tugged him toward the store. "I'd better take advantage of you while you're in a giving mood and your credit card isn't totally smoked out."

"I'm a glutton for punishment."

"I'll thank you later."

She did.

RAYMOND WALKED INTO the studio where he was to make the second voice-over commercial for his new car sponsor. To his surprise, he found Kathryn kissing the afternoon drive-time host, Mark Hanover.

They broke apart at his interruption.

"Hi," Raymond said, after an awkward moment. "Or should I go out and come back in again?"

"It's okay, Ray," Mark said. He rubbed Kathryn's arm. "I'll see you later?"

She nodded.

Mark left and Raymond wondered what he should say. He and Kathryn had done one commercial already and had established an easy relationship with each other, their dinner date notwithstanding. Finally, he said, "He's married, Kathryn."

"I know. I didn't plan this. Neither did he. It doesn't matter." She smiled slightly. "I hope you're not saying this because I've misinterpreted your lack of interest—"

Raymond grinned. "No. I just offered the observation as a friend. I am a friend, Kathryn."

"Thanks. I may need one. I tend to gravitate toward already-attached men." She shrugged. "You were attached, weren't you, when you asked me out?"

"I guess so. My...attention was preoccupied."

"I must have sensed that and responded to it," she admitted, smiling at him. "It was a nice try on both our parts but it would never have worked out."

As they ran through several takes of the commercial, Raymond acknowledged that in the past he would have considered Kathryn's involvement with Mark to be her problem and kept his mouth shut. Only he did things now that he'd never done before—like buying absolutely use-less and very expensive silver lamé dresses because an elf had a wistful eye for one. Holly had been the most beau-tiful creature in the world when she'd modeled it for him. To say he was "preoccupied" with her was the under-statement of the century.

Everything had been worth it when she'd "thanked" him last night. He couldn't wait to see Holly take out the trash.

What the hell was wrong with him? The more he tried to insulate himself against Holly, the more she wheedled her way inside him. She never got the messages of dis-tancing he had sent thus far. She accepted his protests and warnings, and then totally ignored them.

He should be stronger for her sake, he thought. He would hurt her in the long run. He wouldn't mean to, but he was incapable of a deep relationship. Unfortunately, a second little voice inside him constantly reminded him that she expected to be gone by Christmas. He expected her to be gone by Christmas, too, so why shouldn't he indulge in such a tempting relationship? Yet, it stung when he thought of it ending.

"Raymond."

He focused back onto the commercial-making. "Yes, Kathryn?"

She was in the producer's booth with Karen and some of the staff. All of them were grinning. "You missed the last cue...and a few others besides. Are you okay? Or are you preoccupied?"

It must be like snow melting on a dark roof, Raymond thought, because his emotions were showing. "Sorry."

He managed to pay attention during the rest of the work session. But as he arrived home, his cousins' smug atti-tude came back to him. Why had they seemed to think he was incapable of avoiding love? First, one had to be capable of love in order to be incapable of avoiding the emotion.

Somehow, though, he couldn't find the cynicism he normally had for tender feelings. Maybe Holly and her cockeyed optimism were rubbing off on him. She saw promise in everyone, even an unredeemable man on the street. How could she be that way in such a world as existed now? One needed pessimism just to cross the street anymore.

"Hurrah! You're home!" Holly said, poking out from the living room. In her jeans and tucked-in flannel shirt, she looked like the all-American girl. The only sign of difference were her pointed ears revealed by a French twist, and the two icicles that held her hair in place, geisha-style. Funny how her magic worked now. Some things were normal and some were warped. She added, "Come see what I've done."

"Oh, God," Raymond said, shedding his coat as fast as he could.

"Relax. I've only decorated."

"I'm not sure that's better," he commented, wondering how diverse Holly's decorating might get.

But the moment he entered the living room, he just stared in awe. Red-and-green plaid ribbons intertwined lamps and vases. His windows twinkled with tiny white lights. Garlands draped his curtains.

"It's not nearly done," she said. "But I'm getting there."

Raymond didn't know what to think. He hadn't been happy about the Christmas decorations, but had finally caved in when he considered that she must need a touch of normalcy—her normalcy—after her upheavals. He hadn't bought much, not after acting like King Midas over the dress, but he'd never expected his living room to be transformed. It had such a...holiday air.

Raymond grinned. Now he was making puns. What next? Dancing with a lampshade on his head? He hoped not.

"What do you think?" Holly asked.

"I think it looks great," Raymond admitted.

"Good, although I still think we should have gotten those bathroom towels and the toilet-seat covers." She laughed. "I loved the one with Santa saying 'Ho-ho-ho.'"

"I never would have thought you'd like Christmas tacky," he said, laughing with her.

"I *love* Christmas tacky. It's very mischievous." She put her arms around him and kissed him soundly before standing back to admire her handiwork. She kept one arm around his shoulder. "I'm hungry. Aren't you?"

He was, but not for food. Why couldn't he resist her? He had to get a grip on his control. "So what's for dinner?"

She gazed at him somberly. "Whatever you cook. I'm barred from the kitchen for that job, remember?"

"Just testing." He grinned. "But maybe you ought to have a cooking lesson or two that doesn't involve killing the smoke detector. Simple things like eggs and hamburger."

She patted his shoulder. "Actually, I've given this some thought since my last kitchen experience and, my friend, you just go ahead and keep that job as chef."

Raymond laughed. "You're a chicken."

"Damned straight I am. I don't want to clean up, either."

"Oh, that's still doable."

"No, no. You make the mess, you clean it up."

"You clean it up or you don't eat."

"Rats." She sighed. "Okay, but I'd better get one helluva meal for my cleanup."

"Grilled cheese and soup?"

"Good deal."

After dinner, Raymond sat in the living room and admired the Christmas decorations in the twilight. He remembered her words that the trappings of a celebration made one feel good, put one in the mood. He sipped his beer. "I kind of like them."

"I'd say I told you so but that would be rubbing it in," Holly said, as she sat next to him.

He glanced at her. "That's never stopped you before."

"I know. I thought I'd be subtle about it this time."

He roared with laughter.

She grinned smugly, then grew serious. "Raymond? What turned you off love and home and family? What made you so cynical about those things?"

"I thought you knew everything."

"No. I know things, but not everything."

He shrugged.

"Raymond, please. I'd like to know."

Something in her voice, an earnestness, broke though the already existing cracks in his emotional walls, urging him to tell her. Maybe if he told her, she would understand why he warned her about himself.

"I explained about my father making it clear from the beginning that he didn't want me. And my mother made it clear that I was a meal ticket for her and nothing else. It told me not to trust people, that under the surface, people have motives that are manipulative and you'll be bit in the butt by them if you're not careful—"

"'Bit in the butt'?" she interrupted. Then her face cleared. "An expression. Don't worry. I get it."

He smiled ruefully. "I was raised by my grandparents

for a while besides those summers with the cousins. My grandfather was—I don't know—a precise man about things. Peter got along with him better than anybody. My grandmother was..." He swallowed, remembering. "Soft and sweet. I thought she was what she seemed—a sweet lady who loved me. Then she had an affair, and I knew she wasn't what I'd thought. After that, I knew no one ever would be. Nothing and nobody's ever shown me different after that, Holly."

She was silent for a long time. Finally he could stand it no longer.

"Holly?"

"Just thinking." She grinned at him. "So when do we go get the Christmas tree?"

He gaped at her. "Holly!"

"What?"

"I... Never mind."

She accepted what he'd said without comment. Most people would have had something to say about his view. Holly, however, only said he'd lost his heart. It bothered him that she didn't comment. She ought to be talking him out of his opinion, rather than talking about a Christmas tree. A Christmas tree! He'd poured his heart out and she wanted a Christmas tree.

"So, when do we get the tree?" she repeated.

He began to laugh at the irony of it all.

"What's so funny?" she asked.

"I'm telling you my life story and you want to go Christmas-tree shopping."

"What's wrong with that?"

"You don't care. Anyone else would take a profound moment like that and say something to at least make me feel better."

"But Christmas trees make me feel better so I thought

they'd make you feel better," she said. "Is this irony again? Damn! I feel blind without knowing what you're thinking anymore."

"I feel like I've got my pants on, now that you can't."

"I could say something but I won't." She put her arm around him and kissed his cheek. "I'm sorry, Raymond. I don't know what to say other than I love you and you can trust me. But I didn't think you would accept it, so I didn't say it."

Raymond froze. Every fiber of his being turned to stone at her words. Finally he said, "You're mistaken. You can't love me."

"Oh, no." She sounded and looked very sure of herself. "I know I love you. I think I always have.... I have since I got here. That's why I'm going to work very hard to help you find your heart again. I want you to be happy and loved and loving. It's what you need and it's what I want for you."

"You're an elf. You don't know what love is."

"Romeo and Juliet knew, and they were babies compared to me."

"They're fiction."

"You think so, eh?" She chuckled, even as her gaze grew wet with obvious unshed tears. "I wish it could be me who gets to love you all your life, but that can't be. How can it? You'll have to find her for yourself, but you'll know how by the time I'm through with you. Now can we go get the Christmas tree?"

He rose like an automaton at her bidding, numb from her revelation.

Holly had lobbed an emotional bombshell and he'd been right in the line of fire.

Chapter Eleven

Holly stepped back and surveyed the Christmas tree she and Raymond had bought.

The Douglas fir was full, without a hole anywhere, and it was actually straight in the stand after several hours of cursing on Raymond's part last night. What could one expect from a novice tree-mounter?

"Not perfection," she admitted aloud, but he'd managed it.

"No, I don't think the team's on its way up," Raymond said, his voice coming over the radio. Holly had turned it on the last few mornings in order to eavesdrop on him at work. She liked being in touch with him. Raymond continued, "We've been sold a bill of goods by a showman. Jack Crowley is the president of the basketball team and he did what he had to do to get people in the seats. But he could have had Patos from Kentucky for his coach and general manager. Or Carpetti from University of Massachusetts, or King Jones from North Carolina. But he took an assistant GM from a team with no track record for picking real players, who in turn hired an assistant coach with the same lack of success to coach the team. Now we're seeing the results of Jack's personnel decisions. Hey, Jack! Wipe the slate clean and start again, pal.''

"At least, he didn't call the guy a moron," Holly said out loud, proud of Raymond's restraint. "He's getting better."

Even better had been his lovemaking last night. She could tell he had been reluctant but she hadn't helped matters by kissing him in gratitude for buying the tree and putting it in the stand for her. Their lovemaking had had a poignancy she hadn't felt before. Maybe because she'd confessed she loved him. She felt he needed to hear the words, to know someone truly cared for him with no ulterior motive.

He'd held her all night when he slept, too, as if he didn't want to let her go. The little things like that gave her hope that he would find his heart. She was sure he was getting closer. He had the ability. She would never have been sent if he'd been a lost cause.

What their lovemaking was doing to her magic mattered less and less to her. She found him a drug that overshadowed her common sense. It overshadowed everything except him. But she would accept the aftermath, whatever it might be.

She put up the tree decorations they'd bought. So much green still stared back at her, unfortunately. The tree needed more ornaments; the damn thing was practically bare.

"Sorry," she muttered to the tree for cursing it. Raymond had liked the house decorations, and she had wanted to present him with a gorgeous tree today, but that wouldn't happen now. She knew she would never wheedle another shopping trip to the store out of him. If only she could go without him. If only she had a credit card or the money...

She did know where Raymond kept emergency money. No, Holly thought. It wouldn't be right to use it. Decorations were not an emergency. Besides, she'd promised not to go out without him. She really shouldn't. She would have to walk to the store, for one thing, which immediately made the idea one to forgo. She couldn't pop in anywhere Raymond wasn't.

She was supposed to be helping him find his heart. Now *that* was an emergency. After the screaming and yelling for disobeying him, she just knew that he would find great delight in a fully decorated tree. Maybe she would even get him a Christmas gift, a little something to have under the tree. That would be truly wonderful.

Holly went to the kitchen drawer that had the three one-hundred-dollar bills hidden at the back of it. She'd found them in her quest for cooking utensils that actually did something. Really, she thought, anybody could come upon the money and steal it. Her hand hovered over the bills. All of sudden, she felt like ''anybody.''

''I can justify it under the 'naughty list' rules,'' she said aloud and took the bills. Justifying through those was definite justification.

She put on her jacket, although it wasn't quite as nice as wearing Raymond's. Hers lacked the faint scent of his cologne. She also put on the wide-band ear warmer that so effectively covered her points.

But as she adjusted the band in the foyer mirror, she noticed one ear seemed less pointed. Holly tilted her head and stared at it. She tilted the other way to see the other ear. That one, too, seemed slightly less pointed. It was as if the very tips of the tips had been shaved off.

''God, am I losing it!'' she exclaimed, disgusted with her overactive imagination, and snapped the headband in place.

She shut the front door behind her and began her walk of the three blocks up and two blocks over. Nobody stared at her. She felt as if she fit right in with people.

She smiled proudly when the store loomed tall in the distance. Lord & Taylor was such a lovely name, especially when she found the place all by herself.

Inside, she was once more mesmerized by the women's clothing. She couldn't resist trying on some more. After all, she'd passed over one or two things the other day.

Much, much later, Holly sighed in pleasure as she admired the glittery windowpane jacket and long, clinging black dress in the dressing-room mirror. Of course, she wasn't buying this, either, she acknowledged with a wistful sigh. But she knew what she wanted in the future.

Everything.

She'd tried on everything in her size in Sportswear, Better Dresses and the designer sections—literally everything. But one could not have it all. Too damn bad. Still, she had better get shopping for decorations. Her stomach growled. She had better get food, too.

By the time she left the store, the sun was nearly under the horizon. Holly swallowed at how dark it was. Either a snow squall was coming in or she was very late. The tall clock on the corner read after four-thirty.

"Oh, my Lord!" she exclaimed, horrified that it was the latter. She began racing around the crowds on their way home from shopping and work.

"Hey, lady! Can you spare a dollar for a cup of coffee?"

Holly started as a man put himself in her path. She recognized the same poor man from the other day—with yet another bottle tucked inside his coat. Raymond had been right.

"Shame on you!" she said, shaking a finger in his face.

The large shopping bag dangling from the rest of her hand rattled loudly as decorations banged together. "My friend gave you a dollar to get coffee, and you promised you would use it for that. But did you? No! I see it in your coat. I'm glad I used all my money today and I have no dollar to give you. I wouldn't now. You go and get help. I don't want to ever see you again on this street, begging for money!"

"Lady, *you* need help. You're nuts!" the man said, backing away from her. He turned and fled.

"I need help, eh?" Holly snorted, annoyed with him and herself. This random-acts-of-kindness stuff had its flaws. No wonder Raymond was always skeptical.

She wondered if Raymond had come home at his usual time. She hoped he'd had meetings galore today and was still at them. She raced the rest of the way to the town house.

The moment she arrived, however, she noticed the house lights were on. She cursed roundly at her ill luck.

When she pulled the latch on the front door and it didn't open, she realized she probably would have been caught out anyway because she had no key. When she'd left, she had faithfully shut the door and it had no doubt locked behind her. Now she knew she would have been sitting on the front steps, *waiting* for Raymond. Hell, she would have been caught the moment he saw the extra decorations and the missing emergency money, but she'd known that. At that point, she would have had her beautiful decorations to justify her actions.

Faced with the actual confrontation, Holly admitted that her brilliant idea of the morning was another disaster in disguise—impending, in this case, but a disaster nonetheless.

"Better get it over with," she murmured and rang the doorbell.

Feet pounded to the other side of the door. Holly stepped back, out of swinging range—just in case. The door was flung open. Raymond towered on the threshold.

"Hi," she said casually, in an attempt to brazen it through. "We really need to get me a key—"

"A key!" The air turned blue with Raymond's curses. Holly thought she could actually see the barnyard words hovering around them.

"A key would be nice," she said, then added, "Can I come in?"

He froze in mid-curse. His stare should have turned her to stone. Fear curled in Holly's stomach. No matter how she looked at it, she had done wrong.

He stepped aside. "Get in here."

"I'm sorry, Raymond," she said, her courage deflating. "I did something I shouldn't have, and I don't blame you if you never let me in the house again."

"Get in the damn house before I drag you in."

"Okay." She wasn't foolish. Well, sometimes she wasn't, Holly conceded. Today was not one of those times.

She stepped past him, one shopping bag bumping him as she did so.

The front door slammed shut behind her and a shopping bag was snatched out of her hand. Holly jumped and whirled around.

Raymond waved the bag in her face. "What the hell is *this?*"

"Your Christmas present," she said. "And be careful. It's breakable."

He gaped at her, looking completely dumbfounded. "It's what?"

"Your Christmas gift," she repeated. "I got you a statue of an elf reading a Christmas list. I would have gotten something before but I couldn't afford it."

She took the package from his fingers during the silence.

"Raymond, I'm truly sorry," she added. "I meant to be home hours ago, but I got to trying on dresses at Lord & Taylor, and the next thing I knew, it was four-thirty—"

"Do you have any idea how I felt when I got home and you weren't here?" he interrupted. "You scared the hell out of me and you were off gallivanting through a department store!"

"I didn't gallivant," she said in her defense, although she was pleased he'd been worried about her. "I was shopping."

"Shopping! How did you pay for this?" he asked, as if just waking up.

"Well...that's another thing." She tried to smile but she could feel it die on her lips before it even started. "It was your emergency fund, but this was an emergency. We didn't have enough tree ornaments. I knew how much you liked the house decorations—"

"You took the emergency money? How the hell did you even know where it was?"

"I'm not unobservant," she said. "I found it when I was looking for cooking things that night I burned dinner. You should keep it in a safer place—"

"Safer place!"

"I used it for you," she said lamely. She held out the bags. "You can take every bit of it back and get all your money for it. That'll be like it was never gone from the kitchen drawer. I would like to keep your gift, even though I have no money of my own to pay for it. You should have something under the tree on Christmas morning.''

He closed his eyes, saying nothing.

Holly worried. "Raymond?"

He put a hand up, then walked away from her into the back of the house.

"Oh, boy. I think he's ticked," she murmured.

She set the bags down and went into the living room—after first checking to see if Raymond was there. He wasn't. She glanced at the half-decorated Christmas tree—the cause of all her troubles—and sighed. She'd bought such pretty things with the emergency money. The set of musical-instruments ornaments in gold would delight him. Perfect bubbles made from rainbow-hued glass would awe him. Stuffed bears and Santas... She'd bought lots of Santa ornaments. And she'd purchased an angel for the top, all silver cloth with wings. Holly thought the figure looked a little like herself.

"He'll probably toss it in front of a bus now," she commented and turned on the television. But he had been worried about her. That was very encouraging as far as his heart was concerned.

Her stomach began to complain about the need for nourishment. Holly ignored it, not willing to venture into the kitchen. Raymond was better off alone, anyway. Or rather, he was better off not having his feathers ruffled further.

What a mess she had made of things.

She wouldn't be surprised if the Big Guy stuck her here forever. No, he would probably send her to limbo, she thought. He wouldn't torment Raymond with her presence. Raymond had done nothing to deserve her. Probably every elf still at the pole would have taken care of this job already and been back home by now. But not her.

She sighed and leaned her head against the sofa, closing her eyes and vowing not to move off the piece of furniture morning, noon or night.

"Want something to eat?"

She opened her eyes and turned toward Raymond. He stood next to the sofa, a tray in his hands.

Holly sat up. "Yes, please."

"You sound like Oliver," he said, grimacing. "Do you do it on purpose, to make me feel worse?"

"Who's Oliver?" she asked, while eyeing the plate of sandwiches on the tray. The soda looked yummy, too.

"Some poor kid who never had enough to eat," Raymond replied. "Dickens wrote about him."

"He wrote about everyone, didn't he?" But her attention was on the meal he set before her. She took a ham-and-cheese sandwich and bit into it. "Oh, that's good. Raymond, thank you so much. You're wonderful to me, and I'm a disaster for you."

"I can't argue with that." He sat next to her. "Do you understand what it was like for me to come home and you weren't here? I didn't know whether you'd run away or you were out there lost or you'd been kidnapped."

She giggled. "Raymond, that's silly."

"Not in this day and age. I didn't know if you had left forever without saying goodbye."

The mouthful of food felt like ashes in Holly's mouth. She mumbled around it, "I...I didn't think you would think that."

He smiled wryly. "So I could tell."

She forced the food down to her stomach where it sat like a lump. "I didn't mean to worry you. I thought you'd be more upset about the money."

He snorted. "Hell, I don't give a damn about the money—"

Holly threw her arms around him, ecstatic. "Oh, Raymond, this is wonderful! You cared more about me than about the money!"

"Holly!" He set her away from him. "I'm tired of this 'I am a monster' attitude you have about me."

"I *never* said you were a monster!" she replied, indignant, before waving a dismissing hand. "You never were. But don't you see? You thought with your heart about me. That's a terrific sign that you're getting your heart back."

"Holly, I don't give a damn about my heart," he snapped. "I didn't know where you were and I couldn't even call the cops to report you missing. What the hell could I say? 'I've got a missing elf, about five foot two inches tall with blue eyes and pointed ears—'"

"I think they might be less pointed," she interrupted, tipping her head toward him. "What do you think?"

"I don't give a damn about your ears!" he snapped.

She straightened, contrite. "I know you just don't understand what's happening yet. But I do, Raymond. I'm so happy for you."

"You're making more out of my concern than it is, dammit! I'm responsible for you. You don't know about the world out there. Anything could have happened to you. What if you'd been attacked...or worse—"

"I would have popped out." She chuckled. "I might have caused a lot of excitement wherever you were because that's the only place I can pop to, but I would have been safe."

He gazed at her, his mouth set in clear frustration. "*Can* you pop out?"

"Of course." She popped—or tried to. Panic shot through her when she realized she was going nowhere fast. "Oh, no!"

He nodded. "I had a feeling."

RAYMOND WATCHED AS reality hit home for Holly. "Wait," she said and ran out of the room.

"Where are you going?" he demanded, bewildered by her action.

"Maybe I couldn't pop because you were in the room, so I'm going to pop from upstairs."

She could try, he thought. Sympathy joined his anger. He still couldn't believe she'd been so foolish as to go out without him. He'd been so angry when she'd finally returned home, he'd had to remove himself from her presence until he could calm down and reason with her. Reason was not Holly's forte. She'd said she loved him and yet she had an odd way of showing it. But her declaration was another matter altogether.

When Holly didn't pop in or return by human methods, he became impatient. "Holly!"

Eventually he heard feet slowly trailing down the stairs and knew she'd had no success at popping.

She entered the living room. "I guess that's it, then. No more magic."

"Now, will you listen to me?" he asked.

She nodded. A dispirited Holly disturbed him far more than a bold one.

"It'll be okay," he said, rubbing her back.

She nodded again. "Maybe. You were right, too, about that guy begging for money. He was begging again today and hiding another bottle. I yelled at him."

Raymond chuckled. He couldn't help it. "That must have scared him."

"He told me I was nuts." Her voice held a trace of indignation under the apathy. "Can you imagine? *Me?*"

"I couldn't possibly."

"I guess my ears really are less pointed if I can't pop. Oh, well."

"Let me look," he said.

She tilted her head toward him. He pushed her hair aside and examined her ears. They looked and felt noticeably less pointed. He didn't have the heart to tell her. "They're fine."

"You are a liar of the first water and I thank you."

"It'll be all right," he said again. It had to be, he thought. Now that things were calmer, he asked the question that had gotten to him earlier. "Did you really buy me a Christmas present?"

She grinned, her face lighting up with pleasure. "Of course, I did."

He grinned back. "Damn. I can't remember the last gift I got."

Her pleasure turned to shock. "Surely you get gifts."

He shrugged. "Not really. Karen insists on giving me baked cookies or something else to eat, but I don't have much family. Just the cousins and my mother."

"They give you something. They have to."

"Not the guys. We never did that stuff. My mother... Sometimes she's sent a check. Sometimes she's busy."

"Raymond!"

"It never mattered." He meant it. Lack of gifts hadn't mattered for a long, long time. Why couldn't she see that? "I have my own life."

But her gift touched him and he found that he cared very much about her. The house had been so damned empty this afternoon and it had felt even emptier when he considered that she might be gone forever. He wanted her with him. And he was more confused than ever about her.

"I'm sorry you don't have your magic," he said. "I wish I could give it back to you, whatever happens."

She smiled at him and kissed his cheek. "I think I'm getting something better—and that's seeing you get your heart back."

He wanted to tell her she was all wrong about what his concern meant—that he felt no different than the day she had come into his life—but she'd had enough disappointment today as it was. He vowed to help her make a life here if she was truly stuck on earth. He might not initially have wanted the responsibility but he would see it through, even if her "emergency" shopping had made him nuts.

Better to shop with her than to let her loose on her own, he thought. "Get those tree decorations out and we'll put them up."

"You mean we can keep them?"

"What the hell," he said, shrugging nonchalantly. "Might as well not waste your efforts and my emergency money."

"Thank you, Raymond." She threw her arms around him and kissed him. "You're so wonderful."

He held her and kissed her again, thoroughly. "I am wonderful, aren't I? Kind, considerate, a pushover and general idiot."

"Oh, yes." She gave him a last hug, then began dragging ornaments out of the bags.

"I got them on sale," she said excitedly. "Everything was forty-percent off. Wasn't that terrific?"

He laughed. "Honey, you are gonna fit right in with the shopping masses."

"You know, I felt that way today."

"We've created a monster."

He looked at the growing mound of decorations,

amazed at the amount she had bought with the emergency money. He supposed he ought to lecture her about that, but she couldn't pop anywhere. That seemed enough of a punishment. Still, he would have to stash future emergency monies in a better spot. No sense tempting an elf further than she could handle. God only knew what she would next decide was an emergency.

She fussed over the ornaments, wanting each in an exactly perfect spot. Raymond just grinned at her and obeyed. He didn't care as long as she was pleased. And pleased with him.

She'd said she loved him. He hadn't wanted to touch that declaration but he could no longer resist. Not that he had physically resisted after she'd said it. He'd made love to her with a passion he hadn't known he possessed. Yet he wondered if she truly meant the words or even understood them. Would it matter if she did? How much would it hurt if she didn't?

He didn't know.

"Oh, come on. You don't have to look so ticked just because I moved the stuffed Santa from the place you put it," she chided.

"Yeah, well..." Raymond cleared his throat. "I was thinking about something else."

"Really?" she said. "You thought? Or am I in trouble again?"

"You're still in trouble for this afternoon."

"I know. But look on the bright side. I walked there and back all by myself." Her voice held pride in her accomplishment. "I didn't buy a single dress, although I did try on a bunch of them."

"Any as good as the silver?"

"Nope. You really liked that one, didn't you?" She didn't wait for an answer, but added, "I got a bunch more decorations, which you *need,* and a gift for you, which you *will* like. And I didn't have to take out the trash, for which I will *not* wear the silver dress."

"You can really cut the heart out of a guy."

She laughed. "Too late, Raymond. You're on your way."

He sobered. "I know what you think are signs, but Holly, they aren't. I don't feel different. I'm not open to people. I don't trust them or their motives. Oh, I'd give money to a good cause but, hell, I've always done that. It means nothing." He stared at her and added, "You say 'I love you,' and I can't even say anything back. I'm so sorry I can't. But because I can't, I'm not on my way to finding anything, especially not my heart."

She held a heart ornament in her hand and she looked so unruffled he wondered if she'd even heard him. "I never expect you to say the words back, Raymond. You don't ever have to. I love you, that's all. But I have seen changes in you. Subtle, but they're there. You *are* finding your heart."

"I wish you hadn't lost your magic," he said. "You would be able to see all the doubts and cynicism in my mind. I think you're imagining what you think you're seeing. It's just not there."

"Nope. You can't shake my faith on this. I know, Raymond, that you're on your way. I just *know.*"

He didn't argue with her further. Holly, when she got a notion, was like a bulldog with a bone. Under his exasperation, he admired her for that trait. Only he wasn't a changed man inside. Holly would eventually learn that she would have to take no for an answer on the subject of his heart.

When they finally finished with all the ornaments, the tree looked beautiful, but still not complete.

"We need something more," Raymond said.

"Like ornaments?" Holly suggested.

"And tinsel." He turned to her. "I will take you out tomorrow afternoon...if you promise not to sneak out on your own tomorrow morning while I'm gone."

"I'll be good," she said, grinning at him.

"It's like wishing on a star," he muttered, skeptical. "One knows it's useless but one keeps doing it."

"Wishing on stars is never useless," Holly assured him. "At the least of it, you will always know what you want."

"But you never get it."

"Oh, you might." She took his hand. "Here. I'll show you."

She led him outside onto the front steps. The chilly air found its way through their clothes. Holly rubbed her arms, then pointed to the sky.

"See that cluster of stars?" she asked.

"Barely," he replied. "Between the pollution and the city lights, most of the night sky gets wiped out."

"You people ought to do something about that," she said. "You're missing a great show from Mother Nature."

"I have no doubt."

"Now..." she said, and closed her eyes. "I wish with all my heart on that star, that you will find your heart by Christmas morning."

Something suspiciously like emotion clogged his throat. He cleared it. She could have wished for anything. Her abilities back. To go home. She was a stranger in a strange land—for her—and she had wished for him.

Holly opened her eyes. "See? Not only do I know what I want but I can now work hard to get it."

"But..." He cleared the lingering hoarseness in his

throat. "I thought you would wish to have your magic back."

"I thought about it, but this seemed more important to me." She gazed up at the sky, then turned to him. "Can I learn to make a cup of tea? I'm freezing."

He wanted to do so many things. Wrap her in his arms and kiss her. Tell the world how wonderful and giving and bewildering she was. Watch the night sky for a star that moved him to wish as freely as she had. Give her a Christmas gift she would never forget, for he would never forget her.

He gazed up at the stars she'd wished on and saw a bank of clouds move over them. Visible stars didn't matter, he thought, as he wished with all the heart he had that Holly would be happy. It didn't matter whether stars were there or not. His wish wouldn't change.

He discovered that she was right. Now he knew what he wanted and could work toward making Holly happy.

"Let's go fix that tea," he said.

Chapter Twelve

Holly reread the recipe for cutout sugar cookies and wondered if she could make them.

Raymond would kill her if she tried.

"When am I *not* in trouble?" she murmured, with impeccable logic.

She smiled. After all, it was Christmas Eve day. She wanted to make this as nice a Christmas for him as she could. That meant cookies—for what was Christmas without cookies? She wanted Raymond to have all the trimmings, for these past few days with him had been idyllic. Okay, so they had argued a few times over decorations and other sundries, but they'd made love every night. She'd grown very close to him.

"What the hell," she said, and got out the ingredients. This time she would make sure she had everything *before* she started the project. Although she still wasn't quite sure whether a "tbs" was a tablespoon or a television station—it couldn't possibly be the latter—she wasn't about to stop now. She would figure it out.

Over the radio, she heard Raymond say, "What was the best Christmas present you ever gave, Tommy?"

Holly paused in her baking.

"What?" Tommy asked, the question clearly unexpected.

"Hey, I thought this was a sports show," Bob said, in his usual whiny voice. His comedy disrupted serious sports talk more than anything else.

"Okay, so there's a play-off game tomorrow," Raymond conceded.

"And our team's in it!" Tommy said.

"I know, I know. They finally made it and that's a great gift to the fans, but I got to thinking about Christmas and other gifts," Raymond replied. "We can take a few minutes to talk about how we tried to express our...caring to our families and friends—"

"You could wear that corset," Bob interrupted.

"When pigs fly," Raymond told him. "Look. I'm just thinking it feels good to give."

"Oh, I've got to get that boy a better present," Holly said out loud, while smiling with pride and love. "He deserves it."

"I think you're nuts, but you've got a point," Tommy said. "I remember standing in line forever when those Flower Patch Dolls went off the popularity charts, years ago. Erica's little face on Christmas morning was incredible, she was so happy. She carried that doll everywhere." Tommy laughed. "It was filthy by March because she played with it so much. To this day, she still says how great Marcia Roberta was."

"Wow," Raymond said, his voice awed.

"Definitely something better," Holly muttered, mixing up the dough.

"I got a chemistry set for Hanukkah one year," Bob said. "It was the greatest thing my parents gave me."

"I said one you *gave,* dingdong, not one you received," Raymond admonished.

"I'm getting to it, Mr. Big Shot!" Bob continued, "I blew a hole in the garage wall with it. Man, that was wild. This year I gave my son a nice shirt. I'm not that dumb. Bobby's worse than me."

Holly laughed.

"What about you, Ray?" Tommy asked. "What was the best gift you've ever given?"

Holly stopped what she was doing, knowing she couldn't miss one word of the answer.

"I think when I gave those toys to that church," Raymond said promptly. "It felt really good. Hey, people! I know it's a busy day for everyone, with last-minute shopping and all the other stuff that goes with tomorrow, but take a few minutes and buy a toy to put in the marine toy collection. Or throw all your change in the Redemption Army pot. Anything to help another human being today. Lots of people out there need help. Let's help them. Mike on the mobile, you're on WRP...."

Holly swallowed against the unshed tears in her throat. Raymond must get the present of his life tonight—even if she had to steal all the emergency-fund money again. No wonder she loved him so much. He was a wonderful, caring man, who only needed to find it within himself. But she had known. She had had faith that he would.

All of a sudden her legs went weak. She managed to reach a kitchen chair before they gave out on her. She sat down heavily.

"I've done it," she said to the mixing bowl. "I've actually done it!"

She knew—*knew*—in her heart that Raymond had found his. Oh, he might not have his own little family yet, but that was a matter of time. She was finished....

Terrible pain shot through her when she realized all the implications.

She would be leaving him and going home. She didn't doubt it. Like knowing about Raymond's heart, she knew about herself. Only she didn't want to go home now. She wanted to be with Raymond. She wanted to be the one to give him his little family.

Holly wiped at the tears rolling down her face. She wished she could blame her emotions on PMS, but she wasn't having any. She knew that well enough.

She bet if she looked in the mirror, she would see that her ear points were back. She bet she could pop in on Raymond again without mishap. She bet a lot of her abilities were returning.

Deciding to find out, she tried one ability and popped into limbo, a place she hadn't been able to reach for days now. The world moved at its usual pace, passing her like a kaleidoscope of humanity.

She popped back into the kitchen. It seemed as though she was back in working order. She wondered why she'd lost her abilities—not that it mattered now. They were back and that meant Raymond was well again.

More tears leaked out as she quoted the old saying, "'Be careful what you wish for. You just might get it.'"

Her ride home would be here sometime after midnight.

Holly sat for a long while in the kitchen, in her own "nonlimbo limbo." She thought a lot about what she wanted and what would be. She considered trying to go back home now, to plead that they leave her with Raymond. But she knew they would deny her; she was not human. She could not stay. If she managed to make it home this time, they might not even let her come back to Raymond to say goodbye. She didn't want to leave him until she absolutely had to.

After midnight.

Holly wiped the tears from her cheeks. This should be

a happy time, she thought, taking a deep breath. Above all else, she had wanted him to find his heart. It seemed he had. This *was* a happy time, and she would make the most of it. She had cookies to bake, another gift to get and dinner to prepare. She would tell Raymond the good news about his heart later, right before her ride arrived. She didn't want anything to mar her time left with him, for her own sake. The attitude was selfish—she admitted it—but she couldn't help herself.

She also had the Kama Sutra to read. If she was leaving all this behind, she wouldn't miss out on a thing if she could help it.

WHEN RAYMOND CAME HOME after the show, Holly was outside, playing with the local kids. She'd done her extra shopping and had come upon the children playing hide-and-seek. She'd joined them, wanting to savor everything before the night came.

"Okay, Joey, you'll have to be it," she called out to an eight-year-old.

The kids groaned. One yelled to Raymond, "Hey, mister. Can't Holly play more?"

Raymond paused, half-in and half-out of his car.

"I can't, guys. Sorry," she said, before he could answer.

"Sure you don't want to play?" he asked, after kissing her hello.

"Only with you."

"No problem."

She smiled bravely as they went into the house, while hiding all the signs of her impending departure—including her ears. She'd checked and they were pointed again. She'd left her hair unbound to cover them.

"Surprise!" she said, after going into the kitchen and coming back to the foyer with a tray of cookies.

"I hope you bought them from some passing Christmas Girl Scout, even if you borrowed the emergency fund again," he said, shedding his coat while shifting his armload of bags. "Otherwise, it means you went out and bought them, or you baked."

"I baked."

"God help us!" Raymond exclaimed, dumping his coat and bags. "Holly, dammit! You're only up to tea and sandwiches."

"Relax," she said, laughing. She did feel happy and pleased inside—and sad, but she could live forever with this kind of sad. She would have to. "I didn't use any more bowls than the recipe said to. And I didn't get dough on the ceiling, and I didn't beat up the smoke detector again, either. The cookies are a little freaky-looking but they're good. Try one."

He did. First, he held a cookie up before taking a bite. "Hey. It is good. What's it supposed to be?"

"A reindeer, but it looks more like a basset hound. Those cookies stick to the counter when you roll them out and cut them."

"Cut them! I'd better go see the damage."

"O, ye of little faith," Holly intoned. To his back, she added, "Anything in these packages for me?"

"You stay out of them!"

"Oh, goody!" Holly went directly to the packages.

Raymond came back and took her by the waist, steering her into the kitchen. "Oh, no, you don't. No peeking until Christmas morning."

Holly put aside the knowledge that she wouldn't be there in the morning to open her presents and allowed herself to be dragged into the kitchen.

"Okay, so it's a little messy," she conceded at the sight of flour and dough sticking to the counter where she'd done the final work on the cookies. "I haven't had a chance to clean up yet."

"Wow. No dough on the ceiling. I'm impressed." He took another cookie and ate it. "Your basset hounds are delicious."

She giggled. "Then can I make dinner? I really want to."

He shuddered. "That's a scary thought, but I'm willing to live dangerously. What are we having?"

"Food." She grinned. "Probably cookies."

"Works for me." He took the tray out of her hands and set it on the table. "I haven't told you how beautiful you look today."

"Flour all over my shirt and all?" she asked.

"The best part." He took her in his arms and brushed her hair behind her shoulders, taking her by surprise. But her points were still safe from view. He added, "Your hair looks terrific like this."

"If you like it, then I'll wear it like this more often." She would, Holly vowed, to remember him. She pushed the thought aside as she wound her arms around his neck, and he kissed her tenderly, passionately.

"You're in a good mood," she murmured, when he finally ended the kiss.

"I am, aren't I?" He grinned. "Did you hear the show this morning?"

"Of course."

"We were swamped with calls from people who wanted to talk about the best gift they gave. Nearly every caller promised to get a toy for charity or give a donation to a worthy cause. I felt really good, although the football team probably wants to kill us. We barely talked about tomorrow's play-off game.''

"Hey, shame on them for having one on Christmas Day.''

"It's as American as apple pie, Holly." He smiled. "I talked with Marv Gutman, the owner of Kelborn Motors today.''

"Your old sponsor?'' she asked, half remembering the name.

"Right. I've been feeling bad about going with the new people so I called him. I wanted to work something out.''

"And did you?'' she asked softly.

He grinned wryly. "We would have, but he told me that not paying me my fee freed up a lot of cash for him, so he went for a series of ads on all the other radio stations in the area and he's already gotten a better return. He laughed at the irony of it.''

"Hey, it's business." Yet he pleased Holly more for trying to right the wrong he'd done. Business or not, one needed to do the right thing.

He chuckled and slid his hands down her back to knead her derriere. He pulled her tight against his burgeoning arousal. "Feel like an early Christmas gift?''

She nuzzled his neck. "There's a cookie in it for you if you do.''

"Mix those metaphors, girl. I love bribery with my sex.''

They never made it up the stairs to the bedroom; the sofa was a more-than-adequate bed. Holly gave herself up to the wonderful movements of love. She loved him and she wanted him more than ever. If only it would never end.

"I like the way you celebrate Christmas," she murmured as she lay, replete, in his arms afterward.

"You're far too sexy for your own good. And mine," he said, kissing her nose.

He went to tuck her hair behind one ear, but she stopped him before he could. She took his hand and, instead, put it on her naked breast.

"Think you can manage an encore?" she asked, wiggling suggestively under him.

"I think I can manage a lot of things," he said.

She kissed him thoroughly. "Good."

She took so much as they made love again. She gave more back. Holly stored the memories away for herself—the taste and touch and feel and smell and look of Raymond Holiday.

She would need them.

Raymond awoke with a start.

He frowned in confusion, rubbed his eyes and looked around. He lay on his sofa in the middle of the afternoon, naked under an afghan. He felt boneless from making love to Holly. Christmas love.

Sunlight streamed in the gaily-decorated windows, announcing that the Delaware Valley would once again have a green holiday, in the upper forties. Kids all over were probably cursing their luck, he thought in amusement. The area just didn't get a lot of white Christmases. Maybe Holly could do something about that.

Only she wasn't there.

That thought penetrated his musings. Raymond sat up abruptly. "Holly? Holly!"

"Out here," she called from the kitchen.

He rose to his feet and wrapped the afghan around his waist. Picking up the trailing ends, he walked into the kitchen. Holly stood, fully dressed, at the sink.

"What are you doing?" he asked.

"Cleaning up my cookie mess." She turned around. "My, that's a pretty sight. I believe you're hanging through those strategically-placed holes in the afghan pattern."

He looked down at himself. Sure enough, he was showing the family jewels, as the expression went. He grinned at her. "Turns you on, doesn't it?"

She laughed.

"I think I just shrank to oblivion," he muttered ruefully, his libido taking a beating.

She only laughed again.

He went up behind her and wrapped his arms around her waist. He kissed the back of her neck. "Seems to me a while ago you liked that 'pretty sight.' Want to like it again?"

She pressed herself into his hips. "Think you can do something about it?"

"Probably not yet."

"Me, neither."

"Thank God," he said with relief. "I feel like I have Jell-O legs as it is."

Holly turned around. "In that case..."

She kissed him playfully, but he knew it wasn't going anywhere.

It didn't matter. Never had he felt so happy. Something about the last few days had culminated in an excitement and yet a contentment. He knew the source was Holly.

Surely she couldn't be leaving him. She'd lost her magic. How could she go back to a magical world when she no longer had magic? She would violate the first rule.

She must be staying. After all, he hadn't found his heart yet.

Doubts on that score crept into his mind. He forced them out. He still felt no different emotionally toward family, strangers and situations. Maybe he was a *little* more compassionate, but that was Holly's influence. It wouldn't stay if she wasn't here.

"What?" she asked, her expression puzzled.

"Nothing." He kissed her nose. She had a very cute nose. "Tell you what, why don't you wear that silver dress for dinner tonight?"

Her face lit up with pleasure. "You're not tired of seeing me in it to take out the trash?"

He laughed. She had never worn the dress for that purpose, and his taking-out-the-trash comment on the day they'd bought it had become a joke between them. "Not tired yet."

"All righty, then."

"Oh, God. You've been watching *Ace Ventura.*"

"Yes, and I have questions. What was he doing, talking out his—"

The doorbell rang, interrupting her.

"You get it," Raymond said, grateful for the reprieve. Any idiot could guess where her question was going. "I'm not dressed for it."

"No kidding. But you look very cute."

"Thanks."

Holly went to answer the door. Raymond looked down at his makeshift covering and grinned, glad she thought he looked "cute."

A voice in the hallway made him forget all thoughts. Raymond froze the moment he heard it. His mother *couldn't* be here. She lived in Florida.

"How nice to finally meet you, Ann," he heard Holly say. "Raymond's in the kitchen."

His mother *was* here. Before Raymond could move, Ann Holiday turned the corner of the kitchen entryway. Holly was right behind her.

"Raymond!" his mother gasped at the sight of his undress. Her shocked glance focused on his nether regions. Raymond regrouped the afghan to cover himself. Too late. Ann flushed and looked away.

"Merry Christmas?" Holly tentatively suggested into the breach.

"What are you doing here, Mother?" Raymond asked, angry at being caught out.

"I guess I surprised you a little too much," Ann said. "But you're an adult."

She came over to him and hugged him. Raymond almost dropped the afghan at her affectionate gesture. His mother had never been affectionate. A perfunctory kiss usually did the job for her.

A man poked his head around the kitchen entryway— an older man with silver hair and a sheepish smile on his face. He cleared his throat.

"Bill, this is my son, Raymond," Evelyn said. "We seem to have surprised him more than I thought we would." She turned back to Raymond. "I know I should have called, but that didn't seem right. Things have been awkward between us—not that I blame you...."

Raymond felt like the straight man who had just been accidentally smacked in the head with a two-by-four by one of the Three Stooges. Everything was out of whack.

"Why don't you put on some clothes?" Holly told him, very sensibly. "And I'll entertain your mother and her friend in the living room, okay?"

Raymond glared at her. It was a sad day for humankind when an elf was the only one in the room with common sense. She looked entirely too happy about this whole thing as it was.

Holly herded his mother and guest out. A few moments later, his clothes came sailing in from the living room to land in a heap on the kitchen floor. Holly did love to trash a place, he thought.

Raymond dressed, all the while wondering why his mother had shown up. He hadn't seen her in person for *years*. And who the hell was Bill?

This did not bode well, he thought.

He went into the living room. His mother and Bill sat together on the sofa, holding hands and talking with Holly about their drive up from the South. Raymond wondered if they had any clue what had occurred on the sofa earlier. Holly grinned at him from her perch on the chair. She reminded him of the Cheshire cat.

"There you are," she said, cheerfully as if his mother arrived every day for a visit. "Did you put on coffee?"

"Uh...no," Raymond said.

"Good. Then I will." She got up. "Here, you visit with your mother and Bill."

Raymond wanted to tell her she could take the visit and stick it where the sun didn't shine, but he refrained, some remnant of manners surfacing.

He took Holly's place on the chair, while she deserted him and disappeared into the kitchen.

He faced his mother. She looked fit and tanned, a small woman who seemed younger than her years. He sorted through the emotions he had. Under the surprise her visit caused, he still felt the same ambivalence he'd always felt toward her. Buying her the expensive necklace now seemed extravagant, considering their relationship.

"Holly's very charming," his mother said.

"Yes, she is," Raymond replied.

"Does she live with you?"

"Yes, she does."

"I didn't know."

"No, you didn't."

Silence reigned.

Bill cleared his throat. "I married your mother last week. We thought we'd better come and tell you in person."

Raymond stared at the man who had lobbed this latest bomb, stunned by the news. He blurted out the only thing he could think to say to his mother. "But I thought you were living with that Florida millionaire. I thought you said you were never getting married, that it was a waste of time."

"Oh, brother," Holly exclaimed, having entered the room. She had clearly overheard him. "I leave you alone for five minutes and you make a mess of things."

"No, it's okay, Holly," Ann said. Her bottom lip trembled—an incredible display of emotion for his usually emotionless mother. "I did say that, Raymond, years ago. I believed it, too, and I lived with men only for financial security. But then I met Bill and everything changed. I fell in love. Raymond, I actually fell in love. He knows about me, and he doesn't care."

"I'm a bookkeeper for a landscaping business," Bill added. He grinned wryly. "I don't even own it."

"You're kidding!" Raymond exclaimed, knowing his mother's predilection for wealthy men.

"Raymond." His mother's voice had a funny catch in it. "I came to apologize to you, for not loving you the way I should have when you were a child. I was so selfish then. I didn't know." Tears spilled down her face. "I'm so sorry, Raymond."

Raymond felt as though the world had turned upside down.

"Say something, you big dope," Holly said.

He glared at her. "I was about to. Don't you have a kitchen to beat up?"

"Been there, done that," she said, smiling sweetly. Her blue gaze urged him to deal with his mother.

"This is some Christmas," he muttered under his breath. Living without family had its advantages. Louder, he said, "Mother, I don't see why you would come here...."

"Don't crucify her, son," Bill said. "She's trying to do the right thing."

Raymond wanted to tell the man to shut up, that he wasn't about to crucify anyone, but he bit back the impulse. The guy wasn't involved in any of this, and he clearly cared for his new wife.

Raymond wondered what the hell to say. This visit was obviously a catharsis for his mother. It wasn't for him, however. One couldn't stick thirty-six years of emotional neglect under the rug.

"You can forgive," Holly said softly.

Chapter Thirteen

Raymond glanced at her. It was as if she'd answered the question in his mind. No, he thought. She'd lost that ability. Any moron could guess he was hesitant about what to do.

He considered really showing Holly how hopeless her cause was by dismissing his mother. But he realized what had happened in the past really didn't matter. He *had* gotten over it. He didn't care enough to hurt back. That in itself was testament to how little he had changed. Probably it was the best testament.

"It doesn't matter," he said finally. And because it mattered so much to his mother, he added, "Yes, of course, I forgive you."

His mother burst into tears. "Oh, Raymond!"

Bill cradled her in his embrace as she wept. "Thank you. It means a lot to her. To me, too."

Holly smiled at Raymond with pride, tears in her eyes. "You are so wonderful."

Hell, he thought. He hadn't done a damn thing and they were all weepy. He didn't get it. And he didn't want to.

His mother came over to him and hugged him, crying on his neck. Raymond nearly fell out of the chair at her embrace.

"Mother..." he said helplessly, patting her on the back.

"Thank God you're not like me," she told him.

"I'm not what you think, either," he said, not wanting her to have any misconceptions.

His mother sat back and wiped at her eyes. Her makeup was a mess. Raymond decided this was not the time to tell her.

"Oh, I know you have resentments," she said. "You should. I have resentments against my own parents. They had a troubled marriage, all passion and no stability."

"Grandma and Grandpa?" Other than his grandmother's affair, he only remembered them both as being civil, almost cold to each other.

"Yes. I went out of my way not to repeat that. But I went too far the other way. I know that now. I wish I'd realized it much sooner, for your sake. This first step means so much to me." She wiped at more tears.

Raymond felt as if he should have repressed anger to spill out, or vindication to crow about. Instead, he was too dazed to feel anything.

"I'll get the coffee," Holly said. She patted him on the head as she went by. "And some Christmas cookies."

"I'll help," Bill said, getting up and going with her.

"Holly!" Raymond croaked out, not wanting to be left alone with his mother.

Holly just waved at him and was gone.

His mother laughed. "I've become a maudlin old woman and I'm glad."

"Hell," Raymond said. "I don't know what to say."

"Oh, that's all right." Ann looked toward the kitchen. "Isn't Bill wonderful? He's so strong and yet so giving. He has more faith in me than I have in myself. Oh, I know, this is a shock for you. I hope you're not angry that I got married and didn't tell you first."

"You're an adult," he said, eyeing the kitchen entry-way. Where the hell was Holly? If she was blowing up the kitchen while he needed her in here, he would never forgive her.

"As soon as I found love, I knew how wrong I had been," his mother added. "I had no idea that one could feel this way. But you understand, I'm sure, what with Holly. Anyone can see you two love each other. Raymond, thank goodness you turned out normal despite what I did to you."

Raymond stared at his mother. She was dreaming. *He* was dreaming—dreaming this whole thing. That was it, he thought, feeling less confused. He wanted to tell her he wasn't normal, that he had lost his heart. But what would be the sense? She would be hurt over something long past rectifying. But most important, he would wake up and he would be back to the real Normal, with a capital *N*.

"Don't mind my reindeer that look like basset hounds," Holly said, coming in with a tray in her hands. Bill followed with the coffeepot. Holly added, "The damn things stuck to the counter, and I had to practically scrape them off."

"You need a marble rolling board," Ann told her. "You use very little flour and the dough doesn't stick."

"Really?"

A discussion of the merits of marble rolling boards ensued, and Raymond felt as if he had finally and truly entered the Twilight Zone. His mother beamed at Holly. Holly beamed back. Bill beamed, too. Yep. Definitely the Twilight Zone.

His emotions still jumbled around inside him, but ambivalence reigned. He didn't know if that would ever change for his mother. He didn't know if he wanted it to.

"Stay for dinner," Holly urged, bringing him abruptly out of his reverie. She was sitting on the arm of his chair, her fanny practically in his face. Normally, he would enjoy the view. Right now he scowled as she continued, "We'll have a nice little family meal on Christmas Eve and go to church afterward. Raymond needs it." She laughed. "Heck, so do I."

Raymond glanced sharply at her. She must be nuts, he decided. The last thing he wanted was a "nice little family meal" with his mother and her new husband. He wanted Holly in silver lamé. Then he wanted to strip it off her, like opening a Christmas gift. He wanted to make love to her under the tree. He wanted to sin so much with her that church every day of the week would never cure him. It might be the last time.

His mother looked at Bill. They both looked at him. Oddly, Raymond couldn't find the words to say no. He and his mother had never had a normal Christmas together, either.

"Stay," he heard himself say.

Holly took his hand and squeezed it, giving him encouragement. He doubted he would have taken this step without her.

Dinner was a success, although Raymond was privately disappointed in the lack of silver lamé draping Holly's body. Jeans and a sweatshirt depicting elves just didn't have the same effect on his libido. Unfortunately, the elves reminded him that Holly wasn't as human as she looked.

After dinner, Holly said, "Raymond, bring in your parents' bags from the car."

"We have a hotel," Ann said.

"Nonsense," Holly scoffed. "You'll stay with us."

Ann shook her head. "No, dear. Bill and I are already settled in at the hotel. It's our honeymoon, remember."

Raymond said nothing. He would have a lot to say to Holly later. He might have gotten past a few things with his parent, but he was nowhere near ready for a full Christmas with her.

"You'll come back in the morning?" Holly asked anxiously.

"Yes, of course."

"We'll have Christmas breakfast," Raymond added, liking this better than overnight guests.

THEY ALL WENT TO THE midnight, cum eleven o'clock, service, which Raymond discovered was packed with people. He hadn't been to church in years, and he was moved by the experience. Holly patted his right hand at one point, and his mother patted his left at another, both of them obviously feeling emotional. Raymond gave up. This was turning out to be one strange Christmas.

Once he and Holly were alone back at the town house, he could finally set her straight. "Why did you ask them to stay overnight? Are you crazy?"

"It's Christmas," Holly said. "They shouldn't be staying in a hotel. Boy, church wore off you fast."

"It's got nothing to do with church or Christmas. Holly, you pushed it. Don't do it again."

To his surprise, she sighed. "You're right. You're confused enough as it is."

He frowned. "How do you know?"

"Oh…well, anyone can see it in your face. Who wouldn't be confused under the circumstances?"

She had a point. He relaxed and let the lecture on misguided invitations go—not that Holly would have paid much attention. Smiling, he said, "I missed that silver dress tonight."

She smiled back. "Shall I put it on now, or are you too weak from this afternoon?"

"Go put it on, and we'll see how weak I am."

"This is fun." She raced up the stairs.

Raymond climbed the stairs more slowly. *Forget under the tree,* he thought. He couldn't wait that long for Holly. And he wasn't about to get caught with his pants down again. His father might show up after all these years, begging forgiveness, too.

Raymond chuckled, then said out loud, "I forgive you, too, so please stay home."

Might as well send the message out into the universe. It couldn't hurt.

Holly was just pulling the dress up over her nearly naked body when Raymond entered the bedroom. The breath squeezed out of his lungs at the sight of her creamy skin slowly being covered by the silver lamé.

"I think," he said hoarsely, "that I'm about to have a very merry Christmas."

"I think that you are, too," Holly agreed, her voice husky.

He went over to her and brought her against him, the metallic threads of her dress rough against his palms. The flesh of her exposed back was incredibly soft in contrast. His body urged him to remove the dress and rediscover how soft the rest of her was.

"You were wonderful today," she said.

"I was?"

"Mmm." She kissed him. "It was difficult for you, but you were willing to listen. That was good." She giggled. "Your face was priceless when your mother walked in. So was the rest of you."

"I was naked!" he said, then laughed ruefully. "Her timing always was impeccable."

"I thought your butt looked very cute wrapped in that afghan."

Holly kissed him again. It turned from playful to sensual within seconds. When their mouths eased apart, they were both panting for breath.

Raymond lifted her hair to kiss her under her ear, knowing she would melt against him when he did.

"No!" Holly said, pulling away.

But it was too late. He had seen her ear.

"Holly," he said, lifting her hair again to examine her ear better. "Your ear is in a point again."

"I know." She pushed her hair down and refused to look at him.

"You read my mind again earlier, didn't you?" he asked, remembering his thoughts at the time. "Are all your abilities back?"

She nodded. "Pretty much."

He hugged her and spun her around. "Honey, I'm so glad for you. I know how much it upset you not to have them...." Then the implications of her returned magic set in, and he let her go. "What does this mean? What I think it means?"

"I think it means you've found your heart," Holly said.

Unconsciously he put a hand to his chest. Realizing he had, he rubbed his heart area as if to check. "No, I haven't. I don't feel anything different, not even toward my mother."

"But you forgave her. You listened."

"What the hell else could I say without making a huge scene? And it was obvious she was sincere. I got past some old hurts today, but I never felt any rush of love for her. I still haven't. I keep telling you, I *know* I don't feel different.... Holly, does this mean you're leaving me?"

"I...I hope not."

She burst into tears. Nothing had ever hurt Raymond like the realization that she would be gone forever. It was Christmas. She was supposed to be gone by Christmas, or so she'd told him in the beginning. But he didn't have his heart. Maybe the powers that be had decided he was hopeless and they were taking her back anyway.

"Have you tried going back home and asking what the deal is?" He didn't know if he wanted to hear her answer, but the question had to be asked.

"No." She gulped back tears. "I was afraid I'd get there and then they wouldn't let me back to say goodbye. I've spent the day not thinking about it. Do we have to talk about it now? Can't we just be together—?"

"You knew all day and you said nothing!" he exclaimed, furious about her secrecy. "What were you going to do? Say thanks for the roll in the hay and then pop out?"

She straightened, indignant. "I would *never* do such a thing. I don't know what it means, but I didn't want to upset you. Raymond, I love you! I don't want to leave you ever!"

She burst into fresh tears again. All his anger fell away, and Raymond pulled her to him. He held her tightly and knew the final truth.

He loved her.

"SEE?" SHE SAID brokenly, after a long second of silence. She had read his mind—another piece of her magic back. "You *have* found your heart. I told you so."

"But it's for you," he whispered into her hair. "I found it for you."

Faint jingling reached their ears. It seemed to come from above them. From the roof.

"It's too soon!" Holly wailed.

"It's never too soon, girl," a deep voice boomed.

In the next instant, Raymond found he was standing on his roof, its steep pitch no problem in keeping his balance. Neither was the weather a problem. Although the nighttime temperature was in the thirties, he felt as comfortable as if he were in his living room.

A small, intricately carved sled, with a team of live reindeer hitched to it, was perched on his roof's pinnacle. A man stood in the sled. He wore a red robe shot with silver stars and trimmed in white fur. His long white hair and beard blended in with the fur. He was tall, and his body was stocky but nowhere near fat. In fact, he looked very muscular, like a Bulgarian weight lifter. His face had a cheerful expression, as if nothing ever bothered him, and yet his eyes were a fathomless black, as if all the wisdom in the world was contained within them.

"It is, boy," the man said to him.

"Nick!" Holly exclaimed and ran to the wise old man. "We need to talk."

"Later." He swept her up in a huge bear hug. "Holly, you look scrumptious!"

"I've *got* to be dreaming," Raymond said, his legs feeling like a baby's under him. He sat down heavily, trying to make sense of this. Somehow, this visit seemed less bizarre than his mother's visit. He supposed he would have bet he would see Santa before he would ever hear his mother talk about love in glowing terms.

A reindeer face loomed in front of him, its nose the faintest of reds. Raymond gaped at the animal. Recovering, he muttered, "Hell, now I know I'm dreaming."

The reindeer snorted in distinct disgust. Raymond

looked down the front of his shirt in awe. Rudolph—*the* Rudolph—had just used him as a handkerchief.

"No dream, Raymond." Old Saint Nick came to him and lifted him to his feet. Santa's hands were strong and real, firm on Raymond's arm. His touch made Raymond steadier. He patted Raymond on the back, a solid wallop. "You've had one helluva day, kid."

"I don't think Santa curses," Raymond said.

The man roared with laughter.

The reindeer seemed to laugh at him, too. At least, their sudden bleating sounded exactly like a deep "Ho-ho-ho."

"You find, wrap and deliver presents for several billion people and tell me how to do it *without* a good curse or two," Nick said, grinning widely. "This time of year, it's the only way we survive. Right, Holly?"

"Right." Holly grinned back, looking happier than Raymond had ever seen her.

"They miss you back home." Nick winked at Raymond. "She has a deft touch with hope and charity."

Raymond saw the pride in Holly's face at the compliment. He desperately wanted to tell her to forget her old life and stay with him. But he could never offer her better than she already had. What human could? She might think she loved him. Maybe she did. But he hadn't enough to offer in return.

He could never keep her from her old life, he admitted. That would be a mortal sin. She had helped him find his heart. Only now it would break, because he knew he must let her go.

Holly came to him. She wrapped her arms around his waist. He held her, absorbing every nuance of her in his arms, so he would never forget her.

"I love you and I want to be with you always, but I

will gladly go if it means you'll never lose your heart again," Holly said.

"I don't give a damn about my heart," Raymond said. "I love you and I want to be with you, but I will gladly let you go if it means you have your magic back."

"I don't give a damn about my magic," Holly said.

"Well, that's a good thing, then," Nick said. "Because you're not going back, Holly."

They swung around to face him. Nick grinned at them both.

"I'm...I'm not?" Holly asked in a thin voice.

Raymond's heart filled with hope.

"No, you're not," Nick assured her.

"Did I fail my mission?" she asked.

"Ask Raymond."

She looked at Raymond questioningly.

"No," Raymond said. "You are my heart."

"Actually, you're *her* Christmas present, boy."

Raymond gaped at this new twist. "I am?"

"Sure." Nick chucked Holly under the chin. "Way back, when I was the bishop of Myra, I gave poor girls their dowries so they could marry for love. But I ran out of money, and I couldn't save Holly from being sold into a terrible marriage. She died of a broken heart."

"I did?" Holly echoed in bewilderment, then straightened. "Yes! I remembered a little when I first came to Raymond. Things seemed more familiar than they should. Taste and touch. But then that faded."

"We've got to get that matrix fixed," Santa muttered. "You weren't supposed to remember anything. Oh, well. Where was I? When I was...changed, I brought Holly with me, to make up a little for my neglect. I figured I could find her the perfect man. That took longer than I thought. Sorry about that."

Holly and Raymond looked at each other and collapsed in laughter.

"He's the perfect man?" Holly gasped out, while doubled over in amusement.

Raymond paused in his own. "What the hell does that mean?"

"Think about it and tell me why *you* are laughing," she said, still laughing.

Raymond grinned and hugged her.

"Hey, I'm never wrong," Nick said.

The reindeer laughed loudly.

"Keep it up, guys, and you'll get peppermint back at the stables. I'll have to wear a gas mask, but it'll be worth it."

The reindeer shut up.

"And you two stop arguing over the new toy, children," Nick scolded. "You complement each other on many levels—subtle ones, maybe, but they're there."

"So this wasn't a mission for my heart," Raymond said.

"It was," Nick replied. "You had lost a lot of things and you were at a crossroads in your life. Holly did a great job. The best."

"Will I be human now?" Holly asked.

Santa nodded. "That's why you were turning human again. It was your heart's desire coming to the fore as well as your physical attraction to Raymond. You will now be human with all its foibles. That's the price of the gift."

"I'll pay it gladly." Holly rose up on tiptoe and kissed Raymond.

"Wait a minute," Raymond said. He had questions and he knew he would never get answers if he didn't ask *now*.

"How could Holly have been made an elf when she wasn't from magic to begin with?"

"Holly was no longer human," Nick said. "She qualified."

"But how can she be human again?"

"No restriction in the rules for anything to be turned human, boy."

"But she was changing back today to being an elf—"

"She had to accept the gift. If you look, you'll see she's very human, right down to her ears. Now I've got to go. My schedule's already shot to hell and back." Nick put his finger by the side of his nose, then leaped onto the sled. He cracked a whip above the reindeers' heads, and they all flew up into the night sky. As they circled the town house Old Nick called back to Raymond and Holly, "Merry Christmas and good night! Hey, that's what I really said. St. Clement must have had wax in his ears...."

"Say goodbye to Yuri in Wrapping!" Holly shouted.

"Who the hell is Yuri in Wrapping?" Raymond demanded suspiciously.

"Just a nice elf. Relax."

The sled and reindeer sped away, silhouetted for one brief moment against the big pale moon before it vanished from sight.

The boom of reindeer laughter floated back on the wind.

RAYMOND AWOKE ABRUPTLY from the deepest sleep he'd ever had. He knew it as soon as he gained awareness.

Everything rushed back. Holly... His mother... Old Nick...

He realized the other side of the bed was empty, and sat up. "Holly! *Holly!*"

"What? *What!*"

Her exasperated voice, the most beautiful sound he had ever heard, came from downstairs. Raymond's heart pounded in his chest as relief washed through him. He flung back the covers and jumped out of bed. Not caring that he was naked, he ran down the steps to find her.

"Ohh...I guess you want me to decorate that," Holly said, eyeing him provocatively as she met him in the foyer.

Raymond swept her up in his arms. "You're here! I thought you were gone and I had dreamed the whole thing."

"Nope. You heard Nick last night. I'm stuck forever to you."

"I'm glad." He kissed her, tasting her lips and tongue, inhaling her scent of vanilla and spice. Her body, so incredibly real, pressed against his own, fiercely arousing him.

"I was so scared when I woke up and you weren't there," he whispered.

She kissed his neck. I'm sorry. You were snoring away and I wanted to see what I got for Christmas and start the brunch for your mom and stepdad. There's a whole bunch of things under the tree! Come, look."

She led him into the living room. A pile of presents sat under the tree.

"I didn't buy all that." He shivered. "It's cold in here."

Holly sighed loudly. "You must be a nudist at heart. Here." She thrust an afghan into his hands. "Christmas is no fun if we have to wait for you to get dressed."

Raymond wrapped the afghan around his middle and sat down on the floor, next to Holly.

"These new ones are for me," Holly said in surprise, while examining the packages.

"Open them," Raymond urged.

She did. "It's...it's a college diploma. Oh! I just remembered a college education in this time, like someone planted the memories in my head the moment I read the diploma. It's for elementary education. Raymond, I teach kids! How marvelous. And here's a driver's license. I can drive!"

"What is he? Crazy?" Raymond demanded, appalled that Santa would give her such a thing.

"No, I really can drive. I remember lessons and everything, like I've lived now instead of so many years ago. And here's a résumé.... I remember these jobs. And a passport... I've been to Armenia? I *have*. I wonder why.... Well, I'm sure I'll remember a reason eventually. And here's a birth certificate! I'm Holly Jones. Raymond, I am!"

With every gift she opened, she remembered an experience to go with it.

"Old Nick's given you a life in the present," Raymond said.

"I know. So I can survive here and fit in." Holly looked at him. "He always gives us what we need. I wonder what Nick gave you."

"Patience," Raymond replied. "I'm positive of it. How else would I live with you?"

She laughed, then sobered. "I really am a human being now, aren't I?"

"Will you miss being an elf?" Raymond asked. He hoped she would be happy with him, but he could never give her all she'd left behind.

"No." Holly smiled happily. "How could I? I'm with you."

He pushed her hair back from her face. Her ear was

softly round with the barest hint of a tip. "I love you, Holly. Will you marry me?"

"Oh, Raymond." Holly threw her arms around him, knocking him flat on his back in the process of hugging him. "Yes, yes, yes, yes, yes!"

"Thank God you didn't say no," he grumbled, rubbing his aching head. "You probably would have killed me."

"I'm sorry."

"I'm not." He ran his hands down her back as she lay on top of him, marveling that she was real and she was his. "You are the greatest gift I've ever received."

"It's the other way around, dingdong," Holly told him solemnly.

"I don't think so." He grinned and cupped her derriere. "I know what I want for Christmas. *Now.*"

Holly kissed him, then warned, "Your mother's coming in a little while."

"So?"

"I just thought I'd say Merry Christmas, Raymond."

"Merry Christmas, Holly. *You* are my heart."

Epilogue

"I now pronounce you husband and wife. You may kiss the bride."

Raymond kissed Holly amid the cheers of their guests. Their wedding was a small affair on New Year's Day. The judge marrying them was one of Raymond's faithful listeners. Holly wore the dazzling silver lamé dress that he loved so much, and she looked more spectacular than ever.

"Oh, no!" Holly said, when the kiss ended. "I just realized I'm now Holly Holiday."

Raymond burst into laughter.

"I'll live with it," Holly said and kissed him again. "You've got the silliest grin on your face."

"I know." Never had Raymond been so happy. His life *had* been at a crossroads, and he shuddered to think what it would have been like if Holly hadn't come to enrich it. He knew life would never be easy, and as Old Nick had pointed out, Holly was now subject to all its foibles.

Whatever came, he would never lose his heart again. Holly had given that back to him forever.

Raymond was in awe of Holly during the small reception after the ceremony. She greeted guests with aplomb, as if she'd been doing it for years. In fact, she had already adjusted so well that not even he could tell she had ever been anything other than a modern human woman. That must be the last of her magic at work. She was even going job hunting after their honeymoon in Vermont. Holly wanted snow. But the bedroom would be hot, Raymond vowed. *Very* hot.

His cousins cornered him. Peter, Michael and Jared had served as best men. Mary Ellen, Janice and Alison had been Holly's bridesmaids. Janice's kids had stood with Raymond's mother and Bill. Little Amy had declared Holly the lady she had "seen" that night of the party. Raymond had declared her psychic. Everyone had just laughed, and he and Holly had squeaked through a close one.

"You went down faster than the rest of us," Peter said.

"Don't bet on it," Raymond told him, smiling privately.

"Hell, you've known Holly—what?—a few weeks," Jared added. "Even I didn't get married that fast."

"Face it, gentlemen," Michael said. "We didn't have a clue about love before."

"True," the other three agreed.

"Now we do." Raymond held up a glass. "A toast to love."

"The best invention man ever created," Peter said.

"An emotion to be nurtured," Michael commented.

"If you get whacked between the eyes with love, just lie down like a lamb," Jared added solemnly. "It's easier. That'll be the Holiday motto from now on."

"Amen!" They clinked glasses and drank a toast.

"I think I'll go kiss my new wife," Raymond told his cousins.

The four broke up and went their separate ways, all

intent on expressing their emotions to their respective wives. Raymond took Holly in his arms and kissed her thoroughly.

"I love you," he whispered.

"I love you, too," Holly said. She grinned mischievously. "I've been talking to Tommy, who keeps looking at me funny. Bob does, too. I wonder if they've recognized me from those times I couldn't control my pop."

"If they haven't said anything by now, they won't," Raymond said. "Tommy, especially, is very up-front about things."

"I'll say. You definitely have to wear that corset."

"Forget it!" Raymond said.

"Fine. Then *I'll* wear it for your listeners—"

"The hell you will...."

An older couple looked on, unseen by the wedding guests. They smiled in satisfaction that the Holiday men— their grandchildren—were once again as loving as they had been as young boys. The two turned to Cupid, Mother Nature, Justice and Santa Claus.

"Thank you for giving them all back their hearts. We had been so wrapped up in our own problems that we hadn't realized how we affected him. It hurt to see them so unhappy because of us. Thank you."

Cupid laughed. "It was a pleasure."

"A blooming one," Mother Nature said.

"I love it when Justice is served."

Justice smiled at her own inside joke.

"'Tis the season," Old Nick added. "I owed Holly, too."

The four looked at each other and said, "Face it. Everyone loves the Holidays!"

HARLEQUIN WOMEN KNOW ROMANCE WHEN THEY SEE IT.

And they'll see it on **ROMANCE CLASSICS**, the new 24-hour TV channel devoted to romantic movies and original programs like the special **Romantically Speaking—Harlequin™ Goes Prime Time.**

Romantically Speaking—Harlequin™ Goes Prime Time introduces you to many of your favorite romance authors in a program developed exclusively for Harlequin® readers.

Watch for **Romantically Speaking—Harlequin™ Goes Prime Time** beginning in the summer of 1997.

If you're not receiving ROMANCE CLASSICS, call your local cable operator or satellite provider and ask for it today!

Escape to the network of your dreams.

See Ingrid Bergman and Gregory Peck in *Spellbound* on Romance Classics.

As Seen on TV!

Free Gift Offer

With a Free Gift proof-of-purchase
from any Harlequin® book, you can receive
a beautiful cubic zirconia pendant.

This stunning marquise-shaped stone is a genuine cubic
zirconia—accented by an 18" gold tone necklace.
(Approximate retail value $19.95)

Send for yours today...
compliments of ◆ HARLEQUIN®

To receive your free gift, a cubic zirconia pendant, send us one original proof-of-purchase, photocopies not accepted, from the back of any Harlequin Romance®, Harlequin Presents®, Harlequin Temptation®, Harlequin Superromance®, Harlequin Intrigue®, Harlequin American Romance®, or Harlequin Historicals® title available at your favorite retail outlet, together with the Free Gift Certificate, plus a check or money order for $1.65 U.S./$2.15 CAN. (do not send cash) to cover postage and handling, payable to Harlequin Free Gift Offer. We will send you the specified gift. Allow 6 to 8 weeks for delivery. Offer good until December 31, 1997, or while quantities last. Offer valid in the U.S. and Canada only.

Free Gift Certificate

Name: _____

Address: _____

City: _____ State/Province: _____ Zip/Postal Code: _____

Mail this certificate, one proof-of-purchase and a check or money order for postage and handling to: HARLEQUIN FREE GIFT OFFER 1997. In the U.S.: 3010 Walden Avenue, P.O. Box 9071, Buffalo NY 14269-9057. In Canada: P.O. Box 604, Fort Erie, Ontario L2Z 5X3.

FREE GIFT OFFER   084-KEZ

ONE PROOF-OF-PURCHASE
To collect your fabulous FREE GIFT, a cubic zirconia pendant, you must include this
original proof-of-purchase for each gift with the properly completed Free Gift Certificate.

084-KEZR

COMING NEXT MONTH

**Next month, celebrate Christmas with American Romance
as we take you
HOME FOR THE HOLIDAYS**

#705 CHRISTMAS IN THE COUNTRY by Muriel Jensen
Now that he was free, ex-hostage Jeff James wanted nothing more than
to eat Liza deLane's glazed ham for Christmas. But for the woman
touted as the "new Martha Stewart," the *timing* couldn't be worse. She
had a borrowed husband, rented kids...and a very big problem!

#706 MARLEY AND HER SCROOGE by Emily Dalton
When Carl Merrick fell asleep at his desk on Christmas Eve, his business
partner Marley Jacobs made an unexpected appearance in his dreams.
Dressed in a baby-doll nightie, she warned him to change his Scroogelike
ways by the stroke of midnight or someone else would be sharing her
Christmas future.

#707 BELLS, RINGS & ANGELS' WINGS by Linda Randall Wisdom
One minute Libby Barnes idly wished she didn't have to spend Christmas
with her family; the next she wished she'd kept her mouth shut. Because
there was her house, there were her parents, there was her husband Ty—
but nobody knew who *she* was....

#708 THE SANTA SUIT by Karen Toller Whittenburg
Single mom Kate Harmon had always told her twins the truth
Santa Claus didn't exist. So why had they hired detective Gabe Housley
to find him? And why was Kate hoping that Gabe was Santa's answer to
the twins' request for a daddy?

AVAILABLE THIS MONTH:

#701 IN PAPA BEAR'S BED
Judy Christenberry

#703 OVERNIGHT WIFE
Mollie Molay

#702 A DARK & STORMY NIGHT
Anne Stuart

#704 MISTER CHRISTMAS
Linda Cajio

Look us up on-line at: http://www.romance.net

FREE BOOK OFFER!

With every Harlequin Ultimate Guides™ order, receive a FREE bonus book!

#80507	HOW TO TALK TO A NAKED MAN	$4.99 U.S. ☐	$5.50 CAN. ☐
#80508	I CAN FIX THAT	$5.99 U.S. ☐	$6.99 CAN. ☐
#80510	WHAT YOUR TRAVEL AGENT KNOWS THAT YOU DON'T	$5.99 U.S. ☐	$6.99 CAN. ☐
#80511	RISING TO THE OCCASION More Than Manners: Real Life Etiquette for Today's Woman	$5.99 U.S. ☐	$6.99 CAN. ☐
#80513	WHAT GREAT CHEFS KNOW THAT YOU DON'T	$5.99 U.S. ☐	$6.99 CAN. ☐
#80514	WHAT SAVVY INVESTORS KNOW THAT YOU DON'T	$5.99 U.S. ☐	$6.99 CAN. ☐

(quantities may be limited on some titles)

TOTAL AMOUNT	$
POSTAGE & HANDLING	$
($1.00 for one book, 50¢ for each additional)	
APPLICABLE TAXES*	$ _____
TOTAL PAYABLE	$ _____

(check or money order—please do not send cash)

*New York residents remit applicable sales taxes.
Canadian residents remit applicable GST and provincial taxes.

To order, complete this form and send it, along with a check or money order for the total above, payable to Harlequin Ultimate Guides, to: **In the U.S.:** 3010 Walden Avenue, P.O. Box 9047, Buffalo, NY 14269-9047; **In Canada:** P.O. Box 613, Fort Erie, Ontario, L2A 5X3.

HARLEQUIN ULTIMATE GUIDES™
What women really want to know!

Official Proof of Purchase
Please send me my FREE bonus book with this order.

Name: _____

Address: _____

City: _____

State/Prov:._____ Zip/Postal Code: _____

Reader Service Acct.#: _____ **KFZ**

Look us up on-line at: http://www.romance.net   NFPOP